AICKMAN'S
HEIRS

AICKMAN'S HEIRS

EDITED BY
SIMON
STRANTZAS

UNDERTOW
PUBLICATIONS

DEDICATED
TO THE
MEMORY

OF JOEL LANE
1963–2013

CONTENTS

INTRODUCTION

SIMON STRANTZAS

L ET'S GET THIS OVER WITH, RIGHT OFF THE BAT: IF YOU'VE picked up this book because you're a fan of Robert Aickman's fiction and are looking for more of the same, you've come to the wrong place. What follows in these pages are not pastiches of Aickman's inimitable style—they couldn't be: Aickman's fiction straddled so many interwoven lines that the rest of us can hardly keep up. Reserved, yet undeniably sexual; obtuse, yet accessible; surreal, strange, bizarre. Yet funny. Very, very funny, in that odd witty way that sometimes doesn't seem funny until later, after which it becomes chilling. Robert Aickman was a master of what he called "strange stories", and though his fiction has been filed with Horror, it's actually its own beast. Were this book merely a collection of writers doing their best to reproduce something so uniquely Aickman, I'm afraid the book would be interesting only as an example of how mistaken such a direction would have been.

Instead, this book is a sampler of how Robert Aickman's work has become a significant source of inspiration for contemporary writers. Born in 1914, Robert Fordyce Aickman penned only 48 short stories before his untimely death, yet each one of them was drawn deep from the well of his own psyche. A proponent of Freudian psychology, Aickman believed that writing a short story, especially the ghostly sort, was like writing poetry, and the way he practiced the art form involved obeying laws that were less literal than they were subconscious. In this sense, the true key to understanding Aickman's stories existed only in Aickman's head, and since his passing the only hope we have to fully understand them is what we bring to it ourselves. But our own keys do not fit those locks, not perfectly, and as a result some answers will forever remain out of reach.

So if writing like Aickman is so impossible, why does this book exist? Because though Aickman's work was idiosyncratic and unique, the way he worked was and is not. If anything, the influence of Aickman's stories has only grown over the last few years. Less than a decade ago, his name was revered only by a small circle of literate ghost story aficionados, but as time went on there's been an increase not only in authors aware of his work, but in those who cite it as an influence. As we move further away from the horror boom of the last century and its focus on the mainstream appeal of small town horrors, we are encountering successive gener ations of writers open to exploring new avenues of the subtly bizarre, an area Aickman frequently mastered.

What I'd hoped for when inviting authors to be part of this volume was that they might mine their own personal psychology, tap their own subconsciousness, much as Aickman had, and create works that were impossible from another's pen. Each of us learns something different from Aickman; something about ourselves that we hadn't realized was buried until his pen unearthed it. Reading Aickman is like reading the dream journal of a stranger and trying to make sense of its meaning. It's impossible, and yet the joy is in the trying. I hope you get that same joy in reading the pieces in this book, which range in style and subject matter, but all share that same mystery at their heart.

You may not understand what follows. But you will remember it. That is the sort of legacy of which Aickman would be proud.

Simon Strantzas
Toronto, Canada
May, 2015

AICKMAN'S
HEIRS

SEASIDE TOWN

BRIAN EVENSON

I.

In past years, Hovell had simply not bothered to vacation away, but the arrival of Miss Pickaver had changed that. Her arrival had, in fact, changed a lot of things. In the past, Hovell's idea of vacationing had been sitting around in his ratty sweater and khakis in his bedroom, reading the newspaper very slowly, savoring it even, letting his cigarette ash fall where it would, each day like the next until he had to return to work. But then Miss Pickaver had swept into his life and into his bed, and taken him to hand, and slowly taken him to task, and now, yes, he'd been made to understand that, as a vacation, this simply wouldn't do.

"But where would I go?" he pleaded.

"*We*, you mean," said Miss Pickaver, "where would *we* go? Because it isn't just you anymore."

But Hovell didn't care to go anywhere. A man of regular habits, he was an incurious person. He did not care to learn about new things. Even the old things he already knew about he often thought it was better to forget. He still lived in the house he'd been born in, the house he'd inherited when his mother died. And he had some difficulty understanding how it was that Miss Pickaver had suddenly jimmied her way into his life, coming in a matter of weeks to have so much of a say in everything.

"To Europe," Miss Pickaver said decisively.

"Europe?" he repeated, as if confused.

"You have the money. You've never been to Europe. It has to be Europe, James."

It made Hovell wince when she called him by his first name—nobody called him by his first name and even to himself he was simply Hovell, but he had given up correcting her. Miss Pickaver had a first name she used, but he suspected he would always think of her as Miss Pickaver.

And so, Europe. He did not, he was surprised to find, immediately give in. He had the presence of mind to at least let her know that if he had to go to Europe he wanted to stay put, to stay in one place. And once he told her that if she wanted she was welcome to do one of those tours—6 countries in 4 days or some such—as long as he could go somewhere and stay put, she agreed. She'd stay with him for a few days on either end of the trip, she told him, get him established at the beginning and help him pack at the end, but in the middle he'd be on his own. She couldn't help it if he didn't want to make the most of the trip. But no worries, she said: she would be sure to tell him all about everything he missed.

The plane flight from the U.S. alone all but killed him. Though Miss Pickaver had managed to sleep for most of the flight, Hovell had hardly even blinked. When they landed in Paris, Miss Pickaver had delicately stretched and given a little yawn, exposing what had always looked to Hovell like too many teeth, as if she had an extra row of teeth, and then proceeded to lead Hovell implacably through the nightmare that was French customs. Did monsieur have anything to declare? No, monsieur did not. Was monsieur sure? Would monsieur please open his bags? The sight of the officers fingering their way through his carefully folded underthings while Miss Pickaver tittered was too much for him, and when he lost his temper it was only Miss Pickaver's quick action and heartfelt apologies on his behalf that kept him from ending up detained in a back room for hours. When he tried to sleep later, on the train to the seaside town whose name even the French themselves were apparently unsure how to pronounce, she told him no, considering what time it was, he would be better off staying awake until night came. Thus, every time he began to nod off she would nudge him awake.

He arrived at the seaside town half blind with fatigue and disoriented. There were no taxis waiting at the train station, and Miss Pickaver wasn't willing to wait while they figured out how to call one, and so they walked along the road and into town, he pulling both bags while she turned the map over and about, trying to figure out where they were heading.

"But I thought you'd been here before," complained Hovell.

"I have been," said Miss Pickaver. "With that German gentleman I used to know. But he was the one knew the place. I just followed along in his tracks."

"German gentleman?" he asked. "I'm staying in a house you stayed at with some previous lover?"

"Surely I told you about him," she said. "It was years before we met. Well, months anyway." She frowned, smoothed the map over her belly. "And I can't imagine what objection you could possibly have to me taking you to a place that I've been to before and can vouch for," she added, as if the whole reason for her taking a German lover had been entirely for his benefit here, now.

Sighing, he trudged on.

The place was part of a gated community, a little triangle of buildings full of apartments, some of which had motorized metal shutters that could be brought down at night, sealing you in like a tin of preserved meat. The courtyard between buildings seemed deserted—no sign of habitation visible through the windows, and no people out walking on the compound grounds.

Miss Pickaver found the right building, managed to extract a key from the concierge despite she having no French and the concierge having no English. They were on the third floor, room 306. The tiny elevator was too small for him to ride in with the suitcases, and so she went up first, and he sent the bags up one at a time to her.

When, finally, he climbed in, he found it to be even smaller on the inside than it looked from the outside, a kind of lacquered wooden box with a sliding grate for a door. He felt as if he were riding in a coffin.

As the elevator slowly trundled up, creaking, he felt panic beginning to rise. By the time he reached the third floor, he was a nervous wreck.

"Don't be so dramatic," she said. "It's just an elevator."

And true, yes, it was just an elevator, but he had lived fifty years of his life to this point never having to ride in such an elevator as this. Why should he have to ride in one ~~~~

~~~~ She had already turned away, was looking for their apartment. There was one long, dingy hallway stretching away, apartment doors dotted to either side of it, odd on one side, even on the other. They ran out at 305. There was no 306.

"Are you sure the concierge said 306?" he asked.

But the look she threw him made him wish he hadn't asked. Yes, of course she was sure—she was always sure. Even though there was no number on the key fob, she still claimed to be sure.

"It's simply not here," he said.

Stubbornly she went down the hall again, scrutinizing each door in turn with such intensity that Hovell wouldn't have been surprised if 306 did suddenly appear. But, of course, it didn't.

"There must be another third floor," she said.

"Another third floor," he repeated dully.

"Sure," she said. "That you can't get to from this elevator. That you have to get to from another elevator."

He was dispatched to question the concierge, but he refused to take the elevator this time, trudging instead down the tight winding stairs that circled the elevator shaft. The light in the stairwell was dim, and he had to grope, but it was better, even if just a little, than the elevator.

He reached the bottom to find the concierge's lodge locked, and nobody answered when he rang the buzzer. He waited as long as he dared, then trudged back up to deliver the bad news to Miss Pickaver. Miss Pickaver, he knew from experience, did not take bad news well. But when he arrived on the third floor he found only the pile of their bags; Miss Pickaver was nowhere to be seen.

He trudged nervously up the hall and back. He opened the elevator and looked in. And then, quietly, and somewhat hesitantly, he called her name. There was no answer. Maybe she had gotten tired of waiting and taken the elevator down to find him. But surely, if that had been the case, he would have heard the elevator, would likely have even seen her in it when he crossed the first or second floor landing on his way back up. Or at least seen the cable moving.

He knocked again on the concierge's door for good measure. Still no answer. He poked his head out of the building, but it was still just as deserted outside the building as it had been before.

When he finally headed back upstairs, she was there, arms crossed, waiting.

"Where have you been?" she said. "I've been calling for you."

"I was just . . ." he started, and then took off his glasses and rubbed his eyes. He didn't want to fight. But he wasn't sure he could help himself. "Where were you?" he asked, trying not to sound accusatory.

"I," she said, drawing herself up, "was busy finding our place." And then she led him up the dim stairs, up halfway between the third floor and the fourth, where, in the round wall of the stairwell, off one tread, was a small door.

He leaned in close, peered at it in the dim light. He had to squint to read the numbers.

"It says 309," Hovell said.

"That's a mistake," Miss Pickaver said. "It has to be. You saw the hall only went to 305, and there are no other halls."

"I thought you said there had to be another elevator," he said. "Another third floor."

"Don't be difficult, James," said Miss Pickaver. "This is the right room."

But there had been no rooms in the stairwell between the first and second floor, or in the stairwell between the second and third floor. Why would there be a room here? Maybe it was just that he was tired, but it didn't seem right to him.

"It says 309," he insisted.

"Someone must have taken the 6 out and put it in upside down, as a joke."

"What kind of joke is that?" he asked.

She ignored this. Instead she pushed past him, jostling so that he almost slipped and tumbled down the stairs. A moment later the door swung open.

"The key works," she said. "It _____ ____ _____ _____ place.

But even after that, as he hauled the suitcases one by one up the stairs and inside, as he ducked down and made his own way in, as he watched Miss Pickaver opening the windows and airing out the apartment, he still wondered if they were in the right place.

2.

From the window, the courtyard looked not busy exactly, but at least not deserted like it had when they had come in. At a distance, he could hear the sound of the waves. He watched people come and go.

He had slept for hours, had awoken up disoriented with no clear idea of what time it was. Miss Pickaver looked refreshed and relaxed, the exact opposite, he supposed, of how he looked. She had been out to purchase some groceries: olives in a reddish goo, strange tubs of pureed meat, cheese pastes, drinkable yogurts, boxed milk, tins depicting sauerkraut and tiny sausages, dried packets that apparently could be reconstituted into soup or, at least, broth. He stared at it all, as if stunned.

"Feeling better?" she asked brightly.

He nodded weakly. She had done her hair, he noticed now, and had applied a thick, unnaturally dark shade of lipstick. "Are we going out?" he asked.

She gave a peal of laughter. "I've been out, darling. There's no point in your going out, especially not now. It's nearly night again. You slept the sleep of the dead."

The sleep of the dead, he thought now, nursing a bowl of tepid tea as he sat at the window, staring out. The other apartments, the ones on the real third floor, all had balconies, but all theirs had was the window. On one of the balconies below, he watched the backs of a man and a woman, the man holding the woman around the waist as they stared out across the courtyard and through the gap in the buildings to the sea beyond.

He followed their gaze. The light, he had to admit, was beautiful, just as Miss Pickaver had suggested it would be, and if he sat at just the right angle he had a glimpse of the beach. It was littered with bodies. Mostly Eastern Europeans or Germans, he guessed, based on the gold chains they wore and on the fact that the women were blond and seemingly topless. The men, he noticed now, mostly wore nothing at all, lying baking nude in the sun, their flesh leathery, as if being cured.

"Is it a nude beach?" he asked.

But Miss Pickaver, in front of the bathroom mirror plucking her eyebrows, humming softly to herself, didn't seem to hear. He couldn't bring himself to repeat the question. He did not want to be accused by Miss Pickaver of staring at the nudes on the beach. That seemed a humiliation.

When he looked back down at the balcony, the couple were no longer there. He shifted his chair. In the courtyard below, a couple crossed back and forth, their heads bent toward one another. Was it the same couple? He didn't know. The man was about his age, the woman, roughly, the age of Miss Pickaver. There was, now that he thought about it, a physical resemblance as well, both to him and to Miss Pickaver, but they were in the long shadow cast by the building and their faces were turned away, so perhaps that was partly imagined. But when he realized from the cloying smell of her perfume that Miss Pickaver had left the mirror and was standing behind him, he pointed them out to her.

"Like us, no?" he said, and smiled.

She leaned forward and squinted, then drew slowly back. "I don't see the resemblance," she said. Then she kissed him on the top of his head. He imagined the dark stain the lipstick must have left there. "Will you help me carry down my bag?" she asked.

"Your bag?"

"I catch the train in an hour," she said. "For my little tour."

"You're leaving already?" he said, beginning to panic a little.

She crossed her arms, stared at him. "This is what you wanted," she said in a clipped voice. "You wanted to stay put. This is what we agreed on."

But had it been? They'd barely arrived and already she was going. He didn't know the place, he hardly knew how to get to town, but when he voiced these complaints she opened the fridge and gestured at its contents.

"You needn't go to town," she said. "You have everything you need right here." She patiently batted away all his objections until, fifteen minutes later, an ordinary white car pulled into the courtyard below, honked.

"There's my ride," she said.

"But it's not a taxi," he said. "It's just someone's car."

"That's how taxis are here," she claimed.

"But—"

"Who's been here before?" she asked. "You or I?"

Confused, he hauled her bag down the stairs and to the elevator and sent it down. "No point in you coming down. I'll have the driver come in and get it," she said. "You don't need to bother."

He lingered at the window until darkness, and then lingered a little longer. Long after dark there was the noise of the couple walking around below, the gentle murmur of their voices. Though, over time, that murmur became less and less gentle, finally concluding in a shriek from one or the other of them. He kept listening, wondering if he should go down and check on them, but there was only silence. After a while, he closed the window and went to bed.

But he couldn't sleep. His body had no idea what time it was, and he had slept too long during the day, and so he lay in the dark staring up at the ceiling. Perhaps he should have gone with Miss Pickaver. Perhaps he should have done 12 countries in 10 days or whatever it was, expanded his horizons a little—no, this was only nervousness about being left alone. He did not want to see twelve countries. He did not want to see even one country, but now that he was here in this one there was little he could do.

He lay in bed, obsessing, tossing and turning until quite late, one or two in the morning, and then got up and found a book. He tried to read, but the words weren't sticking with him, and after a few pages he had no idea what he'd read. So he turned off the light and went back to the window, resting his elbows on the sill.

There was a moon out now, pale and bitten into, but still casting a fair amount of grayish light. If he leaned far enough out, he could see, below and to the left, the pale white glow of the balcony for the room on the real third floor that was closest to him. There was a dark shape on it, large, though difficult to say whether it was the man or the woman. From time to time it moved a little, or settled in a different way.

Down below, on the paving of the courtyard, a dark blotch of some sort, largish, much bigger than a man. Hard to say exactly what it was, however, and it was in any case motionless. Maybe it wasn't anything at all, a trick of the light. But if it wasn't a trick of the light, what could it be?

He stayed there, staring down, eyes flicking from the shape in the courtyard to the shape on the balcony, until, after a while, close to morning, he began to feel sleepy and went to bed.

3.

When he stumbled awake it was well past noon. He poured out something pink from a jug in the fridge, found it to be slightly sour, but whether it was supposed to be like that he was at a loss to determine. He put it away, poured himself a glass of rusty water from the tap.

Before he knew it he was back at the window, looking down.

Whatever had been in the courtyard the night before had left no sign of its presence. When he leaned out he could see the balcony below, but it was bare, no drink glasses or shoes or bits of clothing to indicate who had been there.

What would he do today? He could find the town, wander through it, just to expend a few hours. Or he could stay here, up in the apartment, read a little, relax, stare out the window.

There was a buzzing sound, unfamiliar but insistent. At first he thought it must be the door, but then it continued and he realized it wasn't coming from the door but from the kitchen, from the telephone on the wall there. *Why bother to answer?* he wondered. It wouldn't be for him—nobody knew he was here, at least nobody who mattered. He would just ignore it.

But it was hard to ignore. It just kept ringing and ringing. After a while he got up and went into the kitchen and stayed there, staring at it. Each time it rang, it shook slightly in its cradle. No, he wouldn't answer it. But it was all he could do not to answer it.

It rang perhaps thirty more times and then stopped. He took a deep breath and slowly let it out and then headed back to the window. By the time he arrived there, the phone had started ringing again.

It might be Miss Pickaver, he told himself this time, less because he believed it and more because of the idea of hearing the phone ring over and over again seemed impossible. *Maybe it is for me after all.*

But when he picked the phone up the connection was odd, thick with static. "Hello?" he said. When he had no response, he added, "Miss Pickaver?"

A voice that sounded very distant said something in another language, maybe French, maybe not. Or maybe it was just the distorted echo of what Hovell had said. He waited a long moment for the voice to say something else. When nothing was forthcoming he hung up the telephone.

Late in the afternoon, he managed to make it downstairs. The concierge was there now, sitting in the lodge just beside the door. It wasn't the same man as yesterday, or at least didn't look like the same. Maybe it was a job shared by two different people, or maybe it was just one person who, depending on what he wore and his mood, could look very different.

Hovell tried to make the man understand what he wanted. *Town* he repeated, again and again, then the actual name of the town, with both pronunciations he had heard, but the concierge just looked blank. The concierge said something back in French, a question judging by the intonation, but Hovell couldn't understand a word of it.

After a while he gave up and went towards the front door. But quickly the concierge was in front of him, between him and the door, gesticulating, pushing him back.

"What's wrong?" asked Hovell. "I just want to go outside."

But when he reached for the door again, the concierge knocked his hand away.

Under normal circumstances this would have been enough to turn Hovell around, send him back up the stairs, but with everything else that had gone on, he was not himself. He reached out and grasped the concierge by both shoulders and moved him out of the way, and then went out the door. This time, the man did not try to stop him.

He crossed the courtyard to find the gate he had originally come through locked, so circled around the edges of the compound until he found a place where the fence met a wall and he was able to climb up and over. Nothing on the other side looked familiar. Immediately he was lost, and when he started out in what he thought might be the direction of the town center he found himself squirreling around small little streets which gradually became larger and emptier, the houses sparser and sparser. He hadn't paid any attention when Miss Pickaver had led them from the train station, he'd been too tired. He should have paid attention. He tried to work his way back to the complex but the streets seemed different going the other way on them, and quickly he was off course. There were streets and houses, but no town center. And then, suddenly, he was at the beach.

He felt immediately conspicuous, dressed as he was in the same khaki trousers and ratty sweater and worn gum-bottomed shoes that he wore to putter around the garden at home. He was over-dressed. The most anyone on the beach was wearing was a thin strip of fabric over their fork, if fork was the right word, and the majority were not wearing even that. Most were nude, scattered in clusters here and there on the beach, and in the few moments he looked out over them none of them moved, as if th———————them to a sort of paralysis.

"Please?" said a voice behind him, in a thick guttural accent. Russian, maybe.

He turned to see a tall, bronzed man who was completely bald and completely nude, greased from head to toe with some sort of oil. A gold watch glinted on his wrist. His eyes were hidden behind a pair of goggles with dark, protective lenses.

"I seem to have gotten lost," said Hovell. It was disconcerting, he realized, to talk to a man naked except for watch and goggles. He felt as if some sort of rule of etiquette was being violated, but wasn't sure whether he or the bronzed man was the one violating it.

"This you can say," said the bronzed man, crossing his arms. "This they all say."

"But it's true," protested Hovell.

"If you care to have your look, we shall have our look too," the man said, and reached out to take hold of Hovell's sweater.

Hovell recoiled, stepping rapidly backward. For a moment the man held on tight and then he suddenly let go. Hovell stumbled and almost went down in the sand. He rushed quickly away, the giddy laughter of the bronzed man ringing loud behind him.

It was nearly dark by the time he found the complex again, which revealed itself to him just at the moment when he'd finally given up looking for it. The gate was still locked and though he rang the buzzer the concierge never came to open it. He circled the complex until he found the place he had climbed over and climbed back in that way. It was more difficult coming back in than going out, and he tore open the knee of his trousers.

In the twilight he crossed the courtyard. The same couple, or a couple very much like them, were there once again tonight, walking arm in arm, heads inclined toward one another, and he thought again of the resemblance of the middle-aged man to himself and of the younger woman to Miss Pickaver. He was tempted to approach them, and indeed had started towards them. But as he came closer he realized that something was happening between them, that what he had taken to be a genial arm-in-arm was the man holding the woman's arm so tightly she couldn't release it. He was pulling her forward, and the reason her head was inclined as it was was because it was hard for her to do otherwise. And yet, the woman did not cry out. Surely if she was in trouble, if she needed him, she would cry out.

Unsure, he drifted toward them anyway until, with a sudden burst of speed they darted away. He stayed there for a moment confused, looking after them, and then went inside. The concierge was there, waiting, and immediately began to wag his finger at him, but whether for climbing the fence or for some other reason, Hovell was at a loss to say. Hovell pushed past him and climbed the stairs.

By the time he reached his own window and was looking out of it, the couple had gone. There were however two men wearing what looked, in the growing darkness, like uniforms. Police perhaps, or people dressed to look like police. What did the police over here dress like anyway? He watched them walk in a unified step across the courtyard and enter his building.

The next hour he spent waiting for them to knock at his door. They did not knock, but knowing they could at any moment was enough to keep him agitated and upset. In his head he imagined what he would tell them about climbing the fence, about accidentally wandering onto the beach. He found his hands moving, gesticulating his innocence to the empty air. He tried for the first time to close the metal shutters over the window, to keep them from seeing him through the window, but though the mechanism made a humming sound the shutters did not come down. Eventually, he took a blanket and a pillow and locked himself in the bathroom to wait for morning. There had been no need to leave the apartment—why had he done it? He would not, he promised himself, leave the apartment again until Miss Pickaver returned.

4.

He was awoken by a narrow strip of light coming under the bathroom door and shining into his eye. He was sore all over from the hardness of the bathroom floor, from having to prop his feet on the bidet as he slept. No, in the light of day, it seemed foolish to have panicked. He hadn't done anything wrong, there was no reason the police would have come for him. He had let his imagination run away from him.

But still, he did not leave the apartment. He moved from room to room, reading, looking idly out the window. He sampled more of the unfamiliar tins that Miss Pickaver had bought, and though he wasn't fully taken by any of it, some of it was at least slightly better than edible. It was good to relax, he told himself. Before long, he would feel like himself again.

Twilight found him at the window watching for the couple, but tonight they were nowhere to be seen. Or, rather, now there was only the man, walking and pacing the courtyard all on his own, in a seemingly agitated state. Perhaps Hovell had started watching for them too late, after the woman had already gone in. Or perhaps the woman was elsewhere tonight. Or perhaps—but no, what other reasonable possibilities were there? No point letting his imagination run away with him.

He would read and then fall asleep, Hovell told himself. No late night for him. Not tonight. But instead he found himself still at the window, the lights of the apartment extinguished behind him so as to see better. How much time went by, he wasn't sure. An hour maybe, or maybe more. And then, suddenly, he noticed again the shape on the balcony, the man there—he was almost sure now it was the man—visible in the moonlight and in contrast to the white metal of the balcony. Another watcher, much like himself, unable to sleep. But what was there to see at night?

And then the clouds shifted and he realized it was there again, on the paving stones of the courtyard: the large black shape, the heap or mound of something. One moment it hadn't been and then now, suddenly, it was. What was it? He felt the hair rising on the back of his neck as his mind darted from terror to terror, offering each as a way to fill the mystery.

But no, it was ridiculous to think this way. He was letting his imagination run away with him again. There must be an explanation. If he went down, he'd find what it was.

He did not move from the window.

The figure on the balcony, he noticed, didn't move either. It must be staring down at the same black heap, just like me. *Unless,* he suddenly realized with a start, *it's staring up at me.*

It was as if the figure had taken this thought of his as its cue. He watched as it clambered onto the rail of the balcony and then, before Hovell could do anything or even cry out, it jumped.

He clattered his way down the stairs, heart pounding, and rushed past the closed concierge's box and out into the courtyard. The body was nowhere to be seen, no human figure was sprawled on the pavement below the balcony. But wasn't the fall enough to kill it? Or him, rather? Maybe he had crawled away.

He moved farther out into the courtyard and thought for a moment he'd glimpsed it, but no, what he saw was too big to be a human figure: it was instead a large, dark heap.

He almost turned and went back but he just couldn't. Now, so close to it, he wanted to know.

He moved forward, wishing he had a tiny flashlight. When he came quite close, he could feel the warmth rising off it, and thought for a moment it was a compost heap or some other form of refuse, but then he came closer still and touched it and felt fur and realized it was a horse.

It was dead, or seemed to be. The body was still warm, but cooling rapidly. It must have been black, or a very dark brown, or he would have been able to see it better from above. But even close to it, even touching it, he had a hard time making it out clearly.

It wasn't possible. It was immense in the darkness, the biggest horse he had ever seen. Where had it come from? And what had the heap been on the earlier night? Surely it couldn't have been the same dead horse on both nights.

But what about the man who had ~~come before him~~

~~He pulled back~~ his hand as if stung and stood up. There, near the door now, between him and the door, stood a figure, apparently a man. At first he thought it was the concierge, but when it began to move toward him with a stuttered, broken stride, he was no longer so sure. For a moment he hesitated, wanting to understand what was happening, to give it a logical explanation. This turned out to be his undoing.

5.

When Miss Pickaver returned she had seen four countries in four days, but since they were not new countries to her, not countries she had not seen before, they hardly counted. What did count was that she had seen them in company with the German gentleman that she used to know, and who had footed the bill. She would not tell Hovell about that—he wouldn't be likely to understand, not in the way he should. But she would tell him about the four countries and what she had seen over the course of those four days. Or, to be honest—which she would not be—*two* days, since she and the German had for the first two days not left his room in town. After all, she had told herself at the time, she was a Miss, not a Mrs.: what she did with her leisure time was nobody's business but her own.

The concierge greeted her with a torrent of French, and gestures she could not understand. She just shrugged and nodded until he either thought he'd gotten his point across or decided to give it up—with the French, how could you know what they were thinking?

Upstairs, she found a man in grubby overalls, a maintenance man of some sort, at the door of their apartment, nailing the 6 in 306 back in place, the right way up, so it no longer could be read as a 9. Inside, Hovell was at the same window he'd been at when she'd left, still staring out into that deserted little courtyard.

"Hello, darling," she said. "Have a nice time?"

He grunted in reply, turned just long enough to give her a wan smile and pat her arm. *Same old James*, she thought. And then, suddenly, he did something that surprised her.

He turned fully toward her. "Shall we take a walk?" he asked, in a voice so confident it seemed hardly his own. "A turn arm in arm in the twilight?" And then he smiled in a way that seemed to her not like him at all. "Come on," he said. "It'll be fun. Nothing to be afraid of."

He stood and put his arm around her and began tugging her toward the door.

NEITHERNOR

RICHARD
GAVIN

I.

Vera was my only cousin and was a distant one in more than the usual way; genetically, yes, but also geographically, emotionally, and, I now see, in the character of what one might call spirit or soul. We had never shared any sort of kinship, or truly any acquaintanceship, to speak of. Best as my holey memory serves, Vera and I had met only a single time, at a stuffy family reunion that had taken place during my tenth Thanksgiving.

To suggest that any sort of foreshadowing had taken place during that soporific feast day would be prevarication of the highest order. I recall only that Vera had worn a plaid skirt and that her hair was very dark and very straight and rather short; not quite as short as I'd worn mine, but nearly. It is dubious that we exchanged any words beyond asking for a condiment to be slung down the chain of hands that lined the long banquet table.

Forearmed with this proem, I hope you might appreciate the dazed reaction I experienced when, on assignment, I came upon her name in conjunction with a tiny art gallery on the outskirts of the city.

"Yes, they're very interesting aren't they? Very interesting indeed. They're made by a local woman, each piece is done by hand and each is one-of-a-kind." This was the voice of the older man who was perched behind the tiny counter. His was the physique of an overfed pigeon and his eyes were large and rheumy. The wooden stool that braced him groaned woefully each time he fidgeted, which was often. His teeth were the grey of cooked mushrooms and they shimmered with saliva when he smiled, which, thankfully, he did but once.

"Unique," I said, hoping that the proprietor would repast with something like 'Oh, yes, very unique' or 'truly unique' so that I could then correct him by saying that the word 'unique' implicitly means something singular and without equal and thus requires no modifiers to enhance it. I enjoy giving these sorts of lessons to my public. Language is so very important, dying though it may be.

But the droopy man's only response was a wet-sounding sneeze. I moved further down the gallery's aisle, pausing to study an especially complex and delicate-looking piece that sat beneath the smudgy glass of a display case.

"That the carousel you're looking at?" the proprietor asked, returning his hanky to the inside of his vest. "A keen eye you've got, sir. I'm fond of that one myself."

I nodded. "Yes . . . yes I suppose it is a carousel at that. Truth be told, I thought it was a scorpion at first."

He chortled. "That's the rub of it. That's Ms. Elan's gift, you see? Your eye's sharper than most, I daresay. She calls this series Neithernor, because they are neither one thing nor the other. One sees two things at once, you might say. Take that one, for example . . . "

He leaned forward on his stool and for a moment I feared he might try to rise, but he merely pointed to the case at the end of the show floor. I moved to it to save him further exertion. I studied the biggish piece featured there.

"For the longest time I thought that one represented a handheld mirror, then a young lady from one of the universities nearby told me that it was most definitely an Egyptian ankh. Now I don't know which it is. I tell you, the funny thing is, when I leave here at night I will often think about Ms. Elan's work, while I'm cooking my supper or lying in bed about to sleep. I think of it, but I can never remember exactly what these pieces look like. Isn't that a puzzler? I sit here five days a week and I study them, trying to memorize every curl and bend, but once I leave this room, my memories change. The pieces become something different than what they were. Talented artist, she is. I'd like to show you my favourite of her creations, a sofa with teeth, but it sold in August."

It was on the tip of my tongue to tell the man about my relation to the artist, but I didn't.

"It's clear she's been successful, given that this gallery showing is all hers."

The man's head drooped as if ashamed. "We're a consignment gallery, sir. We'd pay our artists if we could though. Surely we would."

"She lives locally you said?" I returned, changing the subject.

"Well, her representatives do at the very least. They deliver me new pieces every few weeks or so."

"So her works do sell then?"

"Occasionally. To tourists mostly. Slow time right now, being the off-season."

"Could I trouble you for Ms. Elan's contact information. I'm the arts and culture writer for the Mirror and I'm always looking to educate my readers on the more unique goings-on outside of the city."

"A writer! Well, well, well. But you have me at a disadvantage, sir. Vera is a very private woman."

I nodded. "That's fine. Might I leave you my information so that Vera or her representatives can contact me if they wish?"

"Yes, yes."

I produced my card then made my way to the door.

Prior to exiting, I posed one last question to the owner.

"Yes," the man confirmed, "yes, every piece is, sir. Copper wire and human hair, that's Ms. Elan's medium. As I said, sir, you've a keen eye. Very keen."

———

After I returned to the city and to the echo-heavy building that is the Mirror's headquarters and to my tidy desk that is stationed within it I had every intention of drafting an official proposal concerning a local interest column on my cousin Vera, but two enmeshed events intervened and kept me from forwarding the idea to my editor. The foremost of these was an electrical fire in the annex beside mine, which resulted in irreparable smoke damage to a number of my belongings, including the entirety of my music collection and a suede armchair that was ~~~~~~~~~~~~~~~~~~~~~~~~~~~.

The next was my becoming engaged to a woman named Cara.

I am to blame entirely for this romance. Cara was a clerk at the music shop that sat between the Mirror office and my smoke-damaged home. For a period of a month, perhaps longer, I incorporated a stop at the music store into my lunch hour routine. Cara was not the reason for my frequent visits (though she would likely say otherwise). I was simply trying to not merely replenish but actually improve my lamented record collection and the shop's location was convenient. My guilt in this crime of the heart was ordering Tchaikovsky, which women almost always equate with sensitivity. He is my own concession to the delicate, and it cost me. I have always theorized that women like men who like Tchaikovsky. I am living proof of this theory.

What shall I say about our courtship? We talked and Cara made recommendations for records I did not buy. Somehow we ended up at a cafe and later in her bed and much later in a townhouse that we shared. As to who proposed to whom, my recollection is foggy, but Cara insists that I asked her in a manner that was "endearingly shy." This is the version she tells her friends and her mother, at whose apartment we have lunch every Sunday. I suppose this version is accurate enough.

There were and are obvious advantages to my relationship with Cara. Companionship always puts one more at ease with one's own eccentricities. Alone, one's compulsions can become forces of anguish and alienation. Betrothed, they twist into endearing quirks in the eye of one's lover. This of course is so much easier than the futile quest to entirely remake one's self to fit an ideal.

Also, Cara received an employee discount for any records she purchased, so I was able to rebuild my collection much more quickly and inexpensively than I'd thought.

One Tuesday in November, a most unexpected thing happened. Cara walked through the door shortly after six, smiled, and then handed me a parcel. Its shape and thinness were obvious enough to render the brown paper wrapping a bit superfluous. But then the real question was, exactly *which* record had she gotten me?

I set my magazine aside and said "Thank you, my dove" and pecked her cheek.

The peeled wrapping revealed a cream album jacket. A slate-grey circle with a straight line underneath, akin to an underline used for emphasis, was its only adornment.

"Dear?" I said.

"Scelsi," Cara replied, turning from me to remove her coat. "Put it on."

I broke the seal and heeded.

What came leaking through the speakers was a warbled and creeping harmonic of brass, of strings being tediously bowed. I stood holding the record sleeve. Something cold and shapeless raised the hair on the back of my neck.

"This music," I began.

"Do you like it?"

"It sounds as though it's . . . melting."

"It's called *Anahit*. Scelsi wrote it for Venus. That's why I bought it for you."

I must have been visibly nonplussed, for Cara explained that this music, which I found remote and coldly firm as a headstone, seemed to her to illustrate a kinship between myself and the composer.

"In what way?" I asked, feeling the edge creeping into my voice.

"Just listen. Scelsi felt the same about women as you do."

"Did he?" I asked, now spinning in one of Cara's eddies of insinuation.

"Did he?" she repeated before regressing into the unlit kitchen. A few moments later the scream of a kettle was added to the Italian's razor-wire concerto.

Cara then told me something about Scelsi that I have never forgotten.

It was only natural that I felt impelled to reciprocate her gift, but after a few fruitless hours gazing through boutique windows and pacing the airless labyrinths of antique shop after antique shop I began to question exactly how well I knew my fiancée. Of all the curios I'd spotted, none seemed to represent her. But then, how well did the Scelsi recording represent ... in my candid opinion. I then began down a lane of thought that I admit I'm less than proud of taking. I started to suspect that Cara's motive was less about gifting and more about challenging. The outré concerto was a gauntlet of sorts, a distorted mirror that was designed to confuse me about not only her but also myself.

As I said, I am not proud of the way I searched for Cara's motives in dark corners.

I'm even less proud of the fact that I decided to best her at her own game. But it was as it was. Far be it from me to burnish reality. If the game was to be Presents Beyond the Pale, I knew just the bauble to use as my repast.

3.

I sought the phone number of the little gallery in the little town where Cousin Vera's little creations could be had. I found no listing. My editor had long ago eliminated my off-the-beaten-path travelogues, but the gallery keeper didn't know that. On a Friday I left the office after only a half day and drove north, hoping all the while that the gallery would be open.

I found it closed, permanently.

A cold spring rain began to fall as I stood on the sidewalk, peering into the showroom as though this would somehow alter its condition. Was I expecting the cold potted lamps to suddenly brighten, the showcases to fling back their dustcovers and once again be filled with Vera's fetishes?

Like a petulant child I gripped the entrance handle and shook the door with violence enough to cause the little bell to rattle inside. Then I returned to my post on the sidewalk and tried to think of alternatives.

Had the day not been so gloomy I would likely never have noticed the light that went on in the second-storey window. But notice it I did, beaming like a small amber moon just above me. I took a few paces back and looked upward. The silhouette's frame suggested that it was the gallery clerk. I waved and called hello and prattled something about being the newspaper writer.

The shape disappeared from the window. A few moments later it was standing in the little alley that divided the gallery from the organic bakery next door. My suspicion had been correct, it was the gallery owner. He was dressed in saggy pyjamas, a housecoat and tattered plaid slippers. The umbrella in his dirty fist was designed for a child.

"I wanted to ask you about Vera," I told him after he showed no inclination toward speaking.

"The gallery is no more, I regret to say. I've nothing to sell you."

I wiped the rain from my face and approached him. "Yes, I can see that. But I'm hoping you can call Vera's representatives for me. It's important."

"No way to call *them*," he said. He gave me a beckoning wave and started back down the alley from which he'd emerged. I followed him to a flimsy wooden door, which he pulled back. I squeezed into the tiny landing, holding my breath as the man latched the sad-looking door. "This way," he said. I didn't need to be told this, for the landing only had two exits: the alley door or the bowing stairs of wood so worn it was ice-slick. I climbed with care, for there was no handrail to aid me.

My host unlocked and pressed open the black-stained door at the head of the stairs. I followed him into an L-shaped apartment that smelled of old cooking and cat urine. The room had but two sources of illumination: a skylight of clouded plastic and, unnervingly, a nightlight in the shape of an antique streetlamp that glowed from a wall plug.

"Sit, sit," urged the man. I was reluctant. In way of furnishings there was a tan sofa and a wooden glider chair. The sofa's upholstery was bearded in long cat hair, so I chose the wooden glider. I never did spy the cat. He settled into the sofa and immediately lit a cigarette, producing an ashtray brimming with mangled butts. "What do you fancy?"

I cleared my throat. "I'm looking for a present for my fiancée. One of Vera's sculptures . . . because they are so . . . highly unique."

He nodded and nodded, ~~reclining ~~ smoke into the already cloying atmosphere. This caused his pyjama top to part at the seam. His breastbone was uncannily large and knotty. The sight of it distressed me.

"We was hoping for a newspaper story from you," he returned, rather brashly. I noted that his accent, which had previously suggested the posh air of Knightsbridge, suddenly clanged with an antagonizing cockney lilt.

"Ah, yes. Well, I'm sure you can imagine how it is; editorial bureaucracy and the like. I pitched the idea, but my superiors turned me down." I wondered why I felt the need to explain myself to him. "But I'd still like to purchase a piece, and to be put in touch with Vera if that's the possible." I then revealed my familial connection to her.

"The first bit is, aye. But as to Cousin Vera . . . "

"Nothing's happened to her I hope."

"Why do you say that, eh?"

I couldn't answer. "Um . . . would you happen to have any of Vera's pieces left here?"

The man kept his eyes on me as he extinguished his cigarette. "Cuppa first, yeah?"

"That's not necessary."

"I'm afraid I must insist, 'tis nearly four after all."

"Well in that case . . . "

I scanned the room while my host put the kettle on. The sight of the myriad smudges and smears on the walls gave birth to imagined bugs that crawled coldly across my skin. As I scrambled for a way to politely refuse any food or drink from the whistling man in the kitchenette, my eyes happened upon a plaque that was affixed to the moulding above another door, one that led perhaps to the bedroom or lavatory. The plaque was carved from a wood that was cayenne-red and was so thickly varnished it appeared wet. The word

𝔑𝔢𝔦𝔱𝔥𝔢𝔯𝔫𝔬𝔯

had been scorched into the wood by someone skilled in the art of pyrogravure. Each of the ten characters was modelled in Blackletter script. Given this, regardless of Neithernor's meaning, I obviously couldn't help but hearken back to Alighieri at the Gates.

"Milk and honey?"

I'd grown so lost in my contemplation that I first mistook my host's query as an offering from Paradiso. Glancing sidelong, I discovered that my host was holding a tray upon which both these condiments were standing. I took my tea straight. It was bitter and the cup smelled as though it had been wiped with a dirty rag.

I held my breath while I drank. I might have spewed out some banal chatter, I cannot recall. My next memory was of asking to be directed to the toilet. I was peculiarly hopeful that it existed behind the Neithernor door, but it was at the end of a stout hallway.

Closing the door behind me, I splashed some cold water on my face, and panicked over what my next move would be, for I now felt nothing at all like a visitor and more like a double agent on some life-or-death mission. Using the room for its true purpose, I stepped back into the living room in time to see a bird-like woman pressing the *Neithernor* door shut behind her.

"Vera?" I was surprised at how breathless my voice sounded. She turned to me.

How time had ransacked my cousin. She stood before me dressed in a soiled white smock, hear hair concealed beneath a knitted cap like a patient in the thick of her battle with cancer. Her face had slid from delicate to skullish. Of her complexion and the state of her teeth I shall not speak.

"Come join us for tea, Vera dear," called my host, rising to collect another stinking cup. Only then did it strike me that I did not know his name. The question leapt to the tip of my tongue but died there. The last thing our motley gathering needed was gaucherie.

We sat and sipped and inhaled second-hand tobacco smoke. Vera gave me a lone glance. Furtive and fearful at first, she rectified it, or rather attempted to, by hitching the corner of her chapped mouth into a kind of grin.

Distressed, I asked her bluntly if she was well.

"Oh, yes. Just tired, I suspect."

The response came from the man ~~~~~~ ~~~~~~ ~~~~~~~~~ ~~ a Svengali-like command over my cousin.

"Have you been working on new art, Vera?" I put a heavy emphasis on her name to indicate that I wanted her reply.

"Endlessly," she said. Her voice sounded as I'd feared it might.

"Is that your studio beyond the door there?"

She looked at the man in the sleepwear.

"I should very much like to see it if I may," I added, rising. I moved swiftly so as to carve the bearded man off before he could stop me. Vera did not even attempt to.

Neithernor was not a studio, nor even a room, but a closet. Shallow, lightless, and fragrant with old wood, the recess contained a stout metal stool and, upon the dust-studded floorboards, a spool of gleaming copper wire. Shelves lined either side of the closet and each was stacked with pastry boxes of thin white cardstock, all lidded and bound like caskets awaiting interment. A hatch door was set into the centre of the back wall. It was secured with a latch and padlock, both of which had also been slathered in the same eggshell primer.

A hand reached in front of me and pressed the door shut.

"Neither a studio nor a closet," I said with deliberate impertinence to the bearded man. He stood regarding me with a diamond-hard gaze. His face began to redden and twist. I've no shame in admitting my fear. You too would have been afraid.

"I would like to call on you again, Vera," I called as I reached for my coat. "I am still interested in one of your pieces."

She sat on the sofa like one adrift in dementia. Her mouth moved but I did not hear what she'd uttered.

"We'll have something for you," the man said. I closed the apartment door and took the stairs at a hare's pace. Outside I clung to the street door with one hand while collecting the narrowest wooden slat I could find from amidst the alley's debris. This I used to keep the door from clicking snug into its frame.

4.

I wrestled with whether or not to remain in the little village. My concern for Vera ran deep, regardless of how estranged we were. Sometimes women just need rescuing.

Having nothing in way of a plan, I stopped into a tavern to phone Cara and say that I was chasing a story lead and would not be home until the following day. Her suspicion was palpable.

Night fell and I tried to sort my thoughts into some semblance of a plan. I couldn't even begin to judge whether or not my intentions were pure. Cousin Vera had become swallowed up in a life that I can only describe as leprous. If I could not free her, I could at least confirm that she was not in imminent danger. I believe people have the right to diminish themselves if they so desire.

I buttoned my overcoat against the dropping temperature and once again crossed the little bridge. I stood across the street from Vera's hovel and kept watch. Lamplight shone amber through the second-storey window, but not indefinitely. Shortly after eleven I watched as the bearded man's ugly silhouette extinguished the light. I stood shivering for nearly an hour, affording Vera's keeper time enough (I hoped) to doze off.

Much to my relief, the wedge was still in the door. Scaling those ancient steps noiselessly was arduous and time-consuming, particularly because my most formidable obstacle stood at their summit.

Exactly how I was going to unlock the apartment door was a problem I resolved to simply deal with by whatever means. Ultimately this meant, after attempting to wriggle it loose and to pop the lock using my driver's licence and my lapel pin, kicking the flimsy door open.

The bearded man had been snoring on the sofa where we'd had our dirty tea. The crash of the breached door woke him instantly, but he was too groggy and stunned to prevent me from tearing across the living room and flinging open the door to Neithernor.

As I'd dreaded, Vera was sealed up within the tiny closet. Her slight frame rested on the metal stool and for a beat I thought she was sleeping, until I noticed that her _____ _____ _____ open yet rolled up in her skull like one in an epileptic throe. Her mouth gaped. In her hands she held the spool of copper wire. The glinting strand was taut before her, like a fishing line in the deep. It fed backward above her head and into the tiny hatch. This time the door in the wall was unlocked and ajar. A fat band of shadow concealed whatever was rusting inside that cubby. Whatever it was, it possessed strength enough to tear at Vera's hair, which caused her somnambulistic body to heave up and then drop down again onto the stool. Her scalp was missing much more than the knitted cap.

The bearded man was growling as he grabbed me. Dread and adrenaline made breaking free easy.

Less easy to escape is the memory of those neatly stacked white boxes beginning to rattle and shake and leap from their perch.

Vera was careless or helpless to the whole nightmare. Not even my shrieking flight could lure her from her in-between.

5.

I drove aimlessly for the remainder of the night and when I came home the following morning it was to an empty apartment.

Upon Cara's dressing table, which was stripped clean of the little bottles and brushes and mirrors that littered it, a single leaf of notepaper had been taped:

Forrest—

I will write the things that neither of us has the courage to say aloud.

Where to begin? By suggesting that we have grown apart? No. You cannot separate that which was never together to begin with.

Your phone call yesterday afternoon was the tipping point. There was no story to chase; I called the paper and spoke to your editor. I hope this other woman, whoever she is, is able to give you whatever it is that I couldn't, whatever it is you're lacking. I doubt even you know what that is.

Locking up the townhouse last night I found a parcel on our doorstep. I'm embarrassed to admit that I thought you had left it to surprise me with. But as soon as I opened it and saw the little fetish inside it became very clear to me that you're walking down a road I would never even set foot upon.

Just being in the same house with it last night gave me nightmare after nightmare, when I did manage to sleep that is.

I have nothing more to say. I've gone to stay at Mother's and will arrange to have my things collected. I don't expect this note to shock or pain you in any way, no matter how much I may wish otherwise.

—Cara

p.s.—I left your little bauble for you. You'll find it inside your closet.

I locked the townhouse door behind me and immediately relocated to the only hotel I could afford.

I did not return to the house until the movers I'd hired met me there and carried out the furniture I singled out as being mine. Cara's belongings appeared to have already been collected.

The bedroom closet was never reopened, at least not by my hand. After settling into a small apartment on the far side of the city my first quest was to rebuild my wardrobe to replace the dress shirts, trousers and various other pieces I abandoned for fear of parting the gate to my own little Neithernor.

It seems my life waxes then wanes. For a time my cup runneth over, then is drained, after which I strive and scramble to replenish that which has been lost.

6.

I had noted that Cara had once told ～～～～～～～～～～about Scelsi that I have never forgotten. It is this: the eccentric composer refused to allow his photograph to appear in conjunction with any of musical releases, for he maintained a conviction that his music was much more than a simple outgrowth of his personal imagination. The sounds were a transmission from the greater Soul that transcends all matter and masks. Scelsi was, in his own words, merely a conduit for the music that existed well beyond his own private abilities.

In place of his own visage, distinguished though I later discovered it to be, Scelsi used the symbol (a circle hovering over a straight line) that appeared on the jacket of the recording Cara had presented me with. I have studied that symbol often and with vigour. Cara had always said that for her the image was a cleanly abstract vision of a sinking sun, but to my eye it appears as something else entirely.

LEAST LIGHT, MOST NIGHT

JOHN HOWARD

Why is the sun worshipped, never the arctic cold?
—Sacheverell Sitwell, *For Want of the Golden City*

Mr. Bentley's invitation to Mr Thomas to visit him at home on that Saturday afternoon had come as a complete surprise. Smiling, Bentley had gone on to state the time at which he hoped Thomas could arrive, and given him a piece of paper with his address already written out on it in neat block letters. It was as if he had planned the invitation well in advance, knowing exactly what Thomas' answer would be.

The two men were employed in the same office, and had occupied adjacent desks for several years. But their conversation rarely involved anything other than matters connected with their immediate tasks. If they were aware of each other's first names, they had never revealed any sign of it. Certainly neither had ever referred to the other by his given name. Although it would have been acceptable for Bentley to do so, it would have been beyond the bounds for Thomas to reciprocate. Outside of the office, however, there were no such rules. Nevertheless they were observed.

Until the words of invitation were uttered, Thomas had never seriously speculated on Bentley's home or the life he led there, away from the brightly lit office. He had also assumed that Bentley had no curiosity about his own circumstances. For instance, neither man could be sure whether or not the other was married. For a moment Thomas wondered if that was the reason for the invitation: Bentley was now engaged and wanted to ask the advice, as confidentially as possible, of another man—one younger and presumably more knowledgeable. Thomas hoped not: he was not married. The women he knew—and most of the men for that matter—were complex mysteries to him, and ones he had no desire to unravel and solve.

Thomas left his little house in Turnham Park in order to walk to the bus stop. A damp mist made it seem later than it actually was, and its damp, clinging coldness encouraged him to tuck his scarf in more closely around his neck. During this sort of weather, after returning from his Saturday half day ~~~~~~~~~~~~~~~~ ~~~~~~~~~~~~~~~~~~ ~~~~~~~~~~ ~~~~~ a light lunch, he usually stayed at home. As the afternoon drew on, he would put down his book and light a fire, sipping his tea as the flames danced and flickered. Sometimes he would switch on the radio, listening while the competing steady glow radiated from the perforated panel at the back of the cabinet. Either way Thomas kept himself sheltered in his cozy sitting room.

He had considered going to the trouble and expense of sending a telegram informing Bentley that he had been taken ill, very suddenly, and therefore, regretfully, could not keep the appointment. But that would only cause complications. He dreaded the many complexities that could gather around untruth. For a start, Bentley had seen him earlier and knew there had been nothing wrong then. On Monday he might simply repeat his invitation. Thomas did not wish to court the possibility of offence by a plain refusal, and it would scarcely be credible to invoke illness a second time. Yet again he read the scrap of paper bearing Bentley's address. Bentley had assured him that the bus he specified would carry him almost to the corner of the cul-de-sac where he lived, but as soon as he had reached home he had consulted his street atlas and worked out the route he would take if he were to walk from the bus stop at which he alighted each day he went to work. It had occurred to Thomas that he would, in that case, very likely be following Bentley's own route home. In any case, he wanted to walk. It would help take his mind off the churning anxiety he always felt at a major break with routine. It would also possibly furnish material for conversation, should that turn out to be necessary.

Bentley lived in a part of London that Thomas did not know at all. It was close to home and yet completely unexplored by him. He knew where Brentford was, and where to find Twickenham, but as to what lay between them he had very little idea. His mental map of the region was a distorted parallelogram, featureless, glaring white, with main roads fading out as they reached its indefinite border. He knew that one side of his blank area had the Thames for its boundary, and had supposed somewhere inescapably obvious like Hounslow Heath or London Airport must serve the same function at the opposite, and far, side. The map in the street atlas had narrowed things down and filled some of the gaps. Thomas had worked out that his destination was beyond Brentford and Spring Grove, but not as far as Whitton nor yet quite in Isleworth. If he were to reach the Great Chertsey Road he would have walked too far. The Southern Railway and the Sewage Works were impassable obstacles. If he encountered those he would have to retrace his steps.

The house was a semi-detached villa at the far end of the road by the turning circle. Thomas had dawdled while peering at the house numbers, when visible or existent. But he had found the place without getting lost, and was on time. Behind him, the road vanished into the thickening mist. Bare trees, recently pollarded, wiped the low, milky sky. The world he had come from and walked through was now, at best, remote. It was certainly not possible to look back at it. He shivered, and hoped he would feel warmer inside the house.

After Bentley had taken Thomas' coat and hat and hung them up on the stand in the hall, he indicated that Thomas should precede him up the carpeted stairs. The house seemed no warmer than the street. Thomas was glad he had chosen to wear a thick pullover as well as his usual jacket and tie. He had not wanted to appear too casual, nor yet ignore the fact that the working week had just ended. He was spending time with Bentley voluntarily, and not at the office in his position as a subordinate. Thomas saw that his host had changed out of the suit he had worn that morning. Bentley's concession to the weekend was the donning of a checked shirt and knitted tie, with jacket and trousers that were clearly more casual in cut, the material of each differing slightly.

"After you," Bentley said. "She will bring refreshments in a minute."

Thomas restrained himself from asking who 'she' was. He was sure Bentley had not mentioned a name. Each step up seemed to take a moment longer to release his shoe, and it seemed to swallow light it should.

As he trod warily in the dim light, he wondered if Bentley had meant his mother. Did he still live with his parents? The thought brought back childhood memories of bringing friends back home, out of school hours. Were they going to Bentley's bedroom, as if to play a game or read comics?

"Second door on the left," Bentley said. "I have the entire upstairs. Of course, we share the bathroom."

The front bedroom had been furnished as a sitting room and study, with a worn sofa, armchairs, and a low table. A heavy old desk crouched in front of the bay window. Shelves of dark wood, crammed with books and folders, lined the walls. Bentley flicked the light switch, but nothing more than a vaguely yellow glimmer escaped the lampshade to seep down from the ceiling.

Bentley pointed at one of the armchairs. "Sit you down, Raymond," he said. "Oh—you don't mind if I call you by your first name, do you? Now we are not at work, 'Mr Thomas' and 'Mr Bentley' would seem so unnecessarily formal, don't you think?" Without leaving time for Thomas to reply, Bentley continued, "I'm Gordon. We use first names here. Now I'll see what's happening about those drinks. Please excuse me for a moment."

Left alone in the room, Thomas gazed at the empty fireplace, which gaped like an open mouth. Books and papers were stacked on the mantelpiece, seemingly mocking gravity. On the wall over them was a framed picture, what looked like a drawing, black on white, of a distorted, rimless wheel or giant insect. It was hard to tell, in the congealed light. Whatever it was seemed to possess six spokes or limbs. He looked around, longing to find evidence of a working gas or electric fire, or any sort of portable heater, but there was none to be seen. He wondered what Bentley had meant by 'drinks'. He had certainly not expected anything alcoholic—at least, not this early in the afternoon—and it was surely too cold for lemonade or fruit cordial to be offered. Thomas wanted a cup of hot, strong, sweet, tea. He wanted a cup or mug to cradle in his hands and its heat to warm him through.

The door opened. "Here we are," Bentley said. "It was easier for me to bring them up myself. Edith can be very slow on those stairs. She has to be careful at her age, especially carrying things."

Bentley placed a large tray squarely on the table. There was a plate with a mound of plain, rectangular biscuits, two tall glass tumblers, and a glass jug full of a greenish-grey liquid.

"Ginger beer all right?" Bentley asked, as he filled the glasses. "We don't have hot drinks here. Or hot food either, for that matter."

Thomas dumbly took the glass held out to him, and picked a biscuit from the plate that Bentley also offered.

"Yes, Edith owns this house, and I rent the first floor. It's ideal for our little, well, society, you see, Raymond. At the present time there are but few of us. There should be six in all. Any more than that and it would have to be twelve, formed into a second group. Here we need six. There's the right amount of room for our meetings. Myself and Edith live in this house, and Timothy and Derek join us. Timothy lives in Richmond, and Derek in—oh, I keep forgetting, it's either Feltham or Sunbury. And there's Mr Heldman."

"I thought you said you were on first-name terms," Thomas said, swallowing the last of his biscuit.

"Ah, yes, you caught that. Very good!" Bentley laughed. "Yes indeed, except that Mr Heldman founded and leads our little group so is accorded a small but important honour. We are allowed to use his first name on our festive day."

Thomas took another biscuit from the plate Bentley held out in front of him. "Your festive day?"

"Yes, Raymond, our festive day. It's the Winter Solstice. The shortest day—'least light, most night' as Mr Heldman is wont to remind us. Unfortunately even though the solstice is the darkest day it is not usually the coldest day. We believe that's normally around now, the middle of January. It's certainly when a great number of people seem to be feel at their lowest ebb, if I may put it like that. It's also Mr Heldman's birthday. The seventeenth, that is."

"That's today," Thomas said.

"Yes, it is, isn't it," Bentley said. "Here, let me help you to some more ginger beer. Edith makes it herself."

Thomas leaned forward, putting his glass on the table. He wished he had the courage to stand up, grab his coat and hat, and leave. But he would only have to face Bentley again on Monday morning. He turned his head to look at the picture above the fireplace. The movement caused the frigid air to stir and brush past his face. He clamped his teeth together, in case they should start to chatter. He slipped his hands under his thighs, pushing them between the fabric of his trousers and the rougher material covering the armchair. If he could crush his hands hard enough perhaps his body would try to warm them. He felt heat draining from him.

"We don't have hot drinks or food here, Raymond," Bentley said kindly. "In our little group we have no need of them. Even a little abnormal heat is so unproductive." He poured more ginger beer into Thomas' glass. "There. I did say there should be six of us, didn't I?"

Thomas nodded. Perhaps the effort in the movement could help warm him. The friction of his shirt rubbing against his shoulders and neck: something like that.

"You only named five people," he said.

Bentley took a biscuit, broke it, and crammed both halves into his mouth. He chewed vigorously, and swallowed. Then he gazed at Thomas expectantly.

"You are fast to catch on," he said. "I think you have little difficulty in putting two and two together, Raymond." He reached for another biscuit. "And I am rather hoping you will not end up with four. We are not operating mere calculating machines now! Mr Heldman would be very pleased, I'm sure I may say that much."

The room was silent, except for the sound of Bentley breaking his biscuit into several pieces, which he ate slowly, one by one.

Thomas tried to make it seem that he was not looking anywhere, or at anything, in the room except Bentley. His gaze came to rest on the bay window. The small diamond-shaped panes, held together—or was it apart—by their strips of lead, were a net flung over grey cotton wool. For the first time he realised there were no curtains. The afternoon light seemed to have achieved some sort of equilibrium. It didn't seem to have grown any darker since he had last taken any notice of it.

The other man followed Thomas' stare.

"I remember those old pea souper fogs, don't you, Raymond?" he said. "When you'd step outside and not be able to see your hand in front of your face. Anything could happen, and often did, eh? We agree with all the new measures to cleanse the air. Our London fogs are pretty clean fogs these days, with so much less in the way of dirt and soot contaminating them. I suppose they will be eliminated altogether, one day.

"I always think—and I know Mr Heldman agrees with this—that white fog is colder. It does the job more effectively. White is our colour, you see, Raymond—or is it lack of colour? I'm never sure. Mr Heldman would know. Now it is the coldest, dreariest, lowest time of the year—the most 'immemorial' as Poe might have said of it—but it's the time when the cold mist can glow a spotless white, when the ice can take us beyond all that.

"But no fog at all is the best. One day we, the human race, will never be dreary or 'down' again, because we will be white and clean and frozen through. We will be unmoving and unthinking in an endless worship, clear as crystal and doing nothing but reflecting the light of the sun and moon. And for ever."

Bentley swallowed the last of his ginger beer and stood up. "Raymond, come and look at this."

Thomas followed him over to the empty fireplace. They stood in front of the picture.

"That is the most beautiful thing there can be," Bentley whispered. "A single flake of snow." He paused. "No, Raymond, I'm not quite correct there. The most beautiful sight of all must be an infinitude of snowflakes, dancing in a bright storm or crystallized, at rest in ice or in a snowfield extending to the horizon and beyond. But this one here—that's actually a photograph. Did you know that, Raymond? Out of all the millions and billions and trillions, no-one has ever seen two exactly the same. Did you know that? It was George, our last sixth, who captured that one and photographed it. He reversed the image and expanded it to make the lovely icon we keep here and which I have let you see now.

"Who would have thought that from this dull, ordinary stretch of London the six great arms will ... ... the time is right, and at Mr Heldman's decision, all the infinite number of snowflakes, ice crystals—each one different, Raymond, remember that—will join and their numberless differences will be swallowed. Each unique will join the Unique. There will be safety and security, oneness, and pure, everlasting, rest. And it will be for all."

Bentley's looming proximity and what seemed his increasing bulk brought Thomas out of his reverie. Had he already been frozen in place? The gloomy room was full of a musty dampness: the smell of winter mist and very slightly moist clothing clinging to everything, and impossible not to breathe. His collar felt tighter around his neck; he felt bloated, awkward and misshapen. Sweat broke out on his forehead, despite the chill of the room. Surely it had been Bentley who had eaten nearly all the biscuits and drunk most of the ginger beer. Thomas looked around for the door. When he had finally located it, he moved.

"Please, you must excuse me ... "

"Of course. The door at the top of the stairs. Don't be too long, Raymond. I haven't finished yet."

Soon Thomas did feel better. He stood up. The pale linoleum crackled beneath his shoes. Although he let the hot tap run for as long as he felt he could, there was only icy water for washing his hands. He wiped his face and looked in the mirror. One of its corners was cracked, and forming around the edges was a flaky white discolouration, apparently in the depths of the glass. In the hazy light it seemed to grow slightly even as he leaned in, squinting, to examine it.

He considered he options. No doubt Bentley was expecting that he return to him in the room at the front of the house. Perhaps, even now, Bentley was outside on the landing, waiting to conduct him back to his sanctum. If not, he could attempt to go downstairs and make his escape. On Monday morning he could plead an onset of stomach upset or some other ailment. He would be magnanimous with his conjectures on its origin. But the moment passed, with his resolve. He would have had to take the time to retrieve his coat, scarf, and hat, and Bentley might have come upon him. And there would have been Edith to consider.

Thomas unlocked the bathroom door. The first door on the landing—behind which lay, presumably, Bentley's bedroom—was now ajar, and a sliver of light fell across the increasingly viscid carpet. In contrast to all other light in the house, it was sharp and effective. It actually illuminated. Thomas gently pushed at the door. It rubbed against the carpet with the hiss of the sea gently ebbing. The only other sound, growing into audibility as he continued to push, was a low and monotonous droning. As soon as he had enough space, Thomas put his head around the door, clutching the handle and ready to retreat and pull the door back to how it had been.

The bedroom was as murky as the late afternoon expiring on the other side of the window. The source of the light, and noise, revealed itself to Thomas as a refrigerator, its door flung wide and kept from closing by a pile of books. Rearing up monumentally from the centre of the floor, it dominated the room, pouring forth a tide of bright creamy light. The fridge was unmistakably brand new, straight from the showroom. Its enamelled expanses were still a pristine sparkling white, and its chromium trimmings gleamed. The exposed interior yawned, coated with a thin layer of frost or even ice, but was otherwise utterly empty. The shelves and other fittings had been removed. The motor, hard at work, hummed an unvarying note.

Somehow the sight commanded his respect. Standing as if before a vacated tabernacle, or one as yet bare of a presence, Thomas heard again childhood hymns of the wilderness and holy places. In the desert or waste was all passion stilled. He did not advance any further into the room. Was that frost budding on the carpet? Eventually he backed away and pulled the door closed. He went on to where he knew that Bentley, rejoicing in the stolid patience of a glacier, was still awaiting his return.

More ginger beer and biscuits had been placed on the table during Thomas' absence.

"Ah, Raymond. Better, I trust?"

"Yes. Thank you."

"Good. Now, Raymond, I hope I shall have good news to tell Mr Heldman when he arrives?" Bentley glanced at his watch. "He shouldn't be long now. Then later, when Edith and the others—"

"Mr Heldman? Coming here?"

"Why, yes, Raymond. My dear chap, I thought you had been listening—as well as looking, eh?"

Bentley got up from the sofa and reached out, gripping Thomas' elbow. There was no pain, but he had to move as Bentley moved. They stood, once more, in front of the photograph hanging over the crowded mantelpiece.

"How can you not—"

"It's changed to a new shape," Thomas said.

"What? Oh, yes, very likely it has. I sometimes think so, too, but I can never be certain. I expect it means something—either way."

Thomas wrenched himself free.

"I want to go now," he said. "I have to get home. Forgive me, Gordon."

Thomas walked quickly, stumbling on uneven paving slabs, buttoning his coat as he went. When he reached the end of the road he stopped to adjust his scarf and hat. His breath crystallized. It was dusk. The sky was dirty concrete, with everything beneath it entirely shaded in grey and brown. The mist seemed to have purpose:

poised, about to regather in strength. The only relief came from windows not yet curtained, from streetlights and the headlights of slowly moving vehicles.

In the bus he dug in his pocket for coins to pay his fare. The first he found was a half crown, worn and dull. Clutching it as the conductor made his away along to him, he saw a rime of frost spread like a rash over the smooth metal, engulfing the barely distinct head of a king. He almost dropped his money.

"Sorry, it's the smallest I've got," he told the conductor. The ticket machine clattered and vomited. The conductor poured Thomas' change into his palm. The coins were very new, shiny and warm. Thomas smiled broadly.

"Jackpot," the conductor said, grinning as he moved on.

Thomas thought about staying on the bus past his stop, travelling on until it reached the terminus. Hands in his pockets he relaxed and immersed himself in the warmth and closeness of animated, breathing bodies. He welcomed the chatter and laughter, the banter and grumbles pressing in all around him. The misted windows, dripping with condensation; the garish adverts, the official notices; a bulging shopping bag placed squarely on his foot, which left a dull ache even after the woman, young and harassed, had smiled an apology and moved it: all cheered him. Cigarette smoke drifted across the aisle. There was a wave of coughing. Newspapers and magazines rustled like a gentle rain.

Routine asserted itself, and Thomas jumped off the bus as it started to pull away from his usual stop. He turned off the High Road, walking home along his normal route. As he approached the railway bridge the mist thickened. In the fog he could be anywhere: standing at the end of Bentley's cul-de-sac or still inside the house. Above him, a train clattered out of the station.

Thomas was grateful for the fog. He recognised it as the opposite of everything he had been told about during the afternoon. He strode on. He had never cared for surprises or departures from his tried and tested ways, but now the last of the day had drained away, the idea of further and different days lying in wait—all unformed, arbitrary—held, at last, pure appeal for him.

Later, he thought, he might forsake his little sitting-room with its bookcase and radio, and take the Tube into the West End. On the trains, in the stations beneath the streets, it would again be warm and bright, crowded and noisy. Thomas looked forward to the clamour and disorder—even to the dirt and grime, gathered, unyielding. Anything could happen. Perhaps it would begin to snow.

CAMP

DAVID NICKLE

Before everything, they had to get married.

That had happened just two days prior, at a little woodland bed and breakfast outside South River. There was some family, but it was mostly friends—in from Ottawa and Toronto, and Chicago where James had grown up. They laughed and drank and danced among the black flies and pine trees, the vivid afternoon light that laid the land in such sharp relief. When finally the friends and family went home they swapped out wedding luggage for camping gear from James' sister Evelyn's van, strapped their sea kayaks to the roof of the Honda . . . and James and Paul Berringer headed alone into the northern Ontario high summer.

The truck passed them the first time on a straight-away outside New Liskeard. It was a big silver GM pickup that rode high and was designed for sport more than work. James, driving, gave a polite wave, and Paul had thought he'd been waving at some road-weary toddler. Not so, as it turned out. *Some old bat*, James'd said. More than that it was hard to say, because the truck rode a good two feet higher than the Honda. To show what he meant, James gunned the motor at the next straight-away and sailed past the truck. Paul waved out the window as they passed. He bent to look in the side-view mirror, saw a hand emerge, salute off the top of the cab like it was a captain's hat.

The truck made its next pass on a curve, as the highway cut down close to a lake of tufted islands and wind-warped conifers. Two hands emerged from the passenger window that time, bestowing garlands of air kisses down onto the Honda. Paul tried to return the salute by jutting out his passenger window, propping ass on car door and waving over the top of the roof. But he remembered that the kayaks were there, about the same time as James shouted at him to quit fooling around and put his goddamn seatbelt on.

They laughed and drove, and turned up the music, and turned it down again when they wanted to talk and back up when they'd made their points, as the highway cut through blasted-out shield rock and trees that seemed to hang just over their heads. The truck showed up in the rear-view f̶ but it was gone as often as it was there. After awhile, they stopped checking for it. They were two guys on their honeymoon. They had other things on their mind. Christ.

They stopped, finally, in the late afternoon—at a place called Curt. The town wasn't much more than a co-op grocery store, a liquor store and a filling station, all along the highway. They slowed down and pulled into the grocery store's parking lot. It was late in the afternoon, and things didn't stay open that long up here. And the truck appeared again, pulling into the spot right beside them.

"You two are beautiful," said the man behind the wheel of the truck. "Don't know if you knew that. But you're goddamn beautiful. You're glowing."

Paul leaned out the passenger window and smiled wide and toothy.

"Just married," he said. Beside him, in the driver's seat, James grinned and waved and Paul wondered if that might just be that. The man was about seventy—with close-cropped hair and a deep tan over a heavily lined face. His beard was longer, and it was win-ter-white. Sharp blue eyes twinkled in deep-set lines. His own wife rode shotgun. She was plumper, and more tanned, with reddish hair pulled in a ponytail that reached out the back of her sun visor. *How do a couple like them deal with a couple like us?* Paul wondered.

But when she said, "Honeymooners?" both Paul and James nodded and grinned.

"Honeymooners," he said, and James said again: "Just married."

The old man opened the door and stepped gingerly out of the cab. He was wearing a pair of walking shorts, and his legs were thin as sticks. Sandaled feet crunched on the gravel.

"It's not hard to tell," he said, and grinned. "Did your wedding go well? I don't even have to ask that, do I?"

"Now you're off on an adventure." His wife came out from around the back of the truck. She had a canvas bag that looked like it was stuffed with other canvas bags. "Those are beautiful boats you have on your roof." She and her husband made a show of admiring them.

"They're our wedding gift to each other," said James, and explained that they were just the right size for hauling the two of them and a full camp kit, and how they hoped their camping trip wouldn't be too much of an adventure. Paul started introductions, and it developed that they were talking to Stanley Green and his wife Nancy. Stanley once worked in natural resources. Nancy used to be a compositor for a newspaper. They had been married for 43 years. The last ten, they'd lived up here.

"We bought an old YMCA camp on Scout Lake," said Stanley, and Nancy said, "It was his idea," and Paul said, "Oh, it was like that was it?" and everybody laughed.

Paul leaned on the hood of the Honda, and James easily wended under his arm. It was getting cooler here than they were used to, although the late afternoon sun made the town look lovelier, warmer. Nancy brought out a silver steel thermos and four plastic travel mugs. IF YOU DON'T STAND BEHIND OUR TROOPS, WE CAN ARRANGE FOR YOU TO STAND IN FRONT OF THEM, was written on the side of Paul's.

She set them on the wheel well of the truck, and poured. Paul sipped his. It was Irish coffee, with an emphasis on the Irish. He grinned like a baby. James wasn't as pleased—he had to drive, after all, and they weren't planning on stopping. But like Paul, he liked the Greens. They'd seen a "glow" about them. Where was the harm, really, in a bit more glow from Nancy Green's thermos?

They finished their coffee, gave the mugs back and made it into the store just fifteen minutes before it closed and checked out with a box of supplies five minutes after it closed. Paul looked around for the truck—but it was long gone.

"That's too bad," said James when Paul pointed that out. "They were nice folks. Would have been good to say a proper goodbye." Then he craned his neck, looking at their car, and said, "What the fuck?"

Paul set his box of groceries down on the gravel and pulled the folded sheet of paper from underneath their windshield wiper. He unfolded it.

"It's a map," he said, and held it up. "Scout Tourist Region." James checked it out. The lake was a maze of inlets and islands. It suggested the shape of a horse with a rider. Kind of like an old time scout, Paul thought. There was a big X on one of the islands, toward the western end. The highway was at the east. There was a note in a spot of clear water, written using the same thick pencil as the X.

GREAT MEETING YOU 2! WHY DONT YOU JOIN US AT THE Y? BRING A BEDROLL & THOSE PRETTY KAYAKS— JUST SHOW UP & WE TAKE CARE OF THE REST! XOX YR HWY 11 FRIENDS STAN & NANC

The whiskey in the coffee made James too sleepy to drive and Paul couldn't say he was in any better shape, so they found a little road-side motel twenty-odd kilometers on, and sacked out for the night.

When they settled in, Paul opened up the map on the pine-covered breakfast table and did finger measurements. "Shit," he said. "That's about twelve kilometers in."

"Give or take a thumb," said James. "You're not seriously thinking about this?"

"Scout Lake's a lot closer than Quebec. Just another hour up the highway, the way you drive."

That drew a playful slap, and James bent over the map, made

Paul show him what the route would be. He commented that it looked like a pretty run, but he counted more than twelve kilometers.

"But that's not here nor there," said James. "Fact is, that's a long way in. And we don't know these people."

"Sure we do. Stanley worked in natural resources. Nancy . . . worked in newspapers or something. They carry open liquor in the cab of their truck."

"They pick up glowing men on the highway."

"I'd pick up glowing men on the highway. So would you."

"That's why we're together."

They laughed, but James wondered about that: whether they might just be old-school swingers with a dose of bi-curiosity. "I don't want to go there just to find we have to sponge bath old Stan while Nancy watches on the webcam," he said. Paul thought about that, and agreed: *Yeah, it's possible.* But he didn't take that impression from those two, and cornered on the subject, James admitted that he didn't either. They both took another look at the map.

Depending on the wind, they agreed that, twelve kilometers or fourteen, they could probably make the run in under four hours. Just to be on the safe side, they'd pack some food and a tent—the camp stove—the first aid kit—and the rifle. They could camp out on an island, if it turned out they had to.

The map showed the marina as being right on the highway's edge, but that wasn't how it played out. There was a little sign on the side of the road with an arrow pointing to a long dirt road, which first wound through bush, then dropped on a steep slope between high rounded rocks. Here and there, the dirt road passed a driveway that climbed those hills—and sometimes, Paul could peer up and see parts of houses poking out of the trees overhead. Twice, they had to deal with oncoming traffic: pickup trucks that appeared in front of them with terrifying suddenness and speed.

But they made it. The rocks and trees finally spread, and the marina appeared, in a little natural harbour rimmed with low cliffs and right across from a pair of knuckly little islands. There was a place to park, and a boat launch, and a couple of long docks with outboard motor boats tied up. There was even a little general store that sold wine by the box.

It wasn't an hour before they were in the lake and paddling over still waters, to the sweet space between those first two islands.

After two hours on the lake, they stopped on a little island that seemed to have been furnished for the purpose—with a firepit and a weathered wooden bench for fishing with a toilet seat on it that was not, as it developed, a proper chemical toilet.

The wind was picking up, and they were paddling into it. As they chewed on cold cuts and breakfast bars, James and Paul looked at their maps, and revised their estimated arrival time. Paul wished they could call ahead to say they were coming later—but as James reminded him, Stan and Nancy left no phone number on the map. Just the pencilled-in X.

After lunch, they crossed from the horse's tail to the wide expanse of Scout Lake's belly. Here, the winds were fierce. They moved along the shore, taking shelter in tiny inlets where water lilies grew.

A front blew in from the east and rain came and went, as they crossed the horse's hind legs. This time, they didn't take shelter, and the rain soaked them. The sun came out, and the wind died back, and they poached in their wet clothes as they pushed along low rock faces and cliffs.

"Not far now!" shouted James, and Paul laughed, and James said, "Wow."

"What?" Paul shouted. They were maybe forty feet apart, drifting a moment in the stilled water.

James pointed with his paddle, ahead of them. They were coming onto a promontory—a long tongue of rock and dirt, where a patch of tall, brambled branches—you wouldn't call them trees—clustered. Although it was the height of the summer, their twisted limbs had no leaves. At every crook in the branches, they could see a black speck.

The two kayaks drifted nearer one another as they watched. "Birds," Paul opined, and James added that there were "a fuck of a lot of birds." They dipped paddle and pushed nearer, and although they were as quiet as kayakers could be, before long it was clear they'd set off some sort of alarm. Black wings cut across the water and long sine waves of black-bodied birds emerged from the water. One snaked directly over James' boat, and Paul looked closer and said: "Cormorants!"

They both had a vague idea of what cormorants looked like. There had been a colony of the birds in the city, on some parkland near the lake. The birds were ugly up close, and they ate too much fish, and their shit killed trees, and there'd been a hand-wringing debate about whether to kill them off to save the waterfront and a long segment on the CBC with some breathtaking pictures.

But what did James and Paul know about cormorants, really?

They lifted their paddles from the water and sat still, watching as more of the birds took flight, spun off in lines around them—circling, as if the birds were watching them, making sure they didn't tarry too close. Protecting their nests . . . their families.

Paul wondered about adopting.

"Where did that come from?" asked James—they hadn't talked about having kids, not really—and Paul shrugged.

"It's the future," he said. "It'd be nice, having a son. In the future."

A cloud thinned, and the sun came pale and yellow through it.

"A son?"

"Or a daughter. But if we get to pick—"

"—a son." James considered. "We'd need a bigger place," he said.

Paul thought their place was fine for raising a boy. There were three bedrooms and there could be one for the two of them, another one for the office, and a third for the boy. The place was small and there wasn't much of a yard—but it wasn't much of a hardship, surely it couldn't be much of a hardship.

Paul didn't say any of that, though. He looked back at the shore, watched as the birds returned to their perches—to the bare soil and rock there. They had shapes like vases, standing upright.

James dipped a paddle into the water and started to turn his kayak about. "We should keep moving," he said, and Paul agreed. They both turned the boats away from the colony, and continued further along the shore of the lake.

It was only when they were far away from the birds and their squawks and their black, jagged-looking wingspans, that it occurred to either of them: what a stench the colony carried. It was the foulest thing either of them had ever smelled.

Although neither remarked on it, both of them thought it stank of death.

The sun came out past the noon hour, and all the clouds vanished, and the lake grew quite warm indeed. James stripped off his fleece, and lashed it to the front of the kayak. Paul kept his on just a little longer, and pulled off his and his shirt too, and strapped his life jacket back on over bare skin.

"Okay," said Paul, "you win. No boy right now."

"I didn't say we shouldn't."

"You didn't need to."

They laughed, and Paul asked: "Where are we on the map?"

James fumbled for the paper.

He'd stuffed it in his fleece jacket's pocket, which was lashed to the front of the boat. He raised up, and leaned forward—and took hold of the cloth. The kayak seemed to wriggle as he did so.

Paul thought: *Oh shit*, just as James thought the same. And all at once, the kayak tilted.

James threw himself back, slapped at the water with the flat of his paddle, and tried to twist his shoulders away from the tilt, reclaim his centre of gravity. It was no good. He started to pinwheel the oar, as though he thought he might paddle through air the same as water.

The kayak pitched over. James shouted, maybe screamed, and splashed into the water as the kayak pitched the rest of the way.

It was very still, and hot. The two dry bags that were lashed to the kayak came loose, and bobbed up, one at a time, alongside the kayak's sky-blue hull. James' fleece spread just beneath the water, like a torso-shaped oil slick.

Paul called out James' name: first in the quit-fucking-around tone that James had used the day before, on the highway, when Paul was trying to prop his ass on the edge of the door.

Except for the ripples radiating out from the dry bags, the kayak, the water was a looking glass.

"James!"

Paul shattered that glass with his paddle and drew himself closer to James' still kayak. There had been no struggling, no bubbles, still, as there would have been, if James had pulled himself free of the cockpit, or even if he were trying.

When Paul got close enough, he slid the paddle underneath the hull, where James would be. He might be able to catch hold of it—use it as leverage to pull himself up again, pull himself out. To safety.

Paul didn't let himself consider certain matters: there was no sign of his husband underneath the boat. Even if he were sitting as still as he could, inverted in the kayak, there would have to be some sign of it on the surface: some small stream of bubbles. But how could he be sitting still, under the lake in an inverted kayak? Why would he be sitting still, fully conscious, aware of the fact that he only had so much air, and not struggle to right the kayak—to get out and save himself, before his air ran out and he drowned?

The paddle cut through empty water, and clunked against the plastic gunwales of the little boat, rocking it easily in the water, and this forced Paul to consider: nothing was underneath the boat.

James was not under the boat. He was not, in fact, anywhere.

A dozen cormorants flew so low their feet trailed in the water. They came close to Paul—so close he might have caught one with the blade of his paddle. But he kept still, watched them until they passed, then returned to the water, which he regarded with empty fascination. The air grew cool as the sun fell beneath the line of trees. Insects buzzed in his ear as James' kayak drifted off, the dry bags scattering in their own directions.

As the first star emerged—probably not a star at all, but a planet, maybe Jupiter—in a deepened sky—Paul drew a breath.

He thought it might have been his first.

He dipped his paddle into the water, and drew it to the kayak's bow, and slid backward through the dark water. There was no moon. There were stars, scattering thick across the middle of the sky, but they weren't enough. They left the ~~~~~~~~~~~~~

He paddled backward twice more, and turned himself in another direction—by how much, he couldn't tell—and proceeded. James was gone. The dry bags, the kayak—he left them all.

The night air was cool and numbing, and he warmed himself with exertion—paddling harder and driving the kayak faster across the lake. The water was still as it had been in the afternoon, and the stars reflected in it, dully, stretching infinity below him.

And Paul shut his eyes against even the pale light of the twinning stars, and thought: *It's just me now.*

Did he sleep?

He must have, for when he opened his eyes, it was to a bloody red dawn. The air was hot, and mist rose off the water and swirled about him. He was near a shore, but not one he recognized—this was high, round rock, topped with trees that looked to have been denuded by fire. Nearer the waterline, sharp stumps and rocks like broken teeth rose out of the mist. In their midst . . . a dock lolled, like a grey and splintered tongue, from the base of the rock.

He guided the kayak through the rock and wood, until its tip touched the wood. A moment later, he was stretched on the dock, pulling the kinks from his legs.

He lay back, and looked up the rock-face. It was a strange place to put a dock, for there was no easy way to get up the rock face; it was nearly sheer here, and a good 20 feet up to the remainder of the woods, branches peeking over the lip of the cliff like an untrimmed brow. He felt a smile grow on his face.

And he thought again: *I am alone.*

His smile wavered. He sat up. Looked out through the mist. Its slow swirl fascinated him, and he cocked his head to watch it turn and bend, and as he watched, his smile vanished, as thoughts of speeding down a highway—hanging out the car window, feeling the wind . . . laughing, with him . . .

He bent his head away from the lake, and shut his eyes, and tensed, as a part of him fought . . . fought to return, to remember. He was having a difficult time remembering, anything really.

He gripped his own thighs, and rocked, and his lips struggled with the word, with the name of what he'd lost . . .

. . . of what he'd come for . . .

He opened his eyes, and stood on the dock. The kayak, he saw, was starting to drift off—so he bent over, and reached with his foot. He dragged it back, and took a breath, and put it together, and said it aloud:

"James."

He was losing himself. There had been a second kayak, just like this one—the day before, the time before. As this kayak bumped back against the dock, he considered that moment—James, his husband. And the still water, beneath which he'd vanished.

He tried to hold that in his mind. James. The second kayak. Their wedding.

The long paddle through the night, across the lake of stars . . .

With an effort, he hefted an end of the kayak onto the dock, and hauled it the rest of the way along, until the length of the boat was safe on the dock.

Then, he turned his attention to the rock face.

It was smooth; there didn't seem to be a way to climb it without gear. But it didn't make sense that anyone would put a dock here, if there weren't some way up. Most likely, this was set up to be a portage.

There had to be a reason for the dock. It had to lead to somewhere.

He ran his hands along the stone, and peered into the thinning mist at the base. There was no way up immediately, but there was a slick ledge, at nearly the water's edge, that fell off into the water. Tentatively, he put a toe on it. Maybe there was some stairs, some kind of a ladder, further along. He put a foot on it. He slid into the water, ankle-deep, then came up against a cleft that seemed as though he could balance on.

He put his weight on that foot, and drew the other into the water. It was icy cold, but he could not─

He made his way along the rock face in this way.

And as he proceeded, memory started to become clearer, and his situation clarified—and he thought about James, and the overturned kayak . . . and how he froze, and sat there in his kayak, as his new husband vanished. Why had he not jumped in? Finished the search? Why had he left . . . so easily?

He made it a dozen feet along, so disquieted by these new thoughts that he only heard the outboard motor when it stopped.

"Well hello!"

Stanley Green waved from the back of the aluminum boat, as his wife Nancy sat at the bow, binoculars fixed on him. They were wearing colored windbreakers—Stanley's blue, Nancy's a brilliant yellow. A fishing rod hung over the side of the boat, lure glinting in the mist.

He didn't wave.

"Where's your friend?" said Stanley Green, and Nancy clarified: "Your husband?"

He turned in the water so he faced them, leaning against the rock face. The boat was maybe three dozen yards off, and they had to shout to be heard.

He shouted an answer.

"Oh my!" Nancy said, and Stanley shouted: "Where? Where'd it happen?"

For that, he had no answer. He'd crossed the lake at night, paddled through the stars. It was the other side of *that*.

Stanley and Nancy conferred, and Stanley turned back to him, and shouted that he'd bring the boat in, and get him, and they could go look for his friend together.

He trembled, and slid, and he steadied himself in the water, as Stanley bent over the outboard. What was Stanley doing there, this quiet morning, tugging at a rope on the top of the thing?

There was a terrible coughing sound, and a roar—and it sent his heart pounding . . . and he spun about in the water, and felt it sheathe off his feet, his long and slender legs—

He rested a moment, on top of the rocks, the scoured forest at his back. The view of the lake was more commanding from here; the height made him feel better . . . safer.

The two in the boat were talking to each other. He couldn't understand what they said. But they were pointing at the dock as they spoke. They were confused, and frightened. The boat moved close to the dock, and they both climbed out. He craned his neck over the edge of the rock, peered down curiously at them. She looked up, and pointed, and her husband looked at him too.

Their eyes were wide, and wet, and afraid, and above all—guilty.

And he had enough of it. So he spread his arms wide, and pushed down on the heavy morning air, and left them there on the dock.

Paul finally found James that afternoon, in the cleft between a small rocky island and the shore. It wasn't difficult—he had eyes for this kind of thing, and Paul would recognize James anywhere. He circled twice just to be sure, then narrowed his wings just so, and let the earth pull him down. James flashed silver, as though signalling him, making a perfect target . . . and when the surface of the water broke, Paul took James around the middle, and his gills twitched in recognition, as Paul broke the surface again, and took back to flight.

The two didn't speak after that. There were no words necessary.

They flew in silence, close to the water this time, as Paul guided them both, by prehistoric instinct, to the camp—the place where they were both expected, where hungry mouths waited.

A DELICATE CRAFT

D.P. WATT

His first months in England had been prosperous, maybe even the first couple of years. There was plenty of work, too much really. He had, regrettably, had to turn people away. If only there were so much now. Early on he had regularly sent money home to his mother in Białystok and even to his sister in Łodz. But, now that he was forced to make do with seasonal jobs picking vegetables on local farms, he could barely pay for his little room, with its increasing bills, in the house that he had shared with his four friends that had come over with him from their homeland, back in 2006.

They were all capable tradespeople. Bogdan was the plumber among them and they always joked that he would be the first one to make his million pounds. For most of those couple of years they had worked on construction sites around Nottingham and across Leicestershire. They were a happy team and the regular money, from a decent employer, provided them a good life.

That all ended with the recession. Then, early in 2009, Tomasz, the plasterer, was caught up in a fight in the city centre, whilst trying to protect two girls from what turned out to be their boyfriends. He ended up with a broken bottle through the back of his neck and would be in a wheelchair for the rest of his days. When his family came over to collect him he asked Bogdan to promise him that when he called, to say he'd had enough, Bogdan would fly back to Poland and put a pillow over his face. Thankfully the call had not yet come, and besides he couldn't afford the flight ticket anymore.

Piotr, the electrician, was the next to leave, in 2010. His wife, who had stayed at home in Bydgoszcz, was pregnant and he'd decided that he'd rather bring his child up at home, now that the decent work had dried up. "Nie fantazyjne zbieranie kapusty na resztę mojego życia," he'd said, "pozwól im wybrać własne warzywa, albo głodować, nie obchodzi mnie, który." Maybe he'd been right, Bogdan often thought.

Viktor was originally from Dresden, but his family had moved to Wrocław for work when he was younger. He spoke six languages and had helped them all arrange coming over to England—it had been his idea in the first place. He had studied engineering and always got a good salary for his site management skills. He'd gone back to Germany in 2011, as there was a big contract that needed preparing in Dusseldorf before a team of thirty site managers and technicians headed out to Iraq to build shopping centres. Bogdan did not want to go to such a hot country and neither did Michał, the brickie, the last of the others that was left. It would have been better for him to go, for now he spent his days drinking cheap beer and moaning about the lack of work. Bogdan had tried to get him to come to the farms and work with him but Michał said he hated the countryside of "to zielony i pieprzony nieprzyjemne ziemi" and wanted to work in a factory instead—"ale nie kurwa noc zmiany!" He'd been unemployed for two years now.

On Saturday afternoons Bogdan would manage to muster enough enthusiasm from Michał to go down to their local pub and have a couple of drinks. It was unwise to stay out too late, with all the trouble that happened in the city, always with Tomasz in their minds. At least in their local there was more of a family mood about the place in the afternoons, and they kept their voices down in the corner of the Lounge area, where a few older regulars enjoyed playing cards.

It was in late October 2012 when Bogdan bumped into Agnes, on his way home, having left Michał with a few friends from

Leicester who were celebrating before they went home to Warsaw the following week. It was time he left too, he thought.

Just as he turned into Bottle Lane, his head full of thoughts of home, he bumped into an old lady just coming round the corner. Thankfully she didn't fall over, but her shopping basket went flying and, amid the few tins and packets of a widow's groceries rolling about the pavement a reel of white lace unfurled itself. She yelped in horror as it rolled towards a large muddy puddle in the gutter. Bogdan jumped forwards and tapped it back with his foot, saving it from a rather disastrous and filthy drenching.

"Oh, thank you, *thank* you, thank *you*," she said, with a childish energy, almost jumping for joy. "Oh, that would have been terrible, you know. I've just finished that reel for my friend Nancy's granddaughter's wedding dress trim. It's in two weeks' time and I was just going round to drop it off there now. It would have been ruined if you hadn't saved it. I could never have made another in time."

Bogdan was crouched down reeling the delicate cloth back onto its cardboard spindle. He could feel its intricate pattern trace through his fingers as he wound. It was not a smooth texture, rather more like fine cotton. There was something earthy and real about it, unlike silk.

"There is no need to thank me, madam," Bogdan said, holding the lace up to her as he continued to gather her groceries. "I was not being mindful of where I was going and should apologise to you for almost knocking you into the road."

"Ah, you sweet boy," she said, offering the basket so he could place everything inside. Her hands were contorted and twisted with arthritis and they seemed to wrap around the handle of the basket like wisteria. "There's no harm done is there. Now, I know that accent, don't tell me . . . don't tell me . . . "

Bogdan stood there waiting while she screwed her face up into a very peculiar expression. She stared at him for a few moments and then shut her eyes. He wondered if she might have fallen asleep, standing up with the basket in her hands.

He started to feel a little awkward.

"You're from Poland," she said. The words bursting out of her so rapidly that it startled him.

"Well, yes I am," he said. "My name is Bogdan, and I am a plumber, although now I do not find much of this kind of work anymore. There is not the money for people to afford this so much now."

He had found himself walking along beside her as she headed off down the road.

"I'm very pleased to meet you, Bogdarn," she said. "I'm Agnes, Agnes Cottar. Do you know how I knew where you were from?"

"Er, no Miss, er Mrs Cotter, I do not," he said.

"It's Mrs, although my Alfred's long gone now," she said. "It was Alfred's friend, and his wife, that's how I knew. They were Poles you see. Came over just before the war. My Alfred met him while he was in the RAF, you know. Zeb and Anna. We used to call him Zeb because we couldn't say his full name, couldn't get our tongues round it—Zebigenuf, something like that I think it was."

"Zbigniew," Bogdan said.

"That's it!" Agnes said, stopping abruptly. "We used to go around theirs on a Friday night and drink a lovely cherry vodka he used to make, and play Whist until the early hours. They were a lovely couple. Of course, he had to stay over here after the war because the Russians were arresting all the old officers from before the war and shooting them, or something horrible like that. And their little girl died a year before the war started, so they hadn't got much to go back for anyway. Him and my Alfred even started a little business up in the sixties, doing odd jobs for folks. Didn't come to much though and they both ended up at the Waterworks. Good job that though, and a decent pension too."

They had started walking again halfway through this and Bogdan found he was interested by this old woman.

"So you made that lovely cloth I so nearly ruined?" he said.

"Oh, yes, I've been making lace since I were a little girl," she said, stopping again and turning to him. "My mother made lace and so did my grandmother, of course she used to work in the factories then, my grandmother that is, making it by the yard. But always, as a family, we also did the bobbin work at home. I could show you if you'd like to know how to do it."

This came as quite a surprise to Bogdan. He had only moments to think about it but, why not. She was obviously very kindly and passionate about her hobby. Spending a few hours helping an old lady around her house, and also easing the loneliness he assumed she must suffer, would be fair for almost destroying her handiwork and sending her flying.

"That is a very kind invitation, Mrs Cottar," he said. "I should love to learn a little of this skill from you."

"Oh, none of that *Mrs Cottar* nonsense, it's Agnes," she said, taking a little notebook from her basket. "Now here's my address. You pop round next Saturday afternoon, and we'll have a first go. Sorry I can't do anything before then 'cause I've got the cleaner in on Monday, my hair on Tuesday, and the girls from the club are taking me out Wednesday for Sue's retirement do—although she doesn't half look a cracker for her age, you know. Thursday I've got to finish off a lace order for a company in Stow. They always like the handmade stuff! And Friday I always go for lunch with my friend Arnie, from the market."

"Alright then, Agnes, thank you very much," Bogdan said. Clearly she wasn't in desperate need of company then. "I shall call at your house around midday then."

"That'll be lovely, Bogdarn," she called back at him, having already set off at quite a pace.

"Sorry again for the accident," he called after her. She waved it away in the air as she darted around a corner.

Bogdan looked about him and wasn't quite sure which street he'd ended up in. He soon found his way back home though, smiling to himself about Agnes. It was one of those uplifting encounters that brightens any day.

The next Saturday found him in Agnes' little front room, in a row of old terraced houses, surrounded by the clutter, souvenirs and inscrutable memorabilia of a long life, filled with loves and losses.

He'd already been shown the photograph of Alfred and Agnes with 'Zeb' and Anna down at 'the club' on New Year's Eve 1974. It was thrust upon him almost as soon as he entered the door. He'd also been shown the award Agnes won five years previously for her embroidery—it seemed any work of thread and stitch came naturally to her. Conversation flowed almost as though no time had passed since they had met in the street and he soon found himself in a crumbling paisley chair whose seat was disintegrating and, he thought, barely capable of supporting his weight.

Agnes had prepared scones and jam for him, and even bought a pot of clotted cream which she said she summer. But he was a special guest, she said, and so she had to get him something nice, "as a treat". He didn't want to tell her that cream, or dairy products of any sort, made him feel sick.

"And my grandmother knew Rose and Lucy Hubbard, when they set up their little agency to help all the homeworkers," Agnes said, apropos of nothing, pouring out some tea through a beautiful silver strainer. "Oh, yes, my grandmother knew them very well indeed. Most of her work came from Rose, you know—beyond the factory hours, you know."

Bogdan didn't really know these people that she spoke of, or what factory hours were. He just nodded. Agnes had a beautiful, melodic voice that was just betrayed, with a slight fracture, now and again, due to her age.

"It was a good job too, an' all. What with six children on her hands by that point, and two more to come. Do you take sugar?" Agnes ran the sentences into each other and it took a moment for Bogdan to realise that he had been asked a question.

"Oh, yes, thank you, two sugars," he stuttered. "And I don't take the milk, if you please."

"Oh really, no milk. That's just like my Alfred. He liked it almost as black as coffee, also with two sugars." She ladled two heaped spoons into his cup, her arthritic fingers did not allow her to stir with any precision though and a few slops of tea gushed into the saucer with each stir of the spoon. "Now, there I go again, what a messy pup! I'll get a cloth."

"No please do not trouble yourself," Bogdan said, jumping to his feet. "You tell me where it is and I will fetch it for you. It is very kind of you to invite me here and I must help, if I am able."

"Well, what a polite young man you are, Bodgarn," she said, with a little smile. "There's a tea towel through on the side table in the kitchen."

The kitchen, if such it was, was an education. It belonged in a museum. There was no fridge, or indeed any 'appliance' that might be termed modern. An ageing gas cooker, with an eye-level grill was the only concession to anything like the age they were actually in. An old Belfast sink, set low, had a few plates and saucers in it. A rickety tap dripped into it, perched on the end of a copper pipe caked in verdigris. It's only days before that blows, he thought, I could fix her up a new one some time. But the tap had been there forty years, its demise was either unlikely or imminent.

He found the tea towel and took it back to the lounge. As he handed it to her their forefingers touched and a little electric shock passed between them.

"Oh," Agnes yelped, but began laughing almost instantly. "That's what my dad used to call the 'shockers'. He had a new jumper from my mother, from Woolies, one year—God, their clothes were terrible, I don't know why she got stuff from them, she could make much better herself—and he would rub his hands on it and creep up behind us kids and just touch the back of our ears, and do the "shockers". He only did it to mother once, she clipped him one and split his lip. I used to hate it but my brothers loved it and he'd always end up in a rough and tumble with them afterwards. He was a lovely man, my father. Do you have a name for it, the "shockers"—*you people*, I mean?"

Bogdan had heard this phrase "you people" many times before, normally shouted at him and his friends in the town at night and often accompanied by "go home" or "stole our jobs". He knew Agnes did not mean this though. It was a genuine question—a true care for, and pleasure in, difference.

"No, I do not think so," he said, simply. "If there is such words for this, I do not know them, I am sorry."

"Well, no matter—it must have just been just our dad then, I never heard anyone else call it that either. As I say, you're a very polite young man, it makes a nice change to have someone so polite around, and one interested in the lace. It's rare to find such interest in young people," Agnes said, handing him his cup with a jittery hand that threatened a repeat of the earlier spillage.

"Thank you, I try my best," Bogdan replied. "I am interested in all things that require skill and effort."

"That's lovely, that is, young Bogdarn," she said, pushing aside the tea tray and taking a roll of linen from a basket at her side. She undid the cloth ties around it and opened it on the coffee table before her. There were little compartments within, each with a couple of sticks of turned and polished wood within.

"We're going to learn bobbin lace—and I'm still learning, I can tell you; a very old craft, and it needs its tools, as all such crafts do—tools refined and perfected over generations. Now these are what we call bobbins," she said, taking one of the sticks out of its neat little compartment. It was made of wood, with a dark varnish that had long since worn away in its middle, from years of use. At its base there was a purple bead, threaded on copper wire through a large hole in the wood. "They come in pairs, you see. So that you know which belongs with which."

Bogdan took the thing from her. It was light and simply made, with a few different turns up and down its length, and some basic ridges here and there. He rolled it back and forth in his fingertips, as though assessing its merit. He was well aware of the importance of quality tools and attempted to transfer to this new skill his understanding of his own.

"I find those little ridges very handy now my eyes aren't quite so good," Agnes said. "You can feel which one you have and find its partner, just by touch. Close your eyes and I'll show you."

He did. She placed about six bobbins, of varying lengths, in his other hand and closed his fingers around them. Her skin was smooth and cold.

"Now you find the partner bobbin to the one in your left hand," she said.

Within a moment he had found it.

"You *see*," Agnes chuckled. "This is a work of the *fingers*, as much as the eyes."

He rolled the bobbins back and forth in his hand, coming to know them.

"Lots of people collect these now," she said, with regret. "It's such a shame to think of all of them lying idle about the country in old jam jars, or displayed in cabinets. I admit, they're very pretty, but they were made for making and not for lazing—much like ourselves."

She started a long list of dos and don'ts, along the lines of, "Always use brass pins, so they don't rust in the pillow—that makes an almighty mess of the lace." Bogdan had a job keeping up with the information she was heaping upon him. And then, as though pausing at a point before the crescendo of perfectly scored piece of music she said, "First though we will make your lace pillow."

And so they did. It was a rich blue velvet, with a gold trim around the edge that came from a reel of braid Agnes' Aunt had made many years before. It was Agnes' gift to him. He was pleased with the pillow and the trim, more pleased than he had been with anything in a long time.

Over the coming weeks he learnt the basics of making bobbin lace—the winding of the bobbins; how to prepare a pricking pattern and then to make it; dressing the pillow and how to move the lace across it when working on collars or trim; lengthening and shortening threads; starter stitches: cloth stitch, half stitch and cloth stitch and twist; the differences between Torchon, Cluny, and Bucks Point lace.

The weeks became months. Sometimes he'd go to see Agnes on a Wednesday afternoon, but mostly on a Saturday. He'd stopped going to the pub on Saturday afternoons now, and spent most evenings practicing his lace. Michał didn't notice. He'd become even more withdrawn and bitter. It looked likely they'd both be getting evicted soon as they had been unable to find anyone else to share the house and were very behind on the rent. At that point, Bogdan thought, he'd have to go home, and had started saving the odd five pound note, for a flight back, inside the cover of a book on lace-making that Agnes had lent him—he thought it unlikely that Michał, who he was sure had been rifling through his things for money, would look in there.

During the strawberry season Bogdan had a lot of work, and he was working ten hours a day for almost three weeks, without a break. He'd called at Agnes' house one night after work and explained he would probably not see her until early the following month. She understood and said it was clear that that was the main thing. He grimaced a little and she touched his hand tenderly saying, "Don't you worry dear, I've earmarked a beautiful pattern for us to start once you're ready, it's one of my mother's and I'd been saving it for a special day."

The special day came and she pricked out the pattern on his pillow and guided him through the first turns of the work. Tea flowed but Bogdan's progress was frustratingly slow.

"I would give anything to have the skills you have," he said, draining a cup, and resuming his slow progress on the pattern.

"Really?" Agnes said. "Would you give anything?"

"Oh, yes," he replied, concentrating on selecting the right bobbin to thread over the one in his left hand. "To know something—to truly master it—that is what life is all about isn't it. I want to be well trained at what I do, and you have been a wonderful teacher, but then it will take me many years of practice and hard work to be as accomplished as you are at it."

"Anything at all?" Agnes said, distantly, as though she had not been listening.

"Yes," he said again, firmly.

"Then look at me," Agnes said, taking his hands from their work and holding them in her tiny, deformed fingers.

He did not really understand, but turned to her and looked into her eyes, the colour of which was difficult to discern in the half-light of her front room, and beneath the folds of the wrinkles that gathered around her eyes, threatening to enfold them in darkness.

"May we find this wish heard higher. *These* hands are for *doing*, for *making* and *learning*," she began, as though reciting an old childhood nursery rhyme. She had turned his palms upright and traced a line down each with her thumbs.

"*These* hands are for *nursing*, for *nurturing* and *yearning*," she sang, tracing his forefingers down each of her palms.

"And *between them* they cradle a world full of *knowing*," she gripped his fingers tightly. He could feel every line worn into them, every blemish and callus—pressing harder and harder on his own fingers and then palms. "And none has yet turned the tide of *that flowing*, for age is a *rift* and youth such a *gift*. But the bridge o'er the chasm is built with *desire*."

The room had become hot and airless, and a dull yellow light seemed to have brightened the place, although its source was unclear.

Agnes sank back into her chair, her eyes flaring and her arms shaking. Bogdan made to get up and help her but his legs felt weak, his eyes heavy with sleep and his vision blurred. His hands felt hot and painful. The tiredness was overwhelming and he too fell back into his chair and sank into sleep. The last thing he saw was Agnes rise up, suddenly and swiftly, with a strength he had not seen in her before. She stretched her arms high above her head, a body in the throes of being born again.

Rising from his slumber Bogdan felt his limbs creak slowly into usefulness. His hip ached and his feet were sore and numb. He looked down at his fingers; gnarled and crooked, the nails cracked and dirty. Between a swollen thumb and bent forefinger he held a thin white thread. He traced it back—its fibres further twining together as it trailed through his fingertips—to a delicate bone bobbin that he deftly tucked beneath its partner on a faded blue mat edged in frayed gold braiding that was propped on his lap. His hazy vision could see well enough this close at hand but as he peered around the room he could just make out the forms of ornaments and pictures, each of which sparked half memories of a long life, filled with loves and losses. "Nadszedł czas na herbatę," he thought.

In the narrow street outside a young girl played hopscotch on a hastily chalked grid—as though the late Twentieth century had never happened; her stiff ivory dress was dated; her hair plaited and unfashionably long; her delicate laughter, eternal.

SEVEN MINUTES IN HEAVEN

NADIA BULKIN

A GHOST TOWN LIVED DOWN THE ROAD FROM US. ITS BONES peeked out from over the tree line when we rattled down Highway 51 in our cherry red pick-up. I could see a steeple, a water tower, a dome for a town hall. It was our shadow. It was a ghost town because there was an accident, a long time ago, which turned it into a graveyard.

I used to wonder: what kind of accident kills a whole town? Was it washed away in a storm? Did God decide, "away with you sinners," with a wave of His hand—did He shake our sleeping Mt. Halberk into life? My parents said I was "morbid" when I asked these questions, and told me to play outside. So I would go outside, and play Seven Minutes in Heaven—freeze tag with a hold time of seven minutes, the length of time it takes for a soul to fly to God—with Allie Moore and Jennifer Trudeau. When the sky turned dark orange we would run back to our houses and slam our screen doors, and after my parents tucked me in I would sketch a map of the ghost town by the glow of my Little Buzz flashlight: church on the bottom of Church Street instead of the top, school on the east of the railroad tracks instead of the west. Then I would draw Mt. Halberk, and take a black sharpie, and rain down black curlicues on those little Monopoly houses until every single one was blanketed by the dark. When I got older, and madder, I would draw stick-people too—little stick-families walking little stick-dogs, little stick-farmers herding little stick-cows. And last, the darkness.

When I was in junior high school they told us the truth: the accident was industrial. The principal stood up in the auditorium and said there used to be a factory over there, in *that town*, and one day there was a leak of toxic gas, and people died over there, in *that town*. A long time ago, he said, nothing to worry about now. Some parents were angry; they said kids were getting upset. But gas leak sounds a lot less scary than a volcano, ask any kid.

Nobody would talk about it, except when we needed to dwell on something bad. Some families said a little prayer for the ghost town during Thanksgiving, so they could be grateful for something. My uncle Ben, the asshole, told my cousins he would leave them there if they misbehaved. Politicians in mustard suits pointed across the stage of the town hall and said, "My opponent supports the kind of policies that lead to the kind of accidents that empty out towns like Manfield." That was the ghost's name; Manfield. I lived in Hartbury.

Allie Moore was afraid of bats; she didn't like the way they crawl. Jennifer Trudeau was afraid of ice cream trucks, and nobody knew why. We only knew that when she heard the ring-a-ling song coming around the corner she'd rub her scarab amulet, to remember the power of God.

Me, I was afraid of skeletons. It was mostly the skull, the empty hugeness of the eye sockets and the missing nose and the grin of a mouth that could bite but couldn't kiss. But I also hated the rib cage and the pelvic butterfly and the knife-like fingers splayed apart in perpetual pain. It made me sick to think about what waited for me on the other side: the ugliness, the suffering. My parents took me to church and Pastor Joel promised that there would be none of that in Heaven, when I finally exhausted the cherished life that Almighty God had given me, when I finally decided my seven minutes were up and I was ready to go. "But that won't be for a long, long time from now," he said, patting my head. "So run along."

That was all well and good, but Pastor Joel didn't stop the nightmares. He didn't stop that Hell-sent skeleton from crawling out from under my box spring, clacking its teeth, tearing my sheets and then my skin. I would try to run but could never move, and those rotten bones would clamp like pliers around my neck, squeezing and squeezing until I woke up. I stopped telling my parents; their solution to everything was sleeping pills. The only thing that calmed me down was drawing and destroying Manfield, to remember that I wasn't dead like them.

It was Miss Lucy who stopped the nightmares. Miss Lucy loved Halloween, and come October she decked the classroom in pumpkins and sheet-ghosts and purple-caped vampires. She also hung a three-foot skeleton decal from the American flag above the white board. I could not stop staring at it, because it would not stop staring at me. "I know ol' Mr. Bones is kind of creepy," Miss Lucy whispered after I refused to go to the board to answer a math problem. "But you shouldn't be scared of skeletons, Amanda. You've already got one inside you." Then she reached out her finger and poked me in the chest, in what I suddenly realized was bone. I'm proud to say that I only wanted to dig myself apart for a few gory seconds before I realized that Miss Lucy was right, that a skeleton couldn't hurt me if it was already part of me.

"Memento mori," Miss Lucy said. My parents thought she was witchy, and corrected things she told us about the Pacific Wars—*we never promised that we would help Japan, we never threatened Korea.* She was gone by next September, and a woman with puppy-patterned vests had taken over her class. Mrs. Joan didn't like Halloween. Parents liked her, though.

I was seventeen the first time I went to Manfield. Allie Moore's boyfriend, Jake Felici, decided it would be a hard-core thing to do for Halloween. Jake was a moody, gangly boy who played bass guitar, and Allie's hair had turned a permanent slime-green from years on the swim team. They were the captains of hard-core. Allie invited me and Jennifer Trudeau. Jake invited Brandon Beck, who I loved so frantically that I thought it might kill me. So while other kids in Hartbury were drinking screwdrivers in somebody's base-ment or summoning demons with somebody's Ouija board, we piled into Jake's beat-up Honda Accord and drove down Highway 51, Brandon and his perfect chestnut hair smashed between me and Jennifer Trudeau.

We were expecting something like those old Western gold-miner towns—wood shacks, rusted roadsters, a landscape still dominated by barrels and wheelbarrows. We were expecting something that had been cut down a hundred years ago, when companies were still playing around with chemicals like babies with guns, before regula-tions would have kept them in line. But that was not Manfield. Manfield had ticky-tacky houses and plastic lawn gnomes and busted minivans. There was a Java Hut coffee house, a Quick Loan, a Little Thai restaurant. That is, Manfield looked just like Hart-bury—only dead. Only dark.

We were standing in what had once been the town's beating heart. Jake's flashlight found a now-blinded set of traffic lights. Allie's flashlight found something called Ram's Head Tavern. Taped to the inside of the tavern's windows were newspaper clippings from twelve years back: the local high school had won a track meet; an old man had celebrated sixty years at the chemical plant that would kill them all; and they had held a harvest fair not so different from the one we celebrated in early October. Kids in flannel struggled to hoist blue-ribbon pumpkins, white-haired grandparents held out homemade pies, a blonde girl with a sash that read *Queen of Mount Halberk* waved, smirking, to the camera. Hartbury was the only town on Mt. Halberk now.

"Are you sure this is safe?" asked Jennifer. "What if there's still poison in the air?"

"It's not like it was radiation," said Jake, trying to muster up the certainty to be our Captain Courage. "Gas dissipates, so it's all gone now."

Allie echoed him enthusiastically, but she also pulled her plaid scarf higher up her neck. I looked at Brandon, but he wasn't looking at me. No, Brandon was hanging back with meek, slight, big-eyed Jennifer—telling her that it would be all right, kicking pebbles in her direction. None of it seemed real. I saw the five of us standing like five scarecrows, five finger-puppets, five propped-up people-like things that were, nevertheless, not people. My heart was pounding like a wild animal inside my chest. I wanted to get out—out of Manfield, out of my body. I don't know what I thought was coming after me. I could only feel its rumbling, unstoppable and insurmountable, like the black volcanic clouds I had once drawn descending upon this town.

No one else seemed worried about the fact that everyone had lied about how recently the accident destroyed Manfield, and in the years to come we would never ask our parents why. I suppose we assumed that they had been so traumatized, so saddened by the loss of their sister-town, that they decided to push Manfield backward into the soft underbelly of history. "They never said when it was exactly," Jake said, in their defense, "just that it was a while ago."

A while. All our understanding of time is made up of slipshod words that you can rearrange to cover up the fact that somewhere, somebody was wrong. In a while, Brandon Beck started dating Jennifer Trudeau. In a while, I decided to leave the state for college. For a while, I dreamt of my parents driving five-year-old me to a harvest festival, buying me a pumpkin, crowning me Queen of Manfield, and then leaving me to vanish into a gently swirling fog.

I gave myself an education at Rosewood College. I learned that Seven Minutes in Heaven was not, in fact, a kind of freeze tag, because it was not, in fact, the length of time it took for a dead soul to reach God. I learned that boys would lie to you about hitchhiking across the Pampas to get you to sleep with them, and I learned they probably wouldn't call. I learned that I had no memory of several headliner incidents that took place the year I turned six—not the three-hundred-person Chinese passenger aircraft that was mistakenly shot down over Lake Dover a hundred miles from where I grew up, not the earthquake that killed sixty in Canada, not the Great Northeastern Chemical Disaster that saw a pesticide gas cloud submerge Manfield and then float westward toward Hartbury—and that I actually had no memory of kindergarten at all.

My parents couldn't help me. I would call and they would grunt and hum and rummage through the kitchen drawers; when they got anxious, they needed to fix things. My mother remembered so many of my little childhood calamities—how I once tied our puppy Violet to my Radio Flyer and made her pull me "like a hearse"— but she didn't remember much from the year that Manfield gave up the ghost. So I tried to forget that I'd ever forgotten anything by drinking, making sure I met enough people at this party that I'd be invited to another. I'd eventually cycle through everything and everyone, throw up in every floor's bathroom, memorize every vintage poster for every French and Italian liqueur on every dorm room wall.

I had hoped to get along with my freshman year roommate, a poker-faced redhead named Georgina Hanssen who was also from a small town, but Georgina was not the bonding type. She lived and breathed only anthropology. She had pictures of herself holding spears in Africa and monkeys in Asia, and eventually the truth came out that her parents had been missionaries, and she had been raised Mennonite. Sometimes she ate dinner with me in the white-walled cafeteria, and we would take turns insulting the slop that passed for food, but she didn't give me any ways in, and at night she would turn down hall parties to hunch over her weird yellow books and munch her mother's homemade granola bars. One morning I woke up drunk, half-in half-off my bed, and found her staring at me like a feral animal, like she was seeing me for the first time. "What are you reading," I asked, the only question that could start a conversation with her.

"A History of Forgotten Christianity," she said. Her finger scratched an itch on the open page. "For Professor Kettle's class. I'm on the chapter about cults of universal resurrection." She paused, then started reading. "Cults of universal resurrection have experienced cyclical fortunes throughout American history, typically reaching peak popularity during periods of economic depression.

An estimated three hundred and fifty such communities have been documented across the Northeastern region. They are commonly found in small towns with high mortality rates due to exposure to natural disasters, poor medicine, and unsafe industrial conditions."

Something slithered around my shoulders. "So?"

Georgina took a deep breath. "Cult-followers believed that God had bestowed upon them the power to return the dead to life. When an untimely death occurred in the community, church pastors and town elders would quickly perform a ritual to prevent the soul from leaving the dead person's body, holding it in a state of "limbo" until the more elaborate resurrection ritual—often involving a simulated burial and rebirth—could be performed. Although resurrection rituals varied, all cults of universal resurrection held the dung beetle—famously worshipped by ancient Egyptians for similar reasons—in high symbolic standing, as the insect's eggs emerge from a ball of its waste. Rather than Christ the divine worm, cultists worshipped Christ . . . "

"Christ the divine scarab," I finished. Yes, I had learned that line in Sunday school, along with *God bestows the gift of life unto those who have faith*, and yes, we hung scarabs on our Christmas tree, but only as a reminder that God was all-giving and we were His life-possessing children, and I had no idea what *that* had to do with bringing people back from the fucking dead.

"So? What happened to them?"

"During the Great Evangelical Revival, they were mostly pressured to convert to mainstream Christianity." A fingernail scraped a page. Something tore inside me. "*Mostly.*"

I left school after my freshman year. There didn't seem to be much point in staying. I went into the city, because I couldn't go home—not to that town full of the walking dead. Not to Pastor Joel and whatever he had done to us on the night of the gas leak. Not to my parents. Before I burned their pictures I would search their frozen smiles for some sign, some hollowness, some fakery, some *deadness* in their eyes. Depending on how much time I'd spent with Brother

Whiskey and Sister Vodka, I sometimes found it, sometimes didn't. Regardless, I took their money—I had to, what with the economy and the price of liquor. They sent me Christmas cards with green-and-gold scarabs on them, and on the off chance that they had the right address I burned those cards along with a lock of my poisoned bleached hair, because Lily Twining said she was a witch and that was how you severed family ties. "Doesn't purify your blood, though," Lily warned me, cigarette jammed between her teeth. "Believe me, I've tried."

When I was twenty-three my Aunt Rose, wife to Uncle Ben the asshole, died of a stroke. My ~~~~~~ ~~~~ ~p at the bus station with glassy eyes and the old red pick-up, and oh how I longed to slide back into a gentler, dumber time when I could simply be their daughter, Amanda Stone, twenty-three years old. It did not work. *Memento mori.* I remembered.

Things had changed in Hartbury. My favorite Italian restaurant on Church Street had gone out of business, replaced by a plasma donation center. Everyone looked like ghouls, the skeletons that we all should have turned to grinning through their sagging skin. And a new dog—a black and white spaniel—came bounding off the porch. "Where's Violet?" I asked.

"Violet died last year," said my mother, without a hint of sadness in her voice.

"Life is cheap," I replied, rubbing New Dog behind its ears.

My parents didn't know what was happening to me. They were frightened by my tattoos: a black outline of my sternum where Miss Lucy poked me, followed by three black ribs on each side. They were worried about Brother Whiskey and Sister Vodka, not realizing that those two had seen me through a lot of darkness. They were embarrassed by how I behaved at Aunt Rose's funeral. They didn't understand why Pastor Joel's numb routine of *o death where is thy sting* and *o grave where is thy victory* made me hysterical with terror and laughter. I went to Manfield on my final night in town, and took New Dog with me—like Violet, this mutt had immediately adopted me, apparently willing to overlook the question of whether or not I was undead. I said I was going to see a friend, as in *hello darkness my old friend*, and my mother asked if I was going to see Allie Felici and her new baby. "Sure," I said, and slammed the screen door.

Manfield looked beaten-up. Windows had been broken into, storefronts had been tagged with unimaginative graffiti—a reversed pentagram here, a FOREVER LOVE there. Another car with an unfamiliar set of self-indulgent high school stickers was already parked at the mouth of the main street, and it didn't take me and New Dog long to find the occupants trudging along in the half-light, posing for pictures while making stretched-out corpse-faces. We crept behind at a safe distance, New Dog and I, just close enough to hear the sharp edges of words.

"You hear about that other town that got hit with the same stuff, except nobody died?"

"Why? They closed their windows?"

"No, joker. Look, my mom was a 911 operator. They got so many calls from Hartbury that she thought the whole town was toast, just like Manfield. But when the rescue workers got there, freaking Hartbury just closed up and told them to go home, said everything was fine."

At Aunt Ruth's funeral, my father told me that I had no respect for the life this town gave me. I said that he had no respect for death. I said that if he respected life so much then why didn't he just dig up Aunt Ruth and bring her back? His face collapsed like a withered orange. "Aunt Ruth was ready to go," he said. I flailed out of his grasp like a wildcat. I ran to the parking lot over the graves of strangers who had decided to stay dead, under the watchful eye of the great green stained-glass scarab in the window of the church. *But I am a scarab, and no man.*

It sounds romantic when you first hear it: seven minutes in heaven, seven minutes for your soul to board its tiny interstellar ship and set the coordinates for God. Seven minutes for you to change your mind. But that time is spent in nothing but the dark. The empty. Just like underneath Manfield's carefully preserved skin, behind the Ram's Head Tavern sign forever creaking in the wind, there's nothing but gas masks and body bags.

The world was changing, very fast. I had stolen food out of children's mouths, helped a man I loved pilfer from plague corpses, thanked God I wasn't pregnant because I didn't want a calcified stone baby at the bottom of my stomach. I'd seen a lot of skeletons, but only on a cross-country bus in the dead of summer did my own return to me—howling, ushered in by smoke. Its bones were just as coarse as I remembered, ~~but i~~ ~~gry was so much deeper~~, that much richer. My skeleton had grown up. That time, I let it win. I unclenched my fists and let go. I let God.

I woke up when we stopped to let new passengers barter their way on in exchange for gas. Outside my window, one man was beating another to death for whatever the dead man had in his bag—soldiers who couldn't have been older than fifteen ran off the survivor, the killer. I might have tried to see what I could salvage from the dead one, as ghouls go after corpses, but was interrupted by an old man on the other side of the aisle with rotting teeth and a black fedora. He called me young lady, though I felt like I'd lived forever, and asked where I was from.

It was a question I hated answering. Sometimes I named the state. Sometimes I lied. Sometimes I said something crazy—"outer space" or "hell" or "beyond." That time I told the truth. *Memento mori*—the skeleton made me. I told him about Hartbury, about the harvest festival. I told him about Seven Minutes in Heaven. I told him about playing dead—laying frozen in time in a bed of fallen leaves, waiting for someone to pluck you back to life.

"Can I tell you a secret? I died there." The shadows of nearly all my bones were tattooed across my body—I wanted to command the world to pay witness to my death. "I've died."

The old man grinned and wiggled deeper into his suit, as if he and I and every other loser on that bus were buckled into a fantastic Stairway to Heaven. "Join the club, living dead girl."

The third time I went to Manfield, I was thirty-four. I walked, because my sponsor was big on cold night walks with a backpack filled with stones, to symbolize the burdens we all carry in our Pilgrim's Progress. I was alone, save for the county dogs that smiled at me with bloody gums as they trotted up and down the cracked remains of the interstate. New Dog, whose name turned out to be Buttons, had been hit by a car on Highway 51. I invited my parents, but they frowned sadly and wondered why on Earth I'd want to go. "That's a dead town," they said.

How strange I must have always seemed to them. They must have spent my life blaming themselves for my choices, wondering why I wasn't more like sweet little Jennifer Trudeau, who had her head wrenched off in a freak accident with an ice cream truck. Seven minutes in heaven can't undo that kind of fatality. "It's peaceful there," I said.

So it was. There was a stillness in Manfield that you couldn't find in Hartbury, because when the blanket of death came for us we kicked it off and were left naked and shivering in the world. But in Manfield there was grass carpeting what had once been the side-walk, vines crawling up Ram's Head Tavern, rabbits nesting in the seats of long-gone drivers. Rehab always stressed peace in our time—there are some dragons you must appease, my sponsor said, because there's no fighting them. And truth's one such dragon.

A new flock of teenagers had landed in Manfield. Two girls, three boys, all on crippled bicycles whose parts had been cannibalized for the war effort. I hid behind a termite-eaten column as they wobbled past.

"You know this place is haunted. My older brother knew a guy who went up here on a dare and saw a ghost . . . a girl with a dog. One of them red-eyed demon hellhounds." In hiding, I smiled. Buttons was going to live forever. "I think that guy got deployed." As had Brandon Beck, his perfect hair shorn down to the scalp before he left for the front. The town used to hold candlelight vigils for his never-recovered body, before his parents passed and so many others followed in his footsteps. "I think he's dead."

Everyone was dead; everyone was alive. A fighter jet roared over-head, right on time for its appointment with the grim reaper. The teenagers stopped their pedaling to watch the angel pass and I took the occasion to run silent and deep, head down, fire in the belly.

INFESTATIONS

MICHAEL
CISCO

It is a bright day, May second. Picturesque white clouds. A helicopter hovers somewhere in the blue sky. They hear it, but they don't see it. They look out the window at the street. A dog barks, the shrill, panicked cry of a small dog. Across the street, they are at work, putting the small housefront there in order with rakes and hoses. A car pulls up in front of the house next door.

A woman comes around the corner and then pauses to check the note she carries in her free hand. Then she scans the front of the nearest building, exposing an unusual, mature face, at once attractive and haggard. She walks uncertainly up the block for a few doors, then turns and crosses the street, brought up short by a car that pivots smartly around the corner the moment she steps off the curb. Now she is across the street, entering the larger brownstone apartment building there with the note held up in her hand like a ticket. Their gaze follows her inside, appraisingly.

Over the city, then at the airport, she thought, "So I *am* back."

The plane comes in low, and she can see the East River, river of disappearances. In the streets of Manhattan, they look up, eyes seeking her out in her seat in the plane as it soars overhead. She disembarks from the plane, from the airport, her drawn face tense, hurrying her step, although she has no reason to hurry, no one is supposed to be waiting for her anymore. They watch as she hurries past. She feels eyes on her. Through the baggage claim, and the picket of men in suits holding signs that say "Robinson

Family" or "Anne Bright." They call after her, offering her a ride into town.

She doesn't want to be spoken to, she wants to be invisible. She insists she is not pretty or noticeable. She is tired from her flight and dreads being forced to speak or to listen, having to learn the contours of some face or other, however briefly, and she feels diaphanous and gigantic, blown up to many times her correct size, too big to hide and too flimsy to put up any resistance.

Across the city, along its streets, resentful faces look her a moment in the eye and say, "I never left. I never stopped watching for you, knowing your face is mine. ...

She has not been to New York for almost ten years. Her mother had uncharacteristically hemmed and hawed before asking her if she would be willing to go back; Miriam had been a close friend of both her parents since before she was born—her namesake—a friendship that lasted decades and remained firm across long distances, and Miriam had no family to call her own. Without intending to, her mother made it sound as if Miriam were still lying dead in her apartment, rotting unheeded on the purple carpet, while now and then a new prospective tenant, pressing a handkerchief to his face, trampled the yielding invisibility of her corpse while touring the rooms. No one else was available; her mother was still recovering from knee surgery, and her father had her mother to take care of and retirement coming.

"Someone has to pack up Miriam's apartment," her mother had said.

With his customary thoroughness, her father had drawn up an exhaustive list of all necessary tasks, with numbered steps, but in her imagination she conceived of her task exclusively as having to do with Miriam's apartment. She was going to New York to scrub away Miriam's traces, so that Miriam's possessions could also be buried and the spell of home could be broken, all in obedience to an obscure, commercial necessity.

She had not seen Miriam often when she lived in the city herself. Her work had naturally kept her busy, but she tended to exaggerate her commitments where Miriam was concerned. She told herself it was because she couldn't stand to confront vivid memories of home, believing that she could manage the city only by stiffening herself in a way that meant shutting out those memories, and hesitantly praised herself for being self-aware, but now she had to admit she'd been lying, that Miriam was boring, and, frankly, very nearly an ugly woman. This was not a thought she could bring herself to formulate honestly, but she could not think of Miriam without a pang of aversion, not so much for her appearance as for the awkwardness involved in knowing someone as plain as that and a latent pain of contrast. Miriam was short, flat, all lines and angles, except for her fleshy nose and cheeks. Her hair was not a bad color, but it was thin, falling lifelessly around her ears and halting in an unkempt fringe above her shoulders; from time to time she would turn up unexpectedly with an elaborate hair-do, a variation on artificial curls, which turned her hair into a bizarre glossy mass of unrecognizable material. She either didn't know or care how ridiculous this made her look, which was to her credit somehow. Miriam was always ready to shower her with affection, to forgive her everything, and she seemed especially to rejoice in her namesake's beauty. The face she turned up in her childhood pictures, for all the goofy expressions and crazy teeth, was never delicate, but showed a kind of animal vitality, sometimes dreamy, sometimes bright. She grew into a Junoesque young woman, solid and delicate, innocently humiliating Miriam.

Her parents and the family's satellites were always pairing the two of them, even now that the elder Miriam was dead this was still happening. They did sound the same. When she was visiting Miriam and the phone rang, Miriam, her hands slathered with butter or up to the elbows in dishwater, would ask her to answer it, and callers could never tell which Miriam they were talking to.

She checks into the hotel, with their eyes on her, takes the key from the desk clerk and goes directly to her room. She unpacks, and, in the bathroom, confronts an unusually complete double of herself in the mirrored wall behind the counter. The bags under her eyes are too hard to miss, the droop that only she would notice, starting at the corner of her mouth. The nose is still firm, the teeth are still bright. Her body is still vigorous enough for the task—tasks—ahead. Perhaps just barely, but still . . . still . . . still . . .

After a brief nap, fully dressed, on top of her bed, she leaves the hotel and, hurrying again, makes her way to Miriam's apartment, the address clutched in her free hand. A neighborhood in Queens; auto body shops, bodegas, laundromats, Chinese take out, liquor stores, nail salons, rooftops like rumpled mattresses painted silver and lacquered with indecipherable tags, slogans, cartoons, and seemingly every conceivable kind of person crowding the battered sidewalks. Women in tops to to exhibit to middle-aged Greek women in suits and heavy jewelry, strictly functional Chinese, Italian Romeos, slouching swaying young men dragging their hoods tight against their heads with both hands plunged in the pockets of their sweatshirts. She enters the building with a key; opens the stale apartment and flings open the windows to let in some of the bright Spring air. Was that a mistake? Not the airing of the apartment, which is stuffy with a smell of rugs and upholstery and soap that is naggingly vague, and which she can't help but think is contaminated with a smell of decay that is purely imaginary: Miriam didn't die here, after all, did she? Miriam died in a hospital, didn't she? The mistake was that she'd felt too conspicuous at the window, as if she were displaying herself to the neighborhood.

The refrigerator is empty. A smell like old ice wafts from the open door on feeble puffs of cold. Nothing in the cabinets, not even the paper liners. She wasn't entirely sure what had happened here after Miriam's death; had someone already gone through the place, throwing away perishables? In that case, they missed those withered flowers, so obvious on the table. Or had Miriam stopped buying food before she died, holed up in this apartment, and run through her supplies?

Remembering the grocery she'd passed on her way here, she decides to go back there and pick up a few things. Miriam had lived in this apartment a long time, and had accumulated a great many possessions. Clearing the place out with proper care will obviously take a while—days.

"But why explain this," she thinks irritably, "And bother with reasons? You're alone, so who are you explaining yourself to?"

They are looking at her chest, not her face, as she buys her groceries.

She clears her throat with needless vehemence.

"Weren't these on sale?" she asks, raising her voice, firmly tapping a bundle of broccoli. She knows the answer of course.

She watches something snap shut across the counter from her. They are startled, and sheepishly push her change in her direction before turning away.

"Were they on sale?" she asks again.

"They were on sale," they reply, without turning, mutely breaking off contact with her.

"Thanks," she says automatically, but with a trace of venom, as she takes up her bag.

"Thanks," they say automatically.

It was as if, she thinks, walking down the street—it was as if her words had been recorded and played back to her in altered arrangement.

She has done this before, anyway. They all knew that, but none of them wanted to say it. They had never done this before, but she had—so, send her. She had been the one to box up Juan's things, and set them out for that embittered viper of a sister he had, who blamed his death on her, could barely bring herself to speak to her, could not stifle a vituperating mutter when they were together. She had been too deeply shocked by Juan's death to notice or care much about his sister, and had gone about the business of closing up his life in a mental haze. She let Juan's sister make off with things that didn't belong to her, distractedly not contesting her false insistence that these had belonged to Juan all along. Somehow, the thought that they might have belonged to Juan, even in the eyes of his blindly vengeful sister, made them enough like actual mementos of him to trigger pain, so those things were better gone. Their absence shone in the unfamiliar silence of the apartment, like the ghostly outlines left by paintings on the wall.

He had parted company with two friends and boarded the ferry to Governor's Island. She was waiting for him on the other side, and, when the boat arrived, she saw the worried looks, the anxiety on the faces, and she did not see Juan. When the last of the passengers had disembarked, and still no Juan, she didn't know what to do. It was typical of her that she would leap immediately to the worst, that she would think at once of death.

Those friends had seen him board the ferry, and he had waved to them as it pulled away. It was the middle of an unseasonably cold and drizzly day, and there were only a few passengers; he was easy to keep in sight, even as the boat pulled out into the channel. He waved, then turned and, raising his jacket collar against the wind, walked toward the rail with his hands in his pockets. They remembered this, because Juan never put his hands in his pockets. He would pull out this or that, of course, but he never simply rested his hands in his pockets.

The next thing anyone knew, he was in the water. No one saw him go overboard. No one saw him bobbing in the water until the ferry was some distance away. No one ever saw him again. His body was never found. He had gone into the water very near the middle of Buttermilk Channel; he was a strong man, in good health—he might have been able to save himself, assuming he was not injured. He might have struck his head against something, tripped and tumbled down the steps leading from the upper deck, and this might have caused him to fall, injured, into the water. The channel currents are strong, but eventually she was told they were nearly at maximum flood tide at the time he went over; had the tide been ebbing, he would certainly have been swept out to sea, but in a flood tide, a strong swimmer would have had a chance to swim to within reach of another boat, perhaps even to shore.

The two of them had quarrelled about a week before it happened, she can't remember about what, but it had been a small thing, she was sure of that, and the air had cleared. He'd accused her of flirting with one of his friends. They'd made love the night before he disappeared, and again the following morning. He had been a little absent during, but he was always that way.

—Not at first, she remembers. At first she thought he would

devour her; she was overwhelmed by his desire; it turned him into a giant, it seized on them both like a storm lashes trees.

She saw the river as the plane came into the airport. Was he still there? Was there still a husband?

He hadn't left a note. He wasn't, though, the sort of person who would, even if he'd meant to die. While he was eloquent when it came to abstract things, and while he read poetry with a gentle fervor that was really beautiful, that complemented the beauty of the words with a kind of grace, Juan always choked on strong emotion. She could see the words, whole sentences, crash together like a logjam in his throat. He would sigh, stare at her, and his hands would rise and fall, rise and fall, as if he were releasing balloons one by one into the void. Each time his hand rose and fell, that was another balked effort to speak.

She could see the river from the window of Miriam's apartment, like an iron slab between two buildings, and thought of him. Now what was he, after ten years in the slime? Have you found the words yet, Juan? Anything you want to say to me now?

The failure to turn up his body meant that they could not formally register his death. Was she still married? That was the question. What was she still married to? She looked out Miriam's kitchen window at the river, an iron slab between the buildings, and thought of it as her husband. She walked along the riverfront and looked at the dark opacity of a swift current, like another element belonging to the city instead of a part of the landscape, like another element apart from water, more like liquid mercury, heavy, poisonous, ice-cold. Cold with an entirely new species of cold. It was like staring at a prison, and at a funeral pyre that freezes and preserves, with grinding slowness, where a fire burns and consumes in a flash . . . and at the same time it was like standing in front of an apartment building watching for the light to come on in a lover's window, wondering if a light will suddenly come on in the riverbed, to show her Juan is there, and just as a lover—or, at least, some figure—will sometimes dart across that window, maybe she will see a light come on in the river, and then see, crossing it, a wasted, sticklike arm. Then there will be a thin figure, lit from behind, walking, inhumanly thin, toward her down a corridor of light out of the river, spanning the way between them.

She's naked when there's a knock on the door. A man's voice booms inside the apartment. She snaps the bedroom door shut with a yelp of alarm and throws on the loose-fitting, more comfortable clothes she'd been changing into, shouting—

"Who's there?" her voice cracking, full of fright and surprise.

Only a distant murmur replying.

She seizes a pair of scissors and opens the door cautiously. When she begins to explore, she catches sight of them quickly, in the mirror, a man in a windbreaker standing just inside the apartment. When they see her, the explanation begins.

Crazily assembled, the disjointed words add up roughly to this: they work at the grocery store, they overheard her disagreement with the checker about a sale item (they hold up a long paper tape, a receipt), they recognized her because they have a friend who lives in this building, and they have come to refund her the sale price of the broccoli, a few coins in their palm, level, beneath the level canopy of a fixed and unblinking gaze.

She remains where she is, fifteen feet away, clutching her scissors.

"Forget it," she says, returning his gaze.

"For-get?" they ask.

"I don't want it," she says.

Then she is rushing—she slams the door.

"I don't want it!" she shouts more firmly, confidently, over the murmur coming through the door. She hooks the chain and tugs at it, testing it. Then she pulls a chair halfway across the apartment to shove it under the doorknob.

...A friend in the building? It seems impossible to her that anyone with that way of looking at anything could be capable of friendship.

How did he know what apartment to try?

She made a good impression on Miriam's lawyer. These sorts of things she seems to have a knack for grasping and sorting out, keeping things separated and in the right order, the most expedient order. They like her long neck, long but not like a stalk, not frail. She has, they would say, a neck like a flying buttress. A firm, silent way. An equine look. A way of keeping up appearances, of charm.

Coming out of the lawyer's office, she pauses at the drinking fountain. From the corner of her eye she sees someone round the corner and stop abruptly, evidently expecting to come in for a quick landing at the fountain only to be brought up short by her presence.

"Excuse me," they say testily, already crowding her, gluing their lips to the spigot almost the moment she stops drinking.

There is only the single, unisex bathroom on this floor. She notices some movement as she slips in the door and shuts it. Sitting on the toilet she is only about four feet away from the door, and she can see the shadows of a pair of legs breaking the glare line under it, as if someone were standing right outside fuming with impatience to get in.

Bang! The flat of a hand swats the door on the other side, startling her, and the shadow moves off.

When she emerges a man in a suit explodes at her—"Look ya bitch I go to the water fountain you're there already I go to the toilet and you're jumping in ahead of me! Now stay outta my way!"

"I'm sorry!" she says, taken aback, her voice shrill, indignant, not apologetic.

They whip past her snatching up the doorknob and bringing it to, but with downcast eyes.

"I'm sorry," they say a moment later. The door shuts. It's too late to dissemble, though, because for an instant they were looking at her, Juan's eyes, and she recognized them.

There is something wrong with the paperwork; the proof of residence in the apartment is missing, and there will be a delay of some days before a copy can be found. Not wanting to waste money on the hotel room, she will simply live in Miriam's apartment for the time being. They check her out of the hotel, they call her a cab, they drive her to the door of Miriam's building. From the windows, the street, they observe her entering the building with her luggage. They watch, and see the light come on upstairs, in Miriam's apartment. They note the bathroom light going on, remaining lit.

She emerges from the bathroom directly into their field of view.

"What—?" she says, her voice faint.

"What?" they say.

They apologize, they didn't know she was there.

"Get out!" she calls, moving back toward the bathroom.

The explanations begin.

She looks around and ——— up a heavy glass ashtray.

"Whoa whoa!" one of them says, raising up placating hands beneath that level unblinking gaze. "We're supposed to be here! This is 315, right?"

"Those are mine," she says, pointing to her suitcase in their hands. They were going to make off with all her clothes.

"Yours?"

"Put that down and get the fuck out!"

"Get the fuck out? You called us. We are supposed to clear the place."

They could simply smile and leave with her clothes, still packed in those suitcases. She'd be trapped in the apartment then. Then they would come back later with friends.

"Get the fuck out!" she screams, the sound of her voice insane, unrecognizable, a wail of desperation and fear.

They smile at each other, setting down her bags but in no hurry.

"We'll get out," they say. "We'll get out."

Casual, infuriating, all smiles, placating a child, they leave through a door hanging wide open. She checks an impulse to rush to it and throw it shut—she might not actually be alone in the apartment—or they could be hiding there, just outside the door, waiting for her to come within reach.

Then there is a child framed in the doorway, staring at her, and the boy's mother—a flash of their eyes, and then the child is hurried down the hallway toward the stairs, and she flings down the ashtray onto the sofa, crosses to the door and carefully shuts it without chaining it, in case . . . in case what? Is she shutting them out, or is she shutting herself in with them?

Feeling ridiculous, she picks up the heavy ashtray again, and searches the apartment.

The river looks back at her with Juan's gaze, and she thinks again about a shrivelled silhouette walking swiftly toward her down a hall of yellow light like a shaft cutting the river. She dares someone or something to do just that—go ahead. She speaks without knowing who listens or whether she means the river or Juan, or some larger, thinner, more diaphanous person, not the city exactly but something like a sail or pall of mist, a conscious membrane that is a by-product of so many people living so close together always more and more separated by another kind of distance, or no, the membrane is the distance feeding on itself, fermenting, growing always thinner with a thinness that is somehow poisonous to itself and to human beings.

Well, Juan? she asks silently, the thought now more clear than words. If he comes for her, if he is looking for her, if he wants to claim her, if he wants revenge, if he is jealous, then there is still some bond that links them—and there is, *there is*—something more than memory and unanswered questions—but if the two of them are still connected he cannot affect her without risk to himself— but what could he still possibly have to lose? Only her.

There is a small yard behind the house, then an alley, then another row of three and four storey apartment buildings. Standing in Miriam's just-darkened bedroom, the lamp embering out behind her, she looks out to the windows opposite, a few of them still lit. Down there, on the ground floor, there is a panel of luminous white, a computer screen, showing a film. Is there anyone there to see it? There must be, but she can see only that screen; the film holds a fixed angle, shooting a room, and there is a figure in the foreground, a very pale figure, moving rapidly up and down, up and down. She turns from the window and leaves the room at once, shutting behind her a door that is normally left open.

The cold weather abruptly gives way to hot. The sky is like honey, the sun eats into it like a caustic eye swimming in orange grease. She is walking back to Miriam's apartment yet again; for some reason, a man calling himself the superintendent of the building needed to see her personally and in the apartment itself.

Distracted, she overshoots her destination and gets off one station farther along. Now she is walking back to Miriam's apartment down unfamiliar streets lined with garages and workshops. The air smells a little like ~~small~~ ~~~~ ~~~~ work chemicals. The streets are raked by searchlights hidden in the sun's glare, picking her out, contrasting her forward in the day. She passes slabs of uncut countertop marble, drums labelled with a droplet dissolving a hand, small knots of smoking men who eye her as she goes by. She passes a school, the yard full of children on the other side of a high chain-link fence, and she can feel their eyes on her too, a she goes by. She adjusts her skirt slightly, makes a half-clandestine appraisal of her appearance to see if anything is amiss, but unless her idea of presentability or decency has become imperceptibly distorted, there is nothing at all unusual about her today. It is hot, after all, and it has only just become hot, and she is not entirely ready to brush through the heat that hangs down from the sky in curtains of wet needles and that pants heavily down on her long hair after so long a cold.

Passing a furniture store she notices a large oval mirror hanging on the wall near the window. The mirror has a smooth, broad frame of darkly-stained wood, and is hung edgewise, looking more like an eye than like a door. It is supposed to hang that way; you know that not only by the placement of the hook, but by the disproportionately small brass eagle that marks the top of the frame with its outspread arms. Theirs had had a funny kind of fish instead of an eagle.

She stops, and the man coming up rapidly behind her, a tall man with a briefcase, collides with her, so that she is toppled a little off her balance and has to take another step as he slides across her.

"Sorry!" he says tersely, and then lunges on down the street.

Startled, and dazed, she looks down the block behind her. An older man in a cloth cap stands watching her with his hands in his pockets, evidently having just come out of his front garden. She walks slowly on, almost blindly, realizing now why what she saw from the window last night had affected her so much more than it should have. She once had just such a mirror as that one. It hung in their bedroom, high on the wall opposite the bed. Last night, she had recoiled, and had shut without thinking a door that was normally not kept shut, because that mirror had been hanging on the wall behind the pale figure in the movie last night she had seen going up and down in the foreground, with darker hands reaching up from below and roving freely over the paler skin.

"What do I . . . ?" she thinks, the phrase starting and restarting.

The cafe she passes is filled with people staring at screens. They might all be watching, and the eyes that linger on her as she returns to Miriam's apartment might be eyes that have *seen*, and who else but him? Who else could it have been, to make it, and to make it public somewhere, but *him*? Or has the film not happened yet? The images rise like smoke out of a human darkness of death, hidden ideas, hidden acts, a great black bank of smoke hiding vanished people, all invisible things, ghosts, the dead, rising up onto screens and into people's eyes, from the darkness outside to the darkness within heads and eyes, and if the future emerges from that darkness, then the film may show what will happen, or may counterfeit it, a double of herself, grinning malevolently, turns on the camera.

Her skirt is suddenly gripped and torn. Her throat shuts as a jolt runs through her whole body. The hallway is empty—the hem of her skirt hangs in two pieces. There is a screw sticking out of the doorframe; it caught the hem as she brushed past it into the hallway on Miriam's floor. Footsteps are coming up the stairs, slow and steady, the footsteps of a tired man, or a wary one. Lift your gaze up as you climb the stairs and you might get a look up at what a woman's dress is very imperfectly designed to hide; had she been seen by the climber down there?

She reaches Miriam's apartment, locks the door and chains it, turns to meet the level gaze of Juan, the man from the grocery store, the man from the bathroom, the man in the cloth cap, the man with the briefcase. The room seems to hold an impossibly enormous crowd, all eyes riveted on her, Juan's gaze fixed on her and multiplied as if she were Juan staring at himself in countless mirrors, and they are all momentarily still, momentarily suspended with a fierce paralysis.

"Has this happened before?" she asks herself uncertainly.

"It has," she thinks a moment later, as the stillness in the room begins to abate, there's a sound of wet footsteps coming up the stairs and the door swings unlocked and a moment later, slowly open again behind her.

In Miriam's bedroom, with the door firmly shut behind her, she undresses and climbs into bed. The door hums with a massed presence that presses against the door like flood water, holding it shut with such force as to threaten to break it apart. She lies naked on top of the sheets and blankets—it's stifling, too warm to cover herself with anything. Sweat trickles down her face. When she feels sweat on her arms, she knows she will have to go to the window and open it. She gets up as quietly as she can, feeling the dark listening for her on the other side of the door, a room full of lightless water. And figures treading in it. She moves, crouching, to the window, using the low wall to hide herself. The window is latched, and her hand is slippery with sweat. She tries to unlatch it while standing to one side of the window, but her hand slips, and now she fills the window and all the other windows facing are dark with silhouettes, something dark dangles before her face now at eye level, protruding from the window though there is no one on the other side of it, no opening in the glass for it to come through. It is only inches from her face, close enough for her to smell, staring at her, following her movement as she recoils from the window into the darkened room, the curtains drop to the floor and all the lamps burst ablaze. A relentlessly steady gaze comes through the door, the wall, she is visible through the walls and ceilings and floors, visible for miles, seen from the river and on every screen.

No longer at the window, now it is in the center of the ceiling where the light fixture used to be, still surrounded by that same light, the same streaks and facets in the light, and directly over the bed, waiting for her, and until she acts, she will be seen and continue to be seen, more and more violently and nightmarishly exposed, even though the act she is being invited to do is an act that will mean an eye is pushed inside her—the only way to escape this gaze is to bury the eye inside, where there is nothing to see but the dim blood and organs at work. The bed now is floating up to meet her, and she watches herself uncomprehendingly stretching on the bed, reaching up now to the end, a crashing eruption as fists pound the bedroom door, which bounces violently in the jam, shedding splinters of wood and splatters of foul, stinking water.

Days later, she found a firm swelling on the left side of her abdomen, well buried in the flesh, and decided to see a doctor about it, but the doctor was unable to determine exactly what it was, in fact, she was very confused.

"I don't know what it could be," she says candidly. "It isn't a sebaceous cyst, it isn't a lump of fat, and while it might be a tumor, I wouldn't want to commit myself one way or another without a biopsy."'

She decided to remain in New York for the operation, living in Miriam's apartment.

It was an ectopic pregnancy. Her doctor is even more baffled—"I have no idea whatever how it could have gotten there." The tiny, mummified foetus was lodged just below the musculature of her abdomen. She asked to see it.

"I'm afraid we destroyed it," the doctor admits.

That was Juan's child. There was no one else.

"It must have been there for years! That would give it enough time to migrate to where we found it. But what could have moved it there? And you say you became aware of it suddenly? . . . Because, you know, there was no sign of any other, you know, damage, no pathway."

"What was it like? Well, we call it a foetus, but in this case it was more like an undeveloped twin, in that it was not a complete body. It was mostly eye."

After being released from the hospital, she sits naked by the window of Miriam's apartment, writing reassuringly to her parents, explaining the operation, the strange outcome, the likely period of recovery, her good spirits and firm health, and that she has decided not to come back home, but to remain here, living in Miriam's apartment. She turns abruptly in her seat, staring into the open bedroom for a moment, listening. The bed creaks. She presses a hand to her scar.

THE DYING SEASON

LYNDA E. RUCKER

At dawn, the leisure resort was still and quiet, prefab cabins and trailers jumbled together and sleeping soundly, and along the harbour all was peaceful. The peace would not last; the unseasonably warm and sunny weather so late in the year as October, and particularly for an English seaside village, meant that soon it would be jammed with dog-walkers and families and couples strolling up and down the concrete seafront, taking in the last of the light and the warmth before winter closed in altogether. It was, on the face of it, an unbeautiful shoreline: massive concrete steps leading in low tide to piles of dead black seaweed washed up between large wooden groins. But the dawn's high tide meant that now the sea lapped the steps, while the colourful sailboats glistened in their moorings, the rows of pastel bathing huts were washed in the morning sun, and the sky was a skein of impossible blue with strips torn for clouds.

Sylvia headed up and away from the concrete harbour and to the nature trail that ran above the estuary. The horizon opened before her as she jogged along the scrubby grasses. Gulls wheeled overhead and the shore below was a wash of late-season pink thrift and purple sea lavender. The sea beyond sparkled.

The wind was stronger here and whipped her hair in her face. There was just the wind and the sound of her own breath, and that was a good thing, the tension that still clutched her body from the previous night draining out of her. Big gulps of the fresh salt air.

She could run forever. She ought to run forever. She could do it, just vanish away; wasn't the seaside magical enough for that? An Anglophiliac childhood in America, raised by an English mother, had taught her as much. Viking longships churn across the waters waiting to attack; Jamaica Inn shutters itself to guests and hides its secrets; Merriman Lyon waits by the standing stones, gazing out to sea. There might still be magic here to spirit her away. There might. If only she could run fast enough to catch hold of it.

"Goddammit," John had said the previous night, shoving his plate away. "Why are you bringing *that* up again?" Today, she couldn't even remember what she'd said to him.

"I wasn't," she said. "I didn't mean—," but of course, she did mean, or he said she had, so what did any of it matter?

She ran harder. The tears leaked out the corners of her eyes and were lost on the wind. Now the rhythm of her run beat out two phrases. *I'm sorry. I didn't mean to.* Over and over, spoiling the morning, spoiling everything. Just like she always did.

"I'm trying to fix things here," said John's voice in her head. "I'm trying to make it up to you. Why won't you work with me a little bit? Why won't you help me out? *What's wrong with you?*"

She wheeled round, heading back. She wasn't alone on the trail anymore; as she ran, she drew even with and passed a couple. They both had jet-black hair, were thin and slight and poorly dressed for the weather, the girl in a filmy dress with bare arms and her companion in an equally diaphanous shirt and thin trousers. Perhaps, she thought, they were tourists from someplace much warmer, tricked by the brightness of the day. The wind must have felt cutting to them, and she made a grimace of solidarity in their direction as she passed but they ignored her.

Back at the leisure park, all of the cabins and trailers looked the same. John had been coming here with his parents since he was a child, so he knew exactly which one was theirs, but she'd had to memorize the twists and turns on the gravel pathway in order to find her way back, and even so, she found herself standing for a long time deciding between two cabins, unable to identify which was the right one. For a moment she had the mad idea that both were, or that she was choosing a destiny: walk into one, make the right choice, walk into the other, make the wrong one. But then she thought she heard music coming through the window of one, something classical that John listened to a lot, and what sounded like a child's voice drifted from the window of the other.

"You're just in time," John said as she stepped in. He was wearing an apron and piling up food on a plate: bacon, sausages, grilled tomatoes, a fried egg, a mound of toast. Her stomach clenched. She wasn't hungry; she hated a large breakfast anyway. He knew that. But she couldn't say. She couldn't be difficult. Not now.

"Thought I'd walk up to the harbour in a bit myself," he said with what she told herself was not a forced casualness as she chewed her way methodically through meat, bread, more meat. "I need to check my email and I can't get a signal in here. The signal's better there."

She was glad her mouth was full because it prevented her saying all the things she wanted to say: *That's funny my signal's fine. Why are you really going to the harbour? Who are you phoning? I'll come with you.*

She ate as much as she could but still knew he was going to be angry at her because it wasn't enough and so despite everything she was relieved when he pushed his own plate away and said, "Right, back in a bit," and headed out. She dumped what was left on her plate in the trash and washed the dishes, then sat for a while on the sofa listening to her stomach rumble unpleasantly.

A hammering at the door startled her so much that she simply stared through the glass for a moment or two at the girl on the other side of it. It was the girl from the nature trail. She'd changed into a shapeless hoodie over leggings, and her stringy dark hair framed a pale narrow face. She smiled in a way Sylvia thought was meant to be encouraging and friendly. It reminded her instead of the bared teeth of a monkey.

"I—hi, can I help you?" Sylvia said through the door, which felt standoffish but the girl gave her the creeps.

"We're just in the cabin over there," the girl said, nodding her head in a vague direction, and Sylvia detected what John would call a posh accent, "and we're wondering if you've any milk we can borrow? Just for coffee."

"Oh! Of course!" She still didn't ask the girl in. She opened the door just enough to pass the mug of milk through, keeping the glass between them, then felt a rush of guilt for being so unfriendly and added, "My name's Sylvia. I think I saw you up on the nature trail? Do you spend a lot of time here?"

But the girl was already turning away, saying something about family friends of her boyfriend. Sylvia watched her walk away up the gravel path but couldn't see what cabin she went into.

She'd had time to shower and dry her makeup by the time John returned. She resisted the urge to ask him something leading like, "Anything good in your email?" but she couldn't help saying, "Something weird happened while you were gone."

"Oh?" He was only half-listening, had picked up the remote and was flicking through a series of unpromising-looking programs.

"This girl came by to borrow some milk, but something about her bothered me."

"Bothered you?" He finally looked over at her. "Did you say someone was bothering you?"

"No, I just mean there was something off about her I couldn't put my finger on. She said she and her boyfriend were staying some-where over that way—"waving her hand as vaguely as the girl had—"and that the place belonged to some family friends of her boyfriend, or something. But you know what I kept thinking? About those horror movies, you know, like the home invasion ones?" John loved horror movies, the more violent and gory the better. Sylvia hated them but watched them with him to appease him. "The ones where they go in and kill all the people and then act like they're the ones who live in the house? I kept thinking the girl reminded me of one of those people."

John kept channel surfing. After a moment he said distractedly, "That's a bit mad."

She said, "I know. I mean, I didn't really think it. It's just what it reminded me of. She seemed weird."

John threw down the remote. "Fuck all on the telly as usual. I'm going to do some work and then let's walk into the village. Get out a little bit."

"Yes," she said. "That's where we went wrong yesterday. Too much time sitting around here getting on each others' nerves."

John said, "What are you talking about? Yesterday was fine." Then he was gone, out of the room, and she heard the shower come on. While she waited for him, she went out on the porch to see if she could see the girl again, or anyone else, but there were no signs of life at the leisure resort at all. Even the child who'd been shouting from the nearby window had fallen silent. They might have been all alone there.

John often worked remotely from his London office and it allowed them the leisure to take off midweek from the city occasionally just as they'd done this time. Sylvia lay in the bedroom and tried to read while he worked, but she couldn't seem to focus on either of the books she'd brought.

She dozed off, and next thing she knew John was shaking her awake and saying they ought to take that walk. As they wandered up into the village and round a few indifferent shops she couldn't get over the feeling that she was still dreaming. There wasn't much to do in town, and she said they ought to pop into the Tesco and pick up something for dinner and head back, but John suggested they stop off at a pub. It was nice enough to sit outside even though the sun was setting. A group of men had commandeered the bar inside, but they were alone in the grassy garden.

"Funny listening to the conversations in there," she said. "The one man was bragging, saying his missus had her own money and he had his and they went out with their friends as they liked when they liked and it wasn't like before with Yvonne."

"It's just local people talking."

"I know," she said. "I didn't mean anything—"

He said, "I know it's not as witty and sophisticated as the things your artist friends talk about but then maybe if you paid a little more attention to what people are really like you'd sell something."

Once she would have bitten back at him in defense, but she had long since learned that such an exchange would be futile. Something passed between them. She thought, *I'm going to leave him.* She wasn't sure yet when or how, but in that moment she knew it in her bones, and the knowledge was as irrevocable as knowing you had cancer or that it was raining outside or that you were another year older. As soon as she thought it, it became immutable truth.

He said, "Shall we have another?" like nothing was wrong, and she agreed. She could do this, she could play this agreeable part as long as she needed to. It was almost liberating, like being somebody else entirely. Send the real Sylvia away for a time and let some acquiescent creature take her place. Then behind her she heard someone say, "Oh, look, it's our neighbours," and she turned and it was the couple again. The girl was back in an unsuitable dress, this time a thin white one far too insubstantial for the chill edging in along with the dark. She had combed her dark hair and made up her pale face so that it was even paler save for the dark smudge of her eyes and ruby lips. The two of them looked like a pair of vaguely out-of-date and out-of-place goths, slumming it.

The girl said, "I'm Lynne and this is Gabriel. Mind if we join you?" Of course they minded, but what on earth was there to say? And then Gabriel bought a round, so they were trapped. Still, Lynne and John appeared to be hitting it off, and John rarely hit it off with anyone. Sylvia leaned forward to Gabriel, who seemed always on the verge of smiling contemptuously at a joke only he was in on, and said, "Lynne was saying something about your cabin belonging to family friends—"

Lynne and John stopped the conversation they were having and fell silent, and Gabriel shrugged and said, "People Lynne's parents know," and Lynne turned that bared-tooth grin on her and nodded. "Just some people," she said. "People we know."

"I was asking," Sylvia said, "because John's been coming here since he was a little boy and it's my first time and I keep getting lost. Do you have that problem? I guess at least if you walk into someone's house around here they're not likely to shoot you like in America."

Gabriel said, "Well, there are a lot of hunters and fishermen around here. Our cabin's full of books about it, and trophies." Was that the hint of a foreign accent she detected in his speech? She couldn't tell. Anyway, they could go now, they'd had their pints, but John wouldn't hear of leaving, he had to get the next round, and the evening passed into a haze just like that, two more pints turning into four more pints turning into who knew how many. Lynne said she was a clothing designer and Gabriel was—what was Gabriel? At first Sylvia thought it was something to do with new media, some kind of managing editor for a music publication online, but later there was something about his recording studio, so she wasn't sure. She thought their circles in London must overlap someplace but when she threw out a handful of likely names they both shook their heads, looking bemused, smiles playing at the corners of their mouths. She was drunk. Why was she trying to make sense of anything?

Then it was last orders and she was laughing and leaning on John and the stars reeled overhead and it was just like things used to be and what had she been so upset about anyway? They should eat something, the four of them, and a Chinese takeaway across the street was still open. They ordered spring rolls and chicken with oyster sauce and chips and staggered back down through the town. John was walking up ahead with Lynne and she was lagging behind with Gabriel but she couldn't think of anything to say to him and then the sea was off to their left and she could hear it, sighing softly, washing up against the shore. She wanted to run away from the three of them and toward it. She imagined it, black and cold and endless under the night sky, unpierced by the sliver of moon high above. Secretive. Safe.

"Aren't you cold?" she called to Lynne up ahead of her, but Lynne didn't seem to hear her, and Gabriel said, "She's just like that, she doesn't feel the cold. She doesn't feel many things, really."

"That's a really odd thing to say," Sylvia said, feeling suddenly much more sober. They turned right into the leisure park, into the maze, and Lynne and Gabriel made noises about inviting them over for a nightcap but John said no, he had a conference call early in the morning. She followed John to their cabin but she couldn't shake the feeling that he was leading them back to the wrong one. He went right at a point where she was sure he should have gone left, and she nearly said something. As he fumbled for the keys, she could see the living room through the glass sliding door just as they'd left it. It looked the same, but something was off about it, she was sure of it, something just outside her conscious memory: a piece of furniture moved a foot this way, a nearly-imperceptibly different shade of carpet. Of course that was silly. Even if she'd been correct about turning left, this place was such a maze that there was probably ~~never~~ ~~way to get back to where~~ you'd come from.

Inside, they set the takeaway on the counter and John kissed her hard and then he was pushing up her skirt and pushing aside her underwear and shoving himself inside her, there in the kitchen with the counter hard against her back. She gasped and lifted her head and that was when she saw Lynne, from the window over the sink, standing some yards away but staring in at them through the window, her pale face ghostly in the dark. Sylvia cried out and shoved him away, and he stumbled back, and it would have been comical if he weren't so angry, but now there was no Lynne to be seen out there. Of course there was not. "What the hell?" John said, and she said, "I'm sorry. I thought I saw someone."

"Don't be stupid," he said, and she said, "I know, I'm sorry," but she'd set off another argument as usual, and then next thing she knew she was waking stiff and sore and tangled in bed sheets. Her head was pounding and for a few awful moments she could not remember where she was. The previous evening after the kitchen was nearly a blank: she could remember arguing, and trying to apologize—her, not John—and then not much after. She went into the kitchen for a drink of water and the plastic bag of Chinese food was still sitting there on the counter, untouched.

A run might clear her head. She headed out into a bright cold morning. This time the wind whipping across the sea had an icy quality to it, more so than the day before. It felt like an abrupt shift in the weather and the season, just as something had shifted in her the previous day. Across the water black storm clouds gathered.

As she ran up beyond the harbour to the nature trail the wind intensified, biting at her face, tearing the moisture from her eyes. It was too much. She turned, cutting the run short.

Back in the leisure village, she tried to retrace their steps from the previous night, turning right where John had when she thought he should have turned left. She ended up in front of a cabin that looked like theirs, but it couldn't be; the way hadn't circled round, it had gone off in the opposite direction, and so she went back the way she'd come. This time she went right. Once again, the cabin looked the same, but now she must have been mistaken, there was something taped to the glass of the front door and there hadn't been before. No, she couldn't be wrong; she had followed this path every morning for the last three after her run.

The thing taped to their door was a note, written in an angry scrawl.

We could hear you last night, everybody could all around with your sex noises, and it was disgusting, this is a family place and we are here with our families not like you filthy people and your fucking. What are we supposed to tell our children?

Sylvia stood stunned, frozen, awash in a stew of emotions: shame, humiliation, fury, despair. She looked all around, as though whoever had delivered the note would be lurking nearby. The cabins all appeared deserted as ever. She went over to the one where she thought she'd heard the child's voice from the window the previous day. Curtains were drawn across the glass door so she could not see inside, and she knocked tentatively. What she would say when someone answered she had no idea, but there was no response. She peeked through a window, which was uncurtained, and jumped back, startled.

The place was a tip; it appeared to have been ransacked, clothing and other items strewn across the floor, plates of rotting food stacked about. It looked as though no one had been in there for a long time.

It also looked much the same as their own cabin, from what she could tell under all the mess: roughly the same furniture layout, the same furniture even. Maybe all the cabins came furnished the same way and people didn't bother to change them around.

Sylvia stumbled back. She ran back to their cabin and burst through the door calling, "John!" only to be confronted by a thunderous look; he was on the phone. Of course, the conference call. He made go away gestures to her like she was an unruly pet. She dropped the note on the carpet and fled into the shower, fled him, fled everything. She turned on the water as hot as she could stand and scrubbed till her skin was raw and it still wasn't enough. Then John was hammering at the door. She cried "I—"

shoved it open anyway, shouting, "What the hell is this?" and when she peeked round the shower curtain he was waving the note at her like it was her fault.

She shut the water off and grabbed her towel, winding it round. "It was on the door. Someone had taped it to the door when I came back from my run. And John, I think there's something wrong in the cabin beside us—"

"What the hell? Who the hell did this?" John rubbed his hand over his face. "How am I supposed to—I know the people here. They know my family. They've known me since I was a child. What am I supposed to do? How am I going to face them?"

She was aghast. "How are they going to face you, more like—John, that note's insane. Who would do something like that? What's wrong with people?"

She didn't want to add that she couldn't remember the previous night at all, after the argument in the kitchen; had they gone straight to bed? Had they been loud? Had they been so loud that people in other cabins could hear them? Her memory was a clear, featureless blank, undisturbed even by fitful dreams.

John slammed the bathroom door, shaking the entire cabin. She waited there for several minutes and then crept out. She scurried across the hall to the bedroom and shut the door where she dressed quickly and began shoving things in her bag, her mind racing. She did not want to spend one more moment in his presence. She could push the bag out the window, stroll past John in the living room and say she was going for a walk, circle round and grab her things, walk into town, bus, train, home, back to their flat before he'd worked out she was truly gone as opposed to vanishing in a sulk for a few hours. She could then get anything important she needed and stay with a friend while she figured out what to do next.

She was still throwing things into her bag when John came in the room. "What are you doing?" he said. "Why are you packing? We're not going to be driven out of here by anyone. We have just as much right to be here as anyone else." She said, "I'm just trying to get organized," but his questions deflated her. She thought of what it would take to run away from him, to leave him. Her head hurt and her body was exhausted and she just wanted to curl up and sleep for a very long time. She said, "Anyway, we need to get back to London soon," and he said, "What for? Some dilettante friend of yours smearing herself with mud and writhing around on stage again?"

"Sarah's not a dilettante," she said, "and anyway it wasn't mud it was—never mind." She shoved the bag off the bed. There were better ways to leave him, better ways to make that plan once they'd returned to London. At the moment she needed sleep. The hangover she'd hoped to clear out with the run had taken hold with a vengeance. She crawled into bed and slipped almost immediately into a dream in which she was running along the shoreline only instead of bathing huts it was lined with the leisure park's cabins and trailers. All of them had fallen into disrepair. Some had their fronts torn off and the furniture inside was rotting and falling through floorboards. She kept thinking she just needed to get past them and up to the nature trail but she seemed to be running in circles, or they were just endless, and something was pacing her, just at her heels, though when she turned her head she couldn't see anything. Then whatever the thing was grabbed her and started shaking her roughly, and John's voice said, "Wake up. We've got a dinner invitation from Lynne and Gabriel," and she swam groggily to the surface. Had she really slept the entire day away? She was starving, and realized she hadn't eaten anything since the unwelcome breakfast the previous morning.

She crawled back out of bed and ran a comb through her hair.

She looked terrible, puffy and worn. She was making herself a cup of tea in the kitchen when John came in and said they were already running late and had to go. "Five minutes," she pleaded. "What, do we have a booking they're going to give away if we aren't punctual enough?" But he kicked up such a fuss that in the end she left her tea there cooling in its mug and followed him out.

She said, "How do you know which one is theirs anyway? I can barely find ours," and he said, "They told me, they stopped by while you were sleeping." She supposed that if you knew the leisure village well enough that certain things must serve as landmarks but as far as she could tell they were just walking past the same cabins. John came up in front of one that was exactly like all of the others and said in a satisfied voice, "Here we are!"

"Welcome!" Lynne said, opening the door to them, and as they went inside she felt vaguely disappointed at how ordinary this cabin was too. Table, chairs, a couple of sofas, a television, a gas fire flickering warmly and a kitchenette off the one side.

She said, "It looks almost exactly like ours."

"Oh, yes, they're all the same," Lynne said vaguely, but there were some differences. Gabriel had mentioned hunting but not taxidermy though it, too, was clearly a hobby of the owner as evidenced by several somewhat worn-looking birds—she identified a pheasant, a mallard—mounted on solid bases on the mantle. A shelf near the fireplace held books on the topic along with manuals about angling and hunting.

"Hope you like curry," Gabriel said from the kitchen, and they all agreed that yes, they liked curry, and Lynne brought them wine and they sat on the sofa and Sylvia drank the first glass much too fast, but afterward she felt calmer. Lynne poured her a second and she sat back. The room was warm and the curry smelled so good and maybe John was right. Maybe she needed to relax. Maybe things were in her head. Maybe she was the problem after all.

She was lost in thought and paying no attention to the conversation around her—this was another thing that drove John mad—when she realized John was reading something. It was the note that had been taped to their door.

She said, "John, don't!" but it was too late, and no one was paying attention to her anyway. Her face flamed at hearing the words spoken, and remembering the shock she'd felt on first seeing it, but the other three did not seem to share her sense of humiliation and outrage, least of all John who'd been so angry in front of her. Lynne turned toward her while they were all still laughing and it occurred to her that what bothered her about Lynne's smile was that all of her teeth were too small. They looked like two tiny, even rows of baby teeth in an adult mouth, an adult face.

She murmured, "Sorry, where's your bathroom?" even though she knew based on the identical layout of their own cabin, but they didn't hear her anyway, so she got up and slipped into the hallway and tried the first door, the one that was the main bathroom in their cabin. It appeared to be locked. Out of curiosity she tried another door, one she knew must lead to a bedroom, and it was locked as well. She stood indecisively for a moment or two in the hallway until their laughter reached her again, and then she tried the third door. She knew from the layout of their own place that it would be a bedroom with a half bath just off of it.

This door opened, and the light switch illuminated a plain room that appeared unused. Just a bed, a bureau and no personal items. There was a shelf above the bed with more books on it about hunting and mounted on the wall above that, dominating the room, the pale skull of something with enormous antlers. It must have been a stag, she thought, with its hollow eyes and jagged opening that she guessed must be the snout, the nasal cavity, but which looked like a shrieking mouth.

Imagine how restful a night you'd have with *that* over your head. In the bathroom, she washed her face and hands and looked at herself in the mirror for a long time. She didn't recognize the face that looked back; her eyes looked as hollow as those of the poor dead stag. The wine and heat had flushed her cheeks but it was an unhealthy, feverish flush. She shouldn't drink any more, certainly not before eating something.

She deliberately did not look in the direction of the skull again, and back in the living room, no one seemed to have even noticed she'd left. Gabriel was dishing up dinner at last, heaps of basmati rice and rich yellow curry, and she fell on it ravenously.

"Easy," John said to her, "it's not going anywhere," and she stopped, embarrassed, and Gabriel tried to smooth it over by saying, "It's nice when someone appreciates your cooking" but that only made her feel more self-conscious. Lynne, poking in a desultory way at her plate with one fork and twirling a wine glass with her other hand, said, "You must not look at goblin men, you must not buy their fruit."

Sylvia said, "What?"

"It's from the Rossetti ———," ———— said. "You know, you aren't supposed to eat fairy food or you'll be trapped with them forever. Lynne and I were working on a project a while ago based around it."

"I hope this doesn't mean we're stuck here at the leisure park for the rest of our days," Sylvia said, and they all laughed. It must have been too much wine on an empty stomach that made her add, "You know, I had the funniest thought when I first saw Lynne. That you two didn't belong here. That you'd done something with the people who really lived here and just made yourselves at home."

As soon as it was out she regretted it, but they were laughing again, thank goodness they all laughed, and Gabriel said, "Not sure you'd have to kill anyone to move into one of the cabins this time of year, it's all pretty easy pickings," and they all laughed more. She joined them though she didn't even know why.

"That reminds me," she said. "One of the trailers near us, I think someone might have broken into it actually. It looks like it was ransacked or something. Is there some kind of security here?"

"The Liddells," said Lynne, and nodded solemnly. "There was some trouble there, actually."

Gabriel nodded. "The father. He went a bit mad—it was awful, the police came and everything. They took him away."

"That surprises me," John said. "I've known the Liddells for years. I'd never imagine something like that from them."

"Well, you know," Lynne said solemnly. "They say you just can't tell with families."

They all sat silently for an appropriate moment or two contemplating the sad fate of the Liddells, and Sylvia said, "What about these people, John?"

"What about them?"

"You know just about everyone around here—do you know Gabriel and Lynne's friends, that this cabin belongs to?"

John looked blank for a moment, then shook his head. "It's a big place. A lot of people are transient. I don't know everyone, just the regulars right around my family's cabin."

"You weren't kidding about the enthusiastic hunting," Sylvia said. "That's quite a trophy, the stag back there," and she inclined her head in the direction of the rest of the cabin.

"Oh, yes, that," Lynne said.

"It's kind of creepy," Sylvia said, and John said, "A stag?" and Lynne said, "You should see it, John. Come on back, I'll show it to you."

Sylvia and Gabriel sat in silence after they had gone. Finally Gabriel broke it by asking if she wanted more curry and she said no, she'd had enough, and they continued to sit there.

"Taking their time," she said with a nervous laugh, "it's not that much to look at," and, "I'm going to see what they're up to" and Gabriel said, "I really wouldn't if I were you."

"What do you mean by that?" It felt like the first honest thing she'd said to anyone in days.

"It makes you look clingy and suspicious," Gabriel said. "I don't think John would like that. I know Lynne wouldn't."

She thought then of all the things she ought to say. Things prefaced by arch remarks like *I beg your pardon* or even a properly-inflected *excuse me*? She did not say anything. She and Gabriel sat there and waited and they looked at each other, and she thought how small and strange he was, imagined his pale face a mask to hide a hideous creature beneath it.

Gabriel said, "What do you think they're doing back there anyway? It's not what you think."

"How do you know what I think?" she said, but even as the words were out she felt like she knew his answer, that he knew exactly what she thought, that he knew everything about her, and John too, that they both did and had since their encounter on the nature trail the previous morning. That she ought never to have looked upon them in the first place, or given them something of hers and John's—the mug, the milk—or eaten their goblin fruit. As soon as John came back they would leave. She would make sure of it. Even if she had to make a scene, a terrible embarrassing scene no one would ever forgive her for, and what did she care what any of the other three thought about her anyway?

She said, "I hate this time of year. Everything coming to an end. It depresses me."

"I guess it all depends on how you look at things."

"What other way is there?"

He shrugged. She guessed that he wasn't really in the mood for conversation.

An unsettling chill had settled over the cabin despite the merrily burning gas fire. Any moment now John would emerge with Lynne and she would insist that they go home. Not just back to the cabin, but home-home, all the way back to London; there was still time to catch the last bus and the last train if they were quick about it. Or—she could just leave.

"I feel sick," she said, and set her wine glass down. "I have to go. Tell John I'll see him back at the cabin." She was entirely done with social niceties, and without another word she stepped out the door into a night so black and cold that it momentarily seized her breath. The moon sliver from the previous night had been swallowed up by clouds and she was forced to make her way nearly blind. She knew she was on the path because she felt its gravel under her feet, but then there was grass, so now she must be wandering between cabins. Then she no longer cared about finding her way back to the cabin at all, only out of the leisure park. If she could get to the main road, and the harbour, and into town, she had her purse with her and she could buy a ticket or even thumb a lift if it came to that.

She dug her phone from her pocket so she could use its light, but the battery icon was red and draining fast. On impulse she thumbed

John's number, but his phone simply rang and rang and his voice told her to leave a message or send a text if it was urgent. Then the screen went black. She could hear the sea nearby, and she moved toward the sound with the certainty that if she could get near enough to the sea, she would be safe, but the sound, or her ears, deceived her, shifting, now behind her, now before her.

When the clouds above parted at last, the feeble light of the faraway moon revealed that she was at the edge of the leisure park. The cabins behind her waited, and across the black strip of road the sea would be surging against the concrete steps of the harbour. She had the idea that she had emerged into some kind of purgatory, that she might wander an eternity among the empty cabins, but then a car's oncoming lights loomed up ahead and she stepped to the roadside and put out her thumb. To her surprise, the car came to a stop. A worried-looking middle-aged woman popped her head out of the window. "You lost, love?" she asked. Sylvia said, "I don't know, I need to get to the train station," and the woman said she was on her way to Colchester and would that do? Sylvia said yes, of course it would.

As they sped away she imagined John might have gone to look for her by now, might have discovered she was not back at the cabin. She felt she owed the woman some explanation, so she said, "Thank you. I had a fight with my partner. I just want to go home now and talk it over with him later," and the woman said, "You don't need to explain, love, these things happen." Sylvia pulled out her dead phone again and looked at it, wishing she could ring John and make sure he was okay. The woman commented that it was very late in the year and hadn't the leisure park shut down for the winter? Sylvia found she could not answer her. She could not speak again at all except to thank the woman who drove her right up to the station, where she bought a ticket with minutes to spare. She ran down the platform to her train, dodging other travellers and their piles of luggage, but she could not shake the feeling that she was no longer real, that if she touched anyone she would vanish like the mist rising off the pavement. She leapt aboard her train and was still making her way down the aisle as it eased out of the station.

Then the lights of the station were behind them, and the sound of the engine was the sound of the sea, and they were gliding into a night that was dark, and secret, and uncharted.

A
DISCREET
MUSIC

**MICHAEL
WEHUNT**

"And how can body, laid in that white rush,
But feel the strange heart beating where it lies?"
—W. B. Yeats

THE DARK BLOODLESS TASTE OF WIDOWHOOD HAD COATED Hiram's mouth for three nights when he awoke at dawn alongside that cold gulf of bed. He knew at once some kind of change had visited as he slept. Two hard knots burned in his shoulder blades, and feathers were strewn like bleached leaves across the sheets. But he looked out the window, away from these things, bleary-eyed and trying to miss Sandra.

It had begun to snow in the night, the last of the Virginia winter. By late morning the flurries would turn thick and settle into blankets, bright against the pallbearers' black suits. Bright against his own.

And he was glad it was Sandra he saw through the window and not that other. He drifted into thoughts of his wife, the kind a fresh widower should have, and the bed held him in its half-empty palm. This same oak frame had supported them every night of their forty-two years, the creaks of Sandra rising from it each day the only alarm clock he'd needed. This same shade of pale blue on the walls. Not much had changed their private architecture.

The phone chirred from the nightstand. Sandra's pillow lay plump beside it, the shape of her head already gone. He reached across to answer the call but his hand fell inches short. Instead he made a fist and eased a dent into her pillow, almost pressed his face there to take in the smell of her hair. He couldn't bring himself to give his guilt that satisfaction.

He looked back out the window and watched a handful of years melt from her, Sandra in her dirt-smeared apron, turning the soil around the hellebores with a spade. She climbed to her feet and dragged the back of her hand across her forehead, leaving a red-brown streak that stood out like a brand. And like a brand, it seemed to Hiram the one image of her that wanted to live on for him. Her hair was twisted into a tight silver bun, and he was able to savor, still after all this time, the thought of her undoing it before bed. Her one vanity freed and plunging down her back, anticipating the comb of his fingers. She was always so quick to gasp at his touch.

Now the front yard lined itself with pews, and somewhere close Hiram walked their daughter, Helen, down the aisle, but the window framed only Sandra in blue chiffon, the gold of her hair then only interrupted by subtle ribbons of gray, like guests she had not invited.

But the streak of dirt was on her forehead still, and he thought of her soon in the earth and turned his head away, squeezing his eyes shut. He'd been a smoker until his sixtieth birthday, while she was the one who used the treadmill he'd bought. How had her heart lurched with a fatal thunder while his crept on? A feather brushed his cheek, pulled a teardrop into itself. His shoulder blades ached like something missing.

Gravel crunched in the driveway. Helen had come to take him to the church. He lay there, for a last moment ignoring the dull pain in his back and the feathers scattered across the sheets. Helen had always had a key to the house. Sandra had never accepted that her little girl had long since left the nest, but since she'd only moved an hour away, maybe Sandra hadn't quite been wrong.

The front door opened and Hiram swept the feathers down the bed, yanking the comforter up to his neck just as his daughter rapped on the bedroom door. "Daddy?" she said. "Are you decent?"

Decent. The word rang dull as a wrapped bell. He didn't respond.

Helen came into the room already wearing a gentle exasperation on her face. She held a plastic cleaner's bag, and Hiram didn't want to see the stark black suit inside. He found himself angry that he saw more of himself than Sandra in that face. As if she, too, was not paying her mother the proper tribute. It was his upturned flare of the nose, his dirty blue eyes flecked with green like an algae-stained pond. He only found Sandra in his daughter's cheekbones, the soft jut of the chin, something faint in the shape of her mouth.

"Daddy, I'm sorry but you can't do this," she said. "Not today."

"I'm not feeling well," Hiram whispered. "Maybe tomorrow."

She sat down on the bed. "It's okay that you didn't go to the viewing, Daddy," she said. "Everybody understands. But the funeral is now, not tomorrow. You know that. You have to come say goodbye to her."

He looked out the window again. Only snow falling in vague lines. "Just give me a minute," he told her.

When Helen had hung the suit on the closet door and left the room, Hiram forced himself out of bed. Three or four feathers were caught in his wake and swirled briefly to the floor.

In the mirror his bloodshot eyes regarded him, the skin sagging below them into little troughs. He stalled the moment as long as he could—knowing Helen wouldn't hesitate to knock on this door too—and turned around, twisted his chin back onto his shoulder. Feathers, a dozen or more matching the strange snowfall in the bed, were stuck to his upper back. He plucked one off and a sharp tugging pain brought a hiss through his teeth. It had come *out*, not off. A trickle of blood ran down from the new wound.

He backed a step closer to the sink. Ignoring the feathers, he saw what was more worrisome: something, a growth or tumor, stretched the skin high on each of his shoulder blades. They leaned away from one another, two inches or so wide and half as long, the skin around them pulled taut. He reached, old muscles complaining at the unnatural angle, and touched the one on the left, baring his teeth against a surge of pain that didn't come. It kept the same low ache and was both cool and hot to the touch.

Hiram caught his gaze in the mirror—wings? The idea felt as distant as tree roots under his skin, or motor oil in his veins. He denied it, shut it all from his mind. This brought Sandra back into it where she belonged, but just behind her, drawing closer in his return to the foreground, was Jim. He most of all did not want to think of Jim, not today, this ghost that had only now demanded that Hiram admit he was haunted.

He whispered into the casket. Its cherry wood was polished to an unnatural shine, but mercifully the undertaker had been sparing with Sandra. She lay muted and worn and beautiful against the pale satin.

"I'm so sorry, love." Hiram stood there and seemed to feel all those stages of grief upon him, ~~~~~~~~~~~~~~~~~~~~~~ purchase. There was a great weight pressed against him, that she could die when he was the less defensible. Her hands were folded across her chest, and he cupped one of his own over the dry cool skin. He would have felt blessed to crawl into the coffin with her, reach up and pull the lid down over the both of them. He drew his hand away and traced the back of a finger along her jawline. A small white feather slipped from his cuff and into the hair behind her ear. He wondered whether to leave it there.

The mutter of the church built slowly behind him. He turned, his shoulders giving a throb beneath the tight seams of his suit coat. For a moment he didn't see the cousins and the friends gathered there, Helen comforting someone whose head bowed under a cloud of white hair. He saw 1981, the last year they had before Hiram quietly doomed himself with Jim Hudson. He saw one summer night, in a canoe he and Sandra had taken out on Parson Black Lake, the moon a bloated joy hanging up there just for them. He heard the cicadas filling the world, and Sandra whispering, "Let's jump in."

Hiram looked back to his wife. She'd been such a smiler. He closed his eyes and reminded himself it was the funeral, not 1981 and not the viewing, either. He had avoided seeing her like this, and now here he was. He felt Helen's presence as she reached him, and before she could grasp his shoulder, the swollen knot there, he turned and took her warm, thriving hand. Let her lead him to the front pew. He sat and thought of that canoe, set adrift by an oar braced against the tree-crowded bank. He thought of how young his hands had been that night, holding the oar, how clean they had been.

"The eye is the first circle." Jim had told him that beside the Missouri River, in the early hours of Hiram's second night in St. Louis. It had always sounded like a quote to Hiram, but in the moment he'd been too embarrassed to ask. The words wouldn't leave his head these past days, so he typed them into Google and learned they were from an Emerson essay. Jim spoke to him all over again as he read. About how the second circle is the horizon seen by the first, and how this shape comes to be repeated through nature and the world, on and on.

He thought about that repetition, outward from the circle of his own vision, first glimpsing the tall black-haired man reaching up to staple a Xeroxed paper to a less-cluttered height of a telephone pole, denim shirt riding up three tanned inches above the thick belt. All those razor-straight horizon lines. The man's sign offered a reward for a lost miniature Pinscher named Otis. Hiram had thought it a kindness, to not cover up the flyers already there. It was the first and last time he ever felt this heat-flash reaction toward anyone. That it was a man disoriented and thrilled him.

They'd shared guilty food and their first guilty kiss under the Arch. Hiram had been sent to Missouri for a week to attend a tech convention, and he wondered how many of the other tourists craning their necks had wives back home. "If that wasn't the gateway kiss, I don't know what is," Jim had told him when their lips pulled apart. They'd held hands through the sparse downtown and let the stares bounce off them. The week had seemed as long as a breath. At the end, the airport, glazed with the awe of what he'd done, he wondered where Otis was. If he'd be found.

Circles. Coming back, always. It was how he had thought about Jim all these years, he realized now, thirty-three of them, thirty-three loops back to the fourth night and a fifth of bourbon in a hotel room. Had the room been on the sixth floor? No, it had been far too dingy a place to stand that tall. There had been a thump and a shout through the thin wall, "Quiet the fuck down." The rattled wheeze of the air conditioner on their sweat-slicked skin. Clenching and pulling, their soft animal sounds. He wondered where that Wild Turkey bottle was now, if it still had the ancient taste of their lips on its mouth, and why was his memory doing this to him?

Sandra had been arranging a bridal bouquet at work when her heart quit on her. She'd gone quickly, the florist blurted out when he called, that strange consolation everyone seemed to fumble for. Hiram had squeezed the phone until its plastic groaned, imagined her on the concrete floor, clipped gardenia stems, her hair come unraveled from its bun and silvering all the vivid color in the shop.

But his second thought, elbowing the first rudely aside, had been of Jim. What Jim might look like now, did he have grandchildren, did they brown in the sun the way he had. The thunderbolt of guilt at that had come, but it had taken a shameful long time.

He remembered all the nights he padded into the bathroom while Sandra slept in her bland peace. His left hand pretending the porcelain ridge of the sink was the corded muscles in Jim's thigh while he thrust himself into the right. The grease spot from his forehead on the mirror as he finished, gritting his teeth against a week that kept falling further into the past. He would stand there so long the covers had cooled when he returned to bed, to stare at the ceiling. These acts had to lead him back somewhere. Surely they did.

And, now, he was thinking of Sandra less and less as the hours pooled in the empty house. He and Helen had argued. She'd wanted to stay another week, get him on his feet and into a routine. Hiram had made her go, just four days after they lowered her mother into the wound in the earth, the day the growths on his back split open and blood-smeared vines reached out. The pain grew teeth then and he knew he couldn't have hidden it from his daughter for long. Advil, salve, nothing helped until he took a weary shower and felt an inexplicable relief once the water hit him.

He was beyond the point of denial—they were wings. Arcing out like snowy antennae from his shoulders, each smooth unfurling feather the length of a hand. They were soft enough for pillows once the blood was washed out and they dried. Another day or two, he sensed, and he could fold them beneath a coat. Afternoons were starting to touch fifty degrees, but still with a thread of ice in the air.

He sat at his desk and scrubbed his face with his hands. He typed 'Jim Hudson' into the search bar, and his finger waited for some sign, fidgeting near the keyboard. There would be thousands of Jim Hudsons, his own hiding in their midst, somewhere. Even in an obituary, he warned himself.

"You should stay through the weekend, Hiram Newell," Jim had said that faraway night, and curled his hand into a tube through which he watched him. Then Jim said it again, only this time it meant, *You should stay longer than that.* But Hiram knew he couldn't. The closest he would get was writing one long, anguished letter two years later, then tearing it into smaller and smaller pieces until his fingers cramped.

Jim had reached across the bed for him, and their bodies made a circle. One that had never, for Hiram, gained any circumference. He wondered how he dared dream of protracting it now, in the wake of his wife's death, when his anatomy was occupied with becoming an angel.

An angel—what gave a man the right? He loved Jim. He was surer than ever, now the bottle was uncorked. He tapped enter and began to sift.

The wings matured entering the second week. He admired them in his wife's standing mirror, reflecting that he'd never had any particular grace in his life. Sandra had always carried enough for the both of them.

But already they felt an organic part of his body. A bunching of the muscles in his back gave the wings a powerful flex and bloom, as if in warning, mating, or yearning for flight, all of which he was trying to ignore. They spanned six feet at this reach, until the elbowed joints bent and he collapsed them down against his back.

Thin, hollow rails of bone extended along the outer edge of each. The feathers stank but he didn't mind, as he now bathed every few hours. His pores thirsted for the comfort of water.

There were moments in which he reveled in the wings. There were moments in which he despaired of them. And in those various moments, either Sandra or Jim. He was delaying both. He'd stopped searching for Jim two days after he'd begun, unable to see how he fit into this new mythology. His wife, or someone of import, wanted him to join her, in heaven, he supposed. Hiram would have to find his own grace now, for angels did great works, lithely, purely.

At last he climbed up on the roof in the tenth night and jumped off. Both wings caught the air but couldn't come close to holding it. He dropped like a stone and heard bones snapping, dry and brittle, the pain red then black. Sometime later he woke shivering on the grass, wet with frost in the building dawn light.

His left wing and arm healed with strange speed. The mild flu he picked up in the damp and the cold faded. The feathers began to spread over his skin just as quickly, emerging down his back and around onto his abdomen. The flightless wings seemed less grand to him now, after the failed attempt at the sky.

And there were other changes to consider. The full head of hair he'd managed to hold onto began to turn white and stiff. A bridge of skin grew between each of his toes. He lay in bed and stared at them, slowly realizing. Slowly accepting. Slowly coming to a decision.

He started hearing music while he lay mending. Distant strains of something circling in on itself, simple melodies that he could almost place. It had the quality of a shy transistor radio in the next room. Later, in spring, he might have assumed it was an ice cream truck, trawling some near neighborhood and carrying through the warming air. But this was more discreet, warm and synthesized, and it both calmed and drove him mad from wishing he could turn the volume up, to climb inside its notes.

Three weeks after the funeral, he resolved at last to find Jim. He swung his legs—which were thinning to the bone, the skin shading a charcoal gray—out of the bed. In the gloom of the hall a shape retreated from him, the twirl of a blue skirt as the figure turned into the kitchen. He followed but the room was empty. Sandra's mother's cast-iron skillet swung gently over the stove, as if it had been hung from its hook a moment ago, or touched in passing.

Sandra kept her distance from him. He woke the next few mornings to sense her pressed into a corner of the bedroom, away from the curtains, and when he stood or even looked toward her, she was gone. "What is it you want, love?" he asked. But her old force of personality had departed, or was slow to return.

He checked the mirror with an obsession. No angel he'd heard of was covered in feathers, as he might soon be. A swan, then. He felt certain that his neck would begin to stretch, the feathers continue to flower, and this old ugly duckling would transcend into something more beautiful. Because the symbolism of it—the very thought of it all told him he was meant to be with Jim.

His days settled into the routine Helen had wanted for him. He ate buttered toast at the dining room table and, from the corner of his eye, watched Sandra in her garden. She would only stand and look down at her flowers, hating them or waiting for spring, it was hard to tell. Her hair fell as golden as it had the afternoon he'd coaxed her virginity from her in her grandfather's apple orchard, their skin likely dusted with alar. And, always just behind this image, he thought of that night on the lake, how she'd tried to coax him into the water.

He stopped wearing shirts so the wings could breathe, so the plumage could have its way with him. When his daughter called, she remarked on the brightness in his voice. He sat at the computer through the afternoon into dark. From his home in Charlottesville he placed a virtual pushpin in St. Louis and worked outward, scanning various links and social media accounts for pictures of Jim.

Sandra crept closer during his hours online, until at last she would stand behind him, still only a hint in his peripheral vision watching him work. "I always knew something wasn't right," was the first thing she whispered to him. "When you'd push into me. When I could even get you to."

"Now that's not true, Sandra." He held his face in his hands. "We had forty-two good years."

"Who is Sandra?" Her cold breath soft on his neck. "All I wanted was a man. I wish I'd known that was what you wanted, too." She was gone when he turned.

Jim lived west of Philadelphia. Hiram broke down into sobs when he found him, first at the proof that he was alive, and then again just to see him, tall and hale in a crisp blazer. Hiram zoomed in on the photo and touched one pixelated cheek. Beautiful, still beautiful.

Below the picture were two thin paragraphs about Jim's retirement last year as principal of a middle school. Hiram had only stopped working three months before that, and it seemed yet another thing to draw them closer. The article mentioned Jim's eighteen years of service to the children of West Chester, Pennsylvania, his community service work, and that he was looking forward to time with his family. Hiram stared at the word *family*, whispered at it, but it would not give up its secrets.

A few more minutes and he had Jim's phone number and address. Nearly two hundred and fifty miles separated them. Hiram stood and went to the window of the living room. Forsyth Street was a sunshone silence through the half-open blinds. He let his wings unfold to their full span, the sound like distant bed sheets being shaken out. Sandra used to do that out back at the laundry line, when they were younger.

The feathers had now claimed him from thighs to collarbones, covered him in layers of warm white. His hands ran up and down his body as the empty street aged past noon.

He wept again, with an elaborate, scared joy. Out at the edge of his hearing was that music. It carried the same elegant distance, and he thought it must be the music of the angel he wasn't going to become. Somewhere in the house Sandra was crying, too.

812 Goshen Road. The address was full of harsh consonants, but Hiram relished each one as he tried to decide how to contact him.

A letter or email would be the sensible thing after all the years, but even a phone call wasn't enough. Not for this. He already knew he'd drive every one of those five hours in taut electrical suspense, just to see Jim's eyes widen into circles of reunion.

"Did you want both of us?" He felt her murmur in his hair.

"I should have told you all those years ago, love, I should have. But you know, swans mate for life. And I did that. We did that."

"You're a creature now." But she fell silent after these words. Hiram packed an overnight bag, sent Helen an email saying he was going on a little trip and she shouldn't worry. He dressed in his best jeans and loosest shirt, buttoning it to the top to hide his feathers, the wings folded tight inside against his back. Sandra kept her quiet even as he eased himself into the old station wagon.

He bought a pack of cigarettes before he turned onto I-66, and the first one tasted like coming home at the end of a long dark trip, not this lustrous beginning. Every cough that scraped out of him was an old enemy making amends.

"Is this your swan song, Hiram?" Sandra whispered as the car passed north out of Virginia. He could see the suggestion of her in the rearview, in the middle of the backseat with her hands folded on her lap. She might have been smiling with her old half-mirth.

"Just let me have this," he said, and stopped checking the mirror. He'd known her for more than two-thirds of his life, and though her humor could bite, her scorn never had. Pictures of how to approach Jim slid through his mind, but he couldn't seize any of them for scrutiny. When he saw him he would know. He lit his fourth cigarette and rasped at its smoke. His throat was raw.

Just over the Pennsylvania line, he pulled into a rest stop. Sandra stood behind the toilet in the narrow stall as he sat there, his spindly blackening legs cocked out to each side. She chuckled soundlessly. From the stall next to him came the staccato clicking of a cell phone.

"You're a creature now," she whispered again, "a thing for cold water."

"You could be just my guilt," he told her. The clicking of the phone stopped at this pronouncement. "Because why would you haunt me? I loved you. We had a good life." Hiram decided his business couldn't be done here with all this attention. He should just go, get past these last few miles.

"I don't know how I got here." And she was gone, in a way that felt different, like the air had sewn itself back together around his guess, where she couldn't fit. The toilet to his right flushed and bright white sneakers passed under the door in front of him. Hiram was left in perhaps true peace.

Jim's house was warm and attractive, a brick split-level with a cavernous garage, openmouthed with invitation. The driveway sloped up briefly, so that Hiram couldn't see inside. He rolled the station wagon a half-block forward and parked. His hands trembled. He held them up. They and his face had been spared this transformation, had gotten him here, ostensibly whole. But he sensed the rest of this would come soon.

Cars pulled into other driveways, home from work, and the sun already touched the top of the tree line, pointing shadows across the asphalt toward where Hiram waited. "Get to him while he'll still know it's you," he said to no one, and got out of the car, the old door creaking. His bones creaked with it. His body cried out to be wet.

He stood at Jim's mailbox and heard that same elusive music drifting out of the open garage. His feathers ruffled at it. His heart thrilled along a scale of breathless emotions. All the warmth folded inside the cold evening air seemed to settle upon him.

Hiram walked up to the garage and there Jim stood, reaching to hang a hammer on a wall peg. The sight of Jim's back, his chambray shirt sliding above worn jeans, overwhelmed him. Here was the great circle, of course it was, and at his gasp, Jim turned. Hiram saw all those years pass across his face, furrows deepening along his forehead and around his eyes.

"Hiram?" His voice even richer than the memory of it. The eyes a hue lighter, perhaps. "How in—is that you?"

"It is." Hiram swallowed, tried not to flex his wings inside his shirt, where they itched to escape. "I just came by to see if you ever found Otis." His smile hurt. He touched his lips and they felt stiff and prominent. There wasn't much time, then. The wonderful music played on, from somewhere in the house.

"Otis? My dog?" Finally Jim stepped toward him, still taller than Hiram by a head, that head as gray as his own had been a month ago. "No, I never found Otis. He just ran off, I guess."

"Like I ran off," Hiram said, and wouldn't let himself look down at the oil stain on the concrete.

Jim grinned. "Yeah, at about the same time, too."

"Well, I came to apologize, Jim. And to tell you things."

"Tell me what things? Wait," he said, and looked past Hiram down to the street with a sigh. "I guess you should come in and have a coffee."

Hiram followed him into the kitchen. He leaned against a counter and watched Jim take two cups down from a cabinet. Still the music was a room away, its tones washing with a kind of mournful hope. "I never was raised with God," he said, a tremor in his voice, "but I had to stay with my wife. I loved her. I don't know how I could love you like I did, the almost terror of it, and still love her. But I found a way, I suppose."

Jim paused with the steel pot over a bright red mug. "Now, Hiram, look." There was a tremor there, too. Hiram heard it shimmer in the middle, in his name.

"When Sandra died I felt—I don't know, but there was a freedom there. And I thought of your circles. You saying the eye is a circle, the first one. I had to—I just had to see you." His fingers fidgeted with his shirt buttons, setting each one loose.

"Hiram." Jim set the pot down on the counter, and the sound it made on the granite was a stark punctuation. "We had something a long time ago, and I still think about you. That's more than I can say about most of the men I've known. But half our lives have passed. I've been with someone for twenty years. He'll be home in half an hour. He's got a fine son who's given us two beautiful granddaughters."

The music hadn't stopped exactly, but Hiram could no longer hear it. "But we're a circle," he said. His fingers opened the next to last button on his shirt.

"You show up after thirty-odd years and expect what from me?" Jim said, looking down toward Hiram's waist. "I asked you to stay, and you didn't. We might've done great things together, but we didn't. It's okay. Not everything circles back. It can't."

Hiram's shirt fell away to reveal his thick vest of feathers. He shrugged it off and the wings burst up toward the low ceiling. "I love you," he said. "I love you," and he stepped toward Jim, cupped a hand on his cheek, and his own lips against the pinched withdrawal of the other man's.

Jim shoved him away and began to speak, but Hiram couldn't hear that either. There was pain in his ears and constricting his face. He saw the white tips of feathers creeping into his field of vision. The room blurred and he ran from the kitchen, through the garage, out of the broken circle.

He sat behind the wheel of the station wagon and wept as night thickened around him, a great urgency rising through the shame and lust. His body throbbed with change. He managed thirty miles south on the highway, until the wings shifted forward and began to take his arms into them, bone knitting into bone. An exit sign loomed and he turned right, coasting down the ramp and grinding the car to a stop on the rutted shoulder.

His neck elongated as he staggered out. His torso bunched into itself, down and back onto his legs. He felt his lips peel outward, fuse together with his nose, and he let the resulting protuberance, a creamy red-orange, point him along the exit.

The surf of traffic noise continued behind him. Lights winked from a gas station down the road. Trees swallowed the rest. At last spring was returning to earth, even this far north. An irrepressible warmth moistened the dark. Time receded from him and he was compelled after it, into the wood full of black oaks and cedars and white pines. Sound came back to him, but the machinery and murmur of the world had somehow fallen away here. There was only the crackle of his shifting bones.

Hiram ached for his two great loves. He longed for Jim but wept more for his wife. She was the one who had kept him. He wished he could resign himself to her all over again. What Jim had told him back in that kitchen was right, but then where was the circle Hiram had spent half his life tracing? What did this transformation ask of him?

He was still endlessly in the forest when dawn threaded through the canopy of crosshatched branches, and the same muted hush coated the world like dew. At last he broke through into a wide and round clearing, within which was held a pond, a nearly perfect circle, its circumference marred only by a tongue of shore penetrating the water. Sandra sat on this tongue, or someone did. Thick bands of dirty light fell upon her there, and her hair shone gold inside of them. A spade jutted from the earth at her feet.

He walked over to the rim of water and looked down at what he had become. Wondrous and graceful and hideous, the long curved neck drooping to witness his culmination. He stood perhaps four feet high with his head bowed. The feathers had long finished colonizing him. Black pebble eyes regarded the beaked head cocking to the left. He reached to touch his face and realized again that his arms had gone. In their place the wings gave an undecided jerk before settling back along his sides.

"Let's jump in," a voice said. A strong dawn voice. He turned and it was not Sandra, had never been, but a young woman, her fine hair falling around her face. No longer a trick of the eye, she grew more firm and full the longer he looked at her.

Hiram worked his way out of what little of his clothes remained. His feet were black fans stretched around his toes. He leaned over and dipped his head into the water, cold as heaven and clearer than heaven could have been. The urge to ride this still mirror rose fierce in his gullet, but he withdrew his head and shook the droplets free. Dozens of circles radiated on the pond's surface.

He turned to her again. "Who are you?" His voice had grown reedy and flat, vibrations traveling along a papery membrane. But they were words he spoke.

"I don't know how I got here," the young woman said, turning to him. "But the water looks so nice, doesn't it?"

He moved toward her. Behind, the sun began to spill more generously into the bowl of trees, and the crooking shape of Hiram fell over the woman. Pictures of Sandra and Jim clenched his stomach in dark hunger, but soon their faces began to drift apart and become the one he now looked upon. He thought of his daughter, and his dismay at Helen fading in his mind likewise faded after her. The circles were getting smaller. The ripples were calming.

"Yes," he answered the woman, this buxom thing that had recently stepped fresh out of still and The street of dirt with life, the streak of dirt on her forehead, all darkened beneath him. She wore a green, crimped smock and a sheer night-blue skirt, which to Hiram appeared to be tented with a man's swollen desire. He stared at the erection and said, "Is this place where the music comes from?"

"It's there." She looked across the water. "You just don't hear it now. You are a god of want."

"What is your name?" His new heart beat in his new breast upon her coming response. Her milk thighs unclasped. She looked delicious inside his shadow, and he shifted closer, as though to taste her.

She half-smiled up at him from her perch, a quiver in her soft wet lips as she answered.

UNDERGROUND ECONOMY

JOHN LANGAN

THAT'S NOT WHAT I WANT TO TALK ABOUT. IF YOU'RE interested in hearing about the day to day of a stripper, there are plenty of books you can read. Some of them are pretty good. Or you could watch *Showgirls*. No, it's not accurate, but it's the kind of movie most of the girls I danced with would have made about themselves. So there's that.

It's a person—Nicole AuCoeur, the girl who told me I should try out at the Cusp, they were hiring and I could make some serious cash. I want to talk about her, about this thing that happened to her.

We weren't friends. We'd been in a couple of classes together at SUNY Huguenot. Both of us wanted to be writers. Nikki said she was going to be a travel writer. I was planning on writing screen-plays. We took the same fiction-writing workshop, and were in the same peer-critique group. I read two or three of her stories. They were pretty good. The teacher was into fantasy, *The Lord of the Rings*, *Game of Thrones*, so Nikki turned in that kind of story. She was that type of student. Figure out what the professor likes and play to it.

I didn't know she was working at The Cusp. She was always late for class, and she always showed up stoned. She drenched herself in some kind of ginger-citrus perfume, to hide the smell, but it clung to her hair. She had long, brown hair that she wore in long bangs, like drapes. If anything, I thought she was some kind of dealer. I remember this one time, in the middle of class, she opened her purse and started to root through it—I mean, frantically, taking stuff out of it and piling it on her desk. The professor asked her if everything was okay. She said, "No, I can't find my stash." The guy didn't know how to respond to that. The rest of us tittered.

Anyway. I ran into her the summer after that class. I was sitting in Dunkin Donuts, making lunch out of a small coffee and a Boston cream donut. Nikki sat down across from me. I hadn't realized she was still in town. I assumed she'd gone home for the summer. She said she'd stayed in Huguenot to work. I asked her what she was doing. She said dancing at The Cusp.

I blushed. E~~veryone~~ ~~knew~~ ~~the~~ ~~place.~~ ~~It~~ ~~was~~ ~~on~~ ~~299,~~ on the way into town, a flat-roofed cinderblock building. We used to call it The Cusp juice bar, because they couldn't serve alcohol there, on account of the girls dancing fully nude. I hadn't known anyone who worked there—well, not that I was aware of—but I knew people who'd known people. Although what I'd heard from them had concerned the professors who were regulars at the place. There was a story about this one old guy who'd paid for a girl to come to his place and pee on him, so I guess I had an idea of the club as one step up from a brothel.

Nikki ignored my blush. She said the money was fantastic, and the place was hiring. If I was interested, there were auditions the following Wednesday. We made conversation for a couple of minutes, then she left.

To make a short story shorter, I tried out, was offered the job, and took it. Money—yeah, the money was better than I could make anyplace else in town without a college degree, and in a lot of cases with one. I had been working part-time as a cashier at Shop Rite, but I couldn't get enough hours to cover the rent, my car—which was a piece of shit that spent as much time at the mechanic's as it did on the road—and groceries. Not to mention utilities. And going out. My dad had wanted me to come home for the summer, and when I didn't, he got pissed and said if I wanted to stay in Huguenot so bad, I could find a way to pay for it.

So I did. I had to shave my crotch, which was no fun, and keep it shaved, to give the customers a clear view of what I was waving in

their faces. The dancing wasn't, not really. It was wriggling around
on stage, teasing I was going to undo my top, wriggling some more,
removing my top with one hand but keeping my boobs covered
with the other, wriggling some more, etcetera, until I was down to
my shoes. Oh, and the garter the guys stuffed their dollar bills into.
The air stank of cigarette smoke, mostly from the dancers. All the
same, I smiled at everyone. Not because I was enjoying myself, but
because it made me more money if the customers thought I was
enjoying myself. It intimidated some of them, too, which did please
me. I wasn't especially nervous working at The Cusp. Probably, I
should have been. But I was sure I could handle any creeps who
tried anything with me. My dad had been a marine, and a martial
arts nut, and I had grown up knowing how to punch an attacker in
the throat, tear off his ears, and gouge out his eyes. Plus, there were
always at least two bouncers in close proximity, in case things in the
private rooms got seriously out of hand.

That was where the real money was. Private dances. Lap dances,
mostly, which were forty dollars for five minutes plus whatever you
could convince the guy to tip you. Some girls could keep a customer
in there for two or three dances in a row. I didn't, not usually. There
was also a room at the back of the club, the Champagne Parlor.
Two-fifty for half an hour with the girl of your choice. And a
complimentary bottle of non-alcoholic champagne. That was
mainly for the guys whose buddies had brought them to The Cusp
for their bachelor parties.

Nikki was the queen of the private dances. She had this routine.
The DJ would announce her as, "Isis," which was the stage name
she used. (Mine was Eve. I know: subtle, right?) She would walk
out onto the stage in a long, transparent gown that trailed along the
floor behind her. She danced to Led Zeppelin, "The Battle of Ever-
more." I think she'd studied ballet at some point. There were a lot of
ballet moves in her routine. She stood on one leg and held the other
leg out in front of her, or behind her, or to the side. She skipped
across the stage on the tips of her toes. She half-crouched, leapt,
and came down in another half-crouch. She twirled, sometimes on
her toes, her arms stretched above, sometimes with one leg bent

behind, her head thrown back, her arms curved in front. The gown floated after, whipped around her. She let it drift away. Underneath, she was wrapped in scarves, each of which she undid and sent fluttering to the floor. Throughout, she went from customer to customer, bending towards them, giving them a closer look at what lay beneath the remaining scarves.

By the end of the song, all she had left on was a pair of fairy wings. I guess that's what you'd call them. They were like something from a Halloween costume, one for adults. Sexy Tinkerbell or whatever. A pair of clear straps looped them around her shoulders. They weren't that big, and they were made of thin plastic. When the lights played over them, they filled with a rainbow of colors that slid about inside them like oil. Something to do with the plastic. They weren't butterfly wings, which is what most fairy costumes come with. They were long, narrow, shaped like blades. Hornet wings, or an insect from that branch of the family. If I thought about them that way, they almost freaked me out. Nikki danced stoned—she did everything stoned, from what I could tell—and the glaze the pot gave her eyes made them resemble the hard eyes of an insect. Together with the wings, they lent her the appearance of an extra from a grade-z sci-fi flick, *Attack of the Wasp Women* or something.

None of the customers noticed this. Or, if any of them did, he had a kink I don't want to think about. Nikki never danced more than one song. As Zeppelin faded away, she was off the dance floor, followed by one and sometimes two guys. Most of them went for lap dances, which took place in one of a row of booths set up opposite the club's bar. Yeah, the juice bar. The booths were basically large closets with small couches in them. The customer reclined on the couch, and the dancer did her thing. Each booth had a camera mounted high in one of its corners. For the safety of the dancers, supposedly, and to ensure no one went from lap dance to out-and-out hooking. Part of the bouncers' jobs was to keep an eye on the video feed; although I never saw any of them cast more than a glance in the monitors' direction. I don't think Nikki ever unzipped anyone's jeans, but there's a lot you can do before you reach that point. To be sure, as far as tips went, none of the rest of us could keep up with her.

Not that she was stingy with her money. If it was a night the club closed early, a bunch of us would head to one of the bars in town, and Nikki would cover our drinks. If we were working a late night, once the last customer was out and the front door locked, she'd produce a bottle of Stoli for us to mix with the juice bar's juices. Those times—sitting around the club, shooting the shit—were better than being at an actual bar, more relaxed. Most of us changed into our regular clothes, jeans, t-shirts, wiped the makeup off our faces. Not Nikki. She stayed naked as long as she could. Except for her wings. She wandered around the club, a drink in her hand, the wings bouncing up and down with each step, clicking together. She would lean against the bar, where I was sitting with a cup of coffee because I had an eight a.m. class I'd decided to stay awake for. We didn't say a lot to one another. Mostly, we traded complaints about the amount of reading we had to do for school. But having her beside me gave me an opportunity to study the tattoo that decorated her back, so I did what I could to keep to keep the conversation going, such as it was.

That tattoo. All of the girls had ink. In most cases, it was in a couple of places, the lower back and the shoulder, say. That's where mine were. I had a pair of coiling snakes on my back, and the Chinese character for "air" on my right arm. There's a story behind each of them, but they're not part of this story. One girl, Sheri, had ink on most of her body, brightly-colored figures that were enacting an enormous drama on her skin. Nikki had a single tattoo, a square panel that covered most of her back. It was difficult to see clearly, warped by the plastic wings lying over it. The artist had executed the image in black and dark blue, with here and there highlights of pale yellow and orange. There was a car in the middle of it, an older model with a narrow grill like the cowcatcher on a train. The headlights perched high on either side of the grill. The car stretched along a foreshortened road, its rear wheels and end dropping behind the horizon. I wasn't sure if the distortion was supposed to represent speed, or just an extra-long car. To the right of the car, a cluster of tall figures filled the scene. There were five or six of them. They were dressed in black suits, and black fedoras. Their faces were the same pale oval, eyes and mouths empty circles. To the left of the car, a steep hill led to a slender house whose wall was set with a half-dozen mismatched windows. Within each frame, there seemed to be a tiny figure, but I couldn't make out what any of them were. A rim of orange moon hung over the scene in a sickly smile. The picture had been done in a style that reminded me of something from *Mad* magazine, exaggerated in a way that was more sinister than comic. It fascinated me. I asked Nikki what it was supposed to be. She said, "Oh, ~~that's~~ ~~just a picture,~~ which could have been true, for all I knew. At the same time, that was a lot of investment in a random image.

The customers didn't mind it. Not that I heard, anyway. Most of them were too timid to say anything. They acted as if they were cool, confident, but it was obvious they weren't. It was as if they were tuning forks, and our bare skin was what they'd struck themselves on. They vibrated, made the air surrounding them quiver. There were exceptions, sure. One guy who was a long-haul trucker. Not too big. Kept his hair short, his beard long. Had on a red flannel shirt every time he entered the club, which was about once a month. He was quiet, polite, said, "Yes ma'am," "No ma'am." But there was a stillness to him. It was what you'd expect from a wolf, or one of the big cats, a tiger. The utter focus of a predator. That I know, he hadn't tried anything with any of the girls before I started at The Cusp. He behaved himself while I was there, too. If I'd heard he owned a cabin in the woods, though, whose walls were papered in human skin, I would not have doubted it. I gave him a lap dance, once, and spent the five minutes planning the elbow I'd throw at his temple or throat when he grabbed me. He didn't, and he tipped pretty well. That said, I wouldn't have done it a second time.

The other exception was a group of guys who squeezed into the club one Thursday night. There were five of them, plus a man who said he was their driver. The bouncer who was working the front door said he saw them pull up in a white van. The five guys were huge, the biggest men I'd ever seen in person. I'm going to say seven feet tall, each, three feet and change wide. Three fifty, four hundred pounds. All dressed in the same khaki safari shirts, khaki shorts, and sandals. They had the same hairstyle, crewcuts that squared the tops of the heads. Their faces were blank, unresponsive. They stared straight ahead, and didn't so much as glance at any of the girls. In the club's mix of white and blue lighting, their skin looked dull, gray. They could have been in their early twenties. They could have been twice that. They stood beyond the front door in a group and did not move. They reminded me of the stone heads on Easter Island. They weren't still—they were inert.

Not their driver, though. He was smaller—average-sized, really. It was standing in front of his passengers that made him appear diminutive. He was wearing a beige, zip-up jacket over a white dress shirt with a huge collar and brown bell-bottom slacks. His hair was black, freshly-cut-and-gelled, but his skin had the yellow tinge of someone with jaundice. He was younger pretending to be older. I figured he was in charge of the five guys. Actually, what I thought was, the five passengers were residents of one of the local group homes, and the driver had decided to treat them to a night out. I know how it sounds, but things like it happened often enough for it not to seem strange, anymore.

The driver didn't waste any time. He spoke to the front door guy, who pointed him to the bartender. She leaned across the bar to hear what he had to say, then motioned to one of the girls who was killing time with a cranberry spritzer to fetch someone from the dressing room. I read her lips: Isis. Nikki. The driver nodded at the bartender, and passed her a folded bill. I'm pretty sure it was a hundred.

Nikki emerged from the dressing room wearing her assortment of scarves, but without the long gown. She looked across the club to where the driver was standing with his hands in his trouser pockets. Her head jerked, as if she recognized him. When she walked up to him, she kept her expression neutral, which only seemed to confirm that she knew the driver. He tilted forward to speak into her ear. Whatever he had to say didn't take long, but she took a while to respond to it. She stared at the driver, as if trying to bring him into focus, then nodded and said, "Sure."

Apparently, what the driver wanted was a lap dance for each of his five passengers, all of them provided by Nikki. He gestured for the nearest of the huge guys to come forward. Nikki took hold of one enormous hand and led the guy to the middle lap dance booth. He had to stoop to enter it; I wondered if he'd fit inside. He did. His four buddies didn't register his departure in the slightest. The driver stationed himself midway between the rest of his passengers and the booth. He gazed into space, and waited.

I didn't see Nikki emerge from the booth with the first giant in tow, because I'd been called to the dance floor. It took me two songs into my three-song rout and customer a private dance. He was a college student. I almost thought I recognized him from one of the big lecture classes. He was free with his money, and it wasn't difficult to keep him in the booth for two dances. We were to the right of Nikki and whichever of the enormous guy she had with her. The walls of the booths weren't thick. All kinds of sounds leaked through from the adjoining spaces. That center booth, though, was silent. I noticed this, but I don't know if it seemed strange to me or not. I'm not sure. I was busy with the college student. I want to say that there was something off about that lack of sound. It was as if it was a gap in sound, a blank spot in the middle of a song, rather than the end of it.

Nikki and I finished our dances at the same time. I didn't notice anything wrong with her, then, standing naked outside the booths. She was flushed, but she'd been working hard for almost thirty straight minutes. She was sweaty, too, which was odd. The club was air-conditioned, in order to keep the dancers' sweat to a minimum. I wondered if the driver was going to ask for his turn, next. He didn't. He passed Nikki the biggest roll of bills I had and have ever seen, collected his giant cargo, and exited The Cusp without another word. Nikki gathered her scarves from inside the booth and retreated to the dressing room.

She didn't stay there long. She dropped the scarves on the floor, stuffed the roll of money into her purse, and returned to the club. The first customer she approached was a middle-aged guy wearing gray slacks and a white button-down shirt. He was sitting back from the stage, so he could watch the show and not have to pay out too much cash. Nikki straddled him in his chair and ground her pelvis against him. Whatever prudence he'd imagined he possessed flew out the window. He trailed behind her to the lap dance booths.

A minute later, he was screaming. The booth's door flew open, and Nikki stumbled out of it. There was blood all over her legs, her ass. She stopped, found her balance, and walked toward the dressing room. As she did, her customer emerged, still screaming. The front of his slacks was dark with blood. Of course I assumed he'd done something to her. His face, though. He was wide-eyed, horrified. One of the bouncers was already next to him. I went to check on Nikki.

She was bent over one of the makeup tables, attempting to roll a joint. The backs of her legs, the cheeks of her ass, were scarlet. Closer to her, I saw that her skin had been scraped raw. It reminded me of when I'd been a kid and wiped out on my bike, dragging my palms or shins across the blacktop. The air smelled coppery. Blood ran down Nikki's legs and pooled on the floor. Blood flecked the bottoms of the plastic wings, the tattoo. She wasn't having any luck with the joint. Her hands wouldn't do what she wanted them to. I pushed in beside her, and rolled the spliff as best I could. I passed it to her with fingers that weren't trembling too much, then held her lighter for her.

I didn't know what to say. Everything that came to mind sounded inane, ridiculous. Are you hurt? Her legs and ass looked like hamburger. Do you need a doctor? Obviously. What happened to you? Something bad. Who were those guys? See the answer to the previous question. I couldn't look away from the ruin of her flesh. When I'd started working at The Cusp, I'd thought that I was entering the world as it really was, a place of lust and money. Now I saw that there was a world underneath that one, a realm of blood and pain. For all I knew, there was somewhere below that, a space whose principles I didn't want to imagine. I mumbled something about taking her to a doctor. Nikki ignored me.

By the time one of the bouncers and the bartender came to check on her, Nikki had located her long gown and tugged it on. She checked her pocketbook to be sure the roll of cash was there, took it in the hand that wasn't holding the joint, and crossed to the fire exit at the opposite end of the dressing room. Without breaking stride, she shoved it open, triggering the alarm. She turned left towards the parking lot as the door clunked shut behind her.

The bouncer, the bartender, and I traded looks that asked which of us was going to pursue her. I did. I hurried along the outside of the club and across the parking lot to where Nikki parked her Accord. The car was gone. I ran back towards the building, which everyone was pouring out of. I could hear a distant siren. Most of the customers were scrambling for their cars, hoping to escape the parking lot before the fire engines arrived and boxed them in. I considered making a dash inside for my keys, and was brought up short by the realization that I didn't know where Nikki lived. I had an approximate idea—the apartments down by the Svartkill—but nothing more. I could drive around the parking lots, but what if she'd gone to the emergency room, or one of the walk-in care facilities? I didn't even have her cell number, another fact which suddenly struck me as bizarre. Why couldn't I get in touch with her? Why didn't I know her address? The strangest sensation swept over me there in the parking lot, as if Nikki, and everything connected to her, had been unreal. That couldn't have been the case, though, could it? Or how would I have found out about the job at The Cusp?

I didn't see Nikki for the rest of the time I worked at the club. I stayed through the end of the fall semester, when I graduated early and moved, first back in with my dad, then down to Florida. The five enormous guys, their jaundiced driver, didn't return during those months. The customer whose pants had been soaked with Nikki's blood did. Less than a week later, he appeared at the front door, insisting he had to talk to her. His face was red, sweaty, his eyes glazed. He looked as if he had the flu. The bouncer at the door told him that the girl he was looking for no longer danced here, and no, he didn't know where she'd gone. The guy became agitated, said he had to see her, it was important she know about the cards, the hearts. The bouncer placed his hands gently but firmly on the guy's chest and told him the girl wasn't here and he needed to leave. The guy broke the bouncer's nose, his right cheek, and three of his ribs. It took the other two bouncers on duty to subdue him, and they barely managed to do that. The cop who answered the bartender's 911 call took one look at the guy and requested backup. The cop said they would transport the guy across the Hudson, to Penrose Hospital, where there was a secure psych ward. As far as I know, that's what happened. I don't know what became of Nikki's last customer, only that I didn't see him again.

Years went by. I left Florida for Wyoming, big sky and a job managing a bank. I bought a house, a nice car. The district manager was pleased with my performance, and recommended me for a corporate event in Idaho. I took 80 west to Utah, where I picked up 84 and headed north and west into Idaho. Somewhere on the other side of Rock Springs, a white van roared up behind me and barely avoided crashing into the back of my rental. I swore, steered right. The van swung wide to the left, so sharply it rose up on its right wheels. I thought it was going to tip over, roll onto the median. It didn't. It swerved towards me. I should have braked. Instead, I stomped the gas. The rental surged past the van. As it did, I glanced at the vehicle's passengers. Its rear and middle seats were filled by a group of enormous men whose crewcut heads did not turn from the road ahead. In the front seat, a driver with black hair and yellowed skin laughed uproariously along with a woman with long brown hair. Nikki. Together, she and the driver laughed and laughed, as if caught by an emotion too powerful to resist. He wiped tears from his eyes. She pounded on the dashboard.

I pulled onto the shoulder and threw the car into park. My pulse was hammering in my throat. I watched the van speed west down the highway until it was out of sight. I waited another half hour before I shifted into drive and resumed my journey. The remainder of the drive to Idaho, and all of the way home, I didn't see the van. But I was watching for it.

I still am.

For Fiona

THE VAULT OF HEAVEN

HELEN MARSHALL

> I am the eye with which the Universe
> Beholds itself, and knows it is divine . . .
> —Percy Bysshe Shelley, 'The Hymn of Apollo'

IT WILL BE OF LITTLE SURPRISE TO THOSE WHO KNOW ME WELL that, as a boy, I was possessed by frequent night terrors. I do not like to speak of them now. It embarrasses me—even as it embarrassed my father once. I was a child: I saw as a child and I spoke as a child but my fears were not those of a child. There was a small window set into the north wall of my bedroom, and from this I would gaze out upon the constellations of lights that burst through the gloom: stories my father told me of heroes and monsters, *there* a dragon, *there* Hercules. To him these were figments, glimmering signs of a bygone age, but me? I saw something more . . . a shape, a glimpse of something, an . . . *extrapolation*—a polished skull, grotesque and leering, a living death mask; it set a hook in my soul and with it, utter panic.

My friends have remarked upon the nervous disposition that has followed me into adulthood, but I do not comment. You may from this conclude that I am a private person. This is not entirely true; my discipline requires collaboration; I have adapted out of necessity—and the company of *some* I value very highly, indeed, if it can be got easily enough, and without those promises of further commitment so often pressed upon bachelors of my stature. But one thing my years at Cambridge taught me—pleasant though they were in most respects—was that those of an academic mind are quick to judge; and, having judged, quicker still to slaughter. It is a hobby of theirs—and mine too, if I am honest, or it was once—so.

It was that greatest of Stagirians, Aristotle, who popularized the notion of the five senses—or the five wits—which may strike one as odd since the Greeks had as many forms of divination—and what is that but another form of seeing?—as they had kinds of love. Why *five* then? It has always been clear that my nervous disposition is the result of some form of *sensitivity* if you follow me. In fact, it has been one of my greatest assets: the ability to behold in my mind the shape of a thing as it was once, its true form, to *sense*—ha ha—its outlines.

I say this all as prelude, a ward against skepticism. In my school days a certain archaist ~~~~~~~~~~~~~~~~ the fashion in these sorts of matters. A necessary inoculation, perhaps. I once visited an excavation of the *bema* at Korinthos. The site had hosted the tomb of an old man of little account, which had been looted for a few trinkets in the ancient city's heyday. The locals were so gripped by the fear of the ghost—and this one was no king masked in gold, no gloried warrior!—that they rededicated the place as a temple to appease him.

I understand skepticism. Ghosts, glamours and curses for those who disturbed the dead: these were what my colleagues and I risked. In the golden hills of Hellas, excavation was a bare step up from grave robbing.

In the summer of '57, my pals had all landed plum positions in Ankara or Amphipolis but several disastrous months at a site in the Peloponnese—this was little more than a set of caves discovered by a goatherd, to be clear—had taught me I had neither the complexion nor the stamina for excavation proper: in proper sunlight I curl up and wither like a slug. I could not embark upon a new career path. My father had made that perfectly clear, and docked my subsistence payout from the trust after a pretty heinous fight. My debts were starting to pile up. One of the symptoms of a nervous disposition is a tendency to drink; one of the symptoms of a Cambridge education is the tendency to drink to excess.

After Trinity College, the archaeological museum at Semos was an undeniable let-down—barely preferable to starvation. Semos was a harbour town in one of those rather forgettable islands that had once boasted some obscure trade—sponge-fishing in this case—that had stocked coffers in the early days before modern industry had changed the game. More recently, the town, with its idyllic views and glass-green waters, had been co-opted as a playground for the Athenian rich. They had funded—haphazardly if not without enthusiasm—a number of cultural projects offering the usual diversions.

The museum boasted an assortment of cracked *pithoi* jars behind glass, nothing in the way of English signage, and a stinking-hot pair of shared offices at the back. Its bureaucracy was riddled by the usual plagues: questionable politics, intermittent corruption, and general ineptitude. The director had pieced together funding for the reconstruction of some hammered bronze fragments, and over-promised regarding the delivery date. The previous postholder had dropped out—a national I did not know, no publication history to speak of—and the clock was ticking. They didn't want an Englishman, not really, and *I* didn't want *them*: but I had—foolishly, I admit—jilted the College secretary, and so many of my applications to better positions had mysteriously gone astray. It was only a call from Cavanaugh that landed me the post in the first place, nepotism and blind luck being the two best friends an academic has.

The head of the administration, it turned out, went by the name Nikolaos Papadiliou, not the unctuous civil servant I had expected, but an impressive figure: tough and brawny, born of a generation of sponge-divers, no doubt. He laughed in short, measured bursts, and I found myself wondering how long he could hold his breath.

"Hey ho and *welcome*," he cried with a meaty handclap. His English was flawlessly, pointedly posh. *I'm a Cambridge man too*, it seemed to say, *I was once a master in your land as you shall never be in mine.*

"Hullo," I said stiffly, removing my fingers from his grasp.

"Come in, come in, *do*. A pleasure to have you here, and at such short notice. Found a place to dig in?"

For eighty a month I had secured a dilapidated two-story, all cracked red tiles and formerly white stucco, along with an ancient peasant woman who devised an endless string of poetic epithets for the broom, the basin, and the bed.

"I do hope to get properly acquainted." His eyes were sharp with mockery. "One such as you, good *pedigree*, Cavanaugh told me, but a hard worker nonetheless. Not likely to disappoint, are you, not if you're one of *Cavanaugh's* bunch?"

"No, sir," I replied, "I know what I'm doing."

"Marvelous!" he said. "You shall understand the nature of our dilemma soon enough. And once you do—" ... ... in the Cavanaugh's *prodigy*. We shall see about that, won't we?"

To the others he barked like a sea captain, but for me it was the familiar mix of silk and sulk of the Senior Common Room.

The staff stared at me, uncertain of what spell I had placed upon their commander.

The chill of isolation set in.

But the work, at least, was what I had expected.

I hadn't caught the entire gist of the assignment from Cavanaugh—he had been pretty tight-lipped before my departure, and I wonder now if he hadn't been knocking on with some of the same girls I had been after—but it didn't seem as bad as I'd feared. I found at my desk a series of half-completed sketches of bronze fragments, most annotated heavily in a ragged hand that took some deciphering. My distinguished predecessor's notes.

The find had been fairly recent. The rains last winter had eroded the soil, and a massive hole had opened up in the local necropolis. The villagers had known about the site for ages—their own cemetery was located next to it—but none bothered themselves until the collapse led to the discovery of a simple shaft grave. But while the archaeologists were preparing to enter, looters snuck in under the cover of darkness and took what they could lay hands on. When it became clear the hoard wasn't gold, as they had anticipated, but rather hammered sheets of bronze, they fled. They thought the prize worthless. A disappointment. It was only in the morning when the archaeologists finally came to see for themselves that they discovered in the earth the remnants of what they believed to be a huge disc— perhaps a cauldron, perhaps the covering of a shield—glinting in hues of sea-green and gold.

Bronze work of that sort was my speciality, and I'd seen plenty of the like before. Griffins and bare-breasted sirens. Birds and oxen. Show me the slit of a hemline, and I can tell you if the figure was man, woman or child, social class, hand position even, on a good day. All in all, this kind of craftsmanship was shockingly pre- dictable. The Greeks had a very definite sense of beauty: repetition, symmetry, proportion—what Plotinus called 'formedness'. They valued it above all else, for to them it represented a link with the godhead: the perfection of form was the perfection of the universe itself. Time distorted but the figures themselves, in the purest sense, conformed.

My sensitivity was often an asset in reconstructions of this sort. If I held a fragment before my eyes, my mind would travel the channels, imagining, filling in gaps, unspooling the thread of time to apprehend the thing as it had been once. And so I sat with the pieces—like ancient tesserae, elusive, perplexing—before me. They appeared to be from the Archaic period, bore some resemblances to the finds in Phidias' workshop in Olympia, which meant they'd either traveled a surprising long way, or else someone had picked up his style. But there were Oriental influences too, more than I would have expected: lotuses, anthemia and tendrils, the hindquar- ters of a . . . lion, the head of a woman, a sphinx? The notes were confused. Or merely confusing. There were wild leaps I had diffi- culty following: a line my predecessor curled when I expected it to straighten, figures conjectured that seemed wildly implausible.

It is difficult to convey the sense of this experience, except that it was disorientating, and yet there was a sense of maddening logic. I felt a faint thrill running through me, though of wonder or terror I cannot say, only that it reminded me of the dreams I had as a child, those shapeless, chaotic images that left me drenched with sweat, wild-eyed. My predecessor's imaginings were nonsense. Of course, they were nonsense. But they were that peculiar breed of nonsense that left an imprint upon the world, gave it depth: the barest glimpse of a whole, inarticulate, dimensionless, without form or substance—but with *force*—something—a prickle of sweat, a widened eye, a tightening in the stomach . . .

My immediate judgment was that he had either been a genius— or an utter crank.

No wonder they had sacked him.

to be sure, but I felt inscribed within a circle whose borders I could not detect and I could not pierce. I tried on several occasions but the results were embarrassing. Nikolaos Papadiliou spoke to me from time to time, but I detected within his false bonhomie— "How are you getting on, *old chap*?"—an edge of contempt.

There were women, of course, the long-limbed daughters of sailors whose speech was so guttural I could not make heads or tails of it. The richer sort came in from time to time, but most of them kept to their villas or their yachts, and though a few cast their eye in my direction, they had the look of those married to powerful men. I didn't have the stomach to play that particular game, not on foreign soil.

It is surprising, then, that I did not notice Pelagia earlier. She was a frequent visitor to the museum. My colleagues seemed to treat her with the same sort of aversion they showed me despite her obviously local breeding. True, there was a plainness to her expression, her lips neither too rounded nor quite angular, her eyes verging on colourlessness yet not extraordinarily pale, her skin fine, taut, but lacking lustre, her other parts pleasing in proportion and symmetry without offering inspiration—*architecturally* satisfying; it made me want to place her in a store room somewhere.

My intentions were largely ignoble, and when she proved susceptible to my basic advances—she would speak to me, or allow me to speak to her in any case—things progressed along a fairly predictable line. She refused a private meeting for several weeks, but I persisted, retreated, showed attention when she visited and then rebuffed her when my presence became expected. After one such absence of several days, I made my play, told her I wanted to practice my Greek, or some such, perhaps I asked her about the history of the island and when she responded with enthusiasm, I pushed forward. We met at a taverna near the harbour where the lanterns of the boats reflected shards of light on the waves; all else was darkness around us, pure and impenetrable. She had dressed simply, no ornamentation, but her black hair was bound into a series of sleek, artfully rendered spirals—some effort at least had been taken for the occasion.

We spoke for some time upon the pretense I had offered, and her speech was mellifluous, her engagement genuine. There was a bright spot of colour high in her cheeks, and it charmed me, though I confess that I followed little of what she said. To hear her speak was enough to enchant; understanding would have only spoiled my mood, tempered her innocence with an edge of unfashionable intellect. I ignored her, mostly, and I think she liked it. Most women do. But as night progressed, she grew bolder. At one point, she seized upon my hand and said, for the first time, in English: "Are you *sophisticated*?"

"What do you mean exactly?" I asked her, a little bit uncertain of the change in pace.

"Are you—charming?"

"Some have called me that," I allowed. Her English was good, better than I would have expected.

"You look nervous."

"Do I?" I realized I was. The night was warm, stifling. I was wearing a suit and dark jacket, but I could feel the wet splotches beneath my arms beginning to annex territory.

"You sweat."

"A natural effect of the sun," I muttered. And then, making an effort: "and—your beauty?"

"Was that charming?" Coquettish now.

"You must be the judge of that."

There was silence for a moment, as she looked at me, at first contemplatively. Her adequately shaped eyebrows arched slightly. I was no sailor, but even I could sense a change in the weather.

"Do you have a woman at home? A wife, perhaps? A—how do you say—*girlfriend*? Are you engaged?"

Her eyes were lively. I thought she might be laughing at me, but I wasn't entirely sure. I have always had a damnable time with the Greeks in situations like this.

I made a gambit. "An arranged marriage."

"How barbaric." Her face fell. Had I overplayed? "It must make you very sad."

"D̶i̶s̶.̶.̶.̶.̶.̶"̶ I̶ ̶.̶.̶.̶.̶

away.

Then: "Shall I seduce you? Would you like that? Would it make you happy?"

She smiled like a sphinx.

So did I.

We made love in my ramshackle two-story. The wind moaned hideously, and when a brief shower burst out of the sky, we could see rain dripping from the ceiling into pots she laid out to catch it. The bed, however, was warm. I found I was inspired to poetical epithets myself as it creaked dangerously beneath us. The springs thrummed like a lyre.

She was still plain, unsheathed, but her plainness I had begun to find beautiful. Galen, I'd read, had discovered the perfect proportion from finger to finger, and of all the fingers to the metacarpal, and the wrist, and of all these to the forearm, and of the forearm to the arm, and so on. I explored her dimensions.

"What are you doing?" she asked me.

"An experiment."

"Stop it. I am not a—*specimen*." Was that the word she used? "Not for you. Close your eyes now. Do it all by touch."

But when I did as she asked, the darkness made a cradle for my brain, and all that spilled forth were images of her: angles and lines uncurling themselves, fixing new positions, shredding the patterns I had learned so well and making something new, provocative, startling. Her body was both hard and delicate, muscled, brightly burnished by the sun. She moved as languorously as oil, and I found myself thinking of something I had read once: "That is the spirit that Beauty must ever induce: wonderment and delicious trouble, longing and love and a trembling that is all delight." I had never been moved by sentiment before, but now I began to shake violently, gripping her shoulder until I printed the shape of my finger upon her and she covered my hand in her own.

"There," she said, "you have been seduced. How does it feel?"

"Wonderful," I gasped, but there was a squirming, nasty sensation in the pit of my stomach. I cried out, and she kissed me, and then it was wonderful, and then it was awful again. "Sleep now," she commanded, and just as instantly, the anguish left me. I curled up beside her, my forehead pressed against the sweet-smelling flesh of her shoulder. In the morning, she would be gone. Regret was an early riser, and it chased most women out the door before I had found my shirt. And so certainty returned. I was still myself, nothing had been lost, nothing abandoned.

But I was not at ease that night.

The old feeling of terror returned: I dreamed the roof of my house had turned to shoddy glass, and above the nigrescent dome of space enclosed me. Beyond it stood a crowd of darkening shades, stripped and fleshless, their bodies glistening with rot, studded with stars, a hideous empty eye and all else collapsed and sunken. And yet, despite their freakishness, there was something familiar about them, the barest hint of memory. My body was brittle upon awakening. I was afraid I must have cried out in my sleep. I was afraid she might have left me.

But when I turned, Pelagia was still there, undisturbed. She had thrust an arm carelessly over her face to shut out the light, and so the dawn's glow fell unevenly upon all of her body except her eyes. I watched how it lit up the various sections of her, as if she was formed from the stone of different quarries. Had I ever looked at a woman in the morning sun? I could not recall. Rain plinked into the copper pots she had placed around the bedroom. It reminded me of the arrangement of *pithoi* in the cave I had excavated. Unnerved, I nudged her carefully.

"Darling." I wondered what the Greek called their lovers.

She arose gradually, first her fingers fluttered, then her toes.

I was at a loss for what to say next. Ought I to be warm? Friendly? Consoling?

"I sleep late in the morning," she said at last.

It was intimate knowledge, different than what we had shared the night before. Previously I had avoided this, but I found myself curious, desirous, eager to share. That phrase—"I sleep late in the morning," was infinitely precious. It demanded reciprocation. If I did not, she would be lost forever.

"Sometimes—" I started, "—I have night terrors."

"It is not so strange," she said. "The darkness holds much. It is—how do you say?—a cauldron? No—" she frowned "—this is too much for cooking. More like—" she made a gesture with her hands. I had learned many words for the shapes of pots, but I could not make out what she meant. "It pours itself out." She had a peculiar way of talking. The sort of poetry only foreigners can make out of the English language. I wanted more. I was suddenly thirsty for her words. How had I ignored her so blithely? How had I not hung on every word, engraved it upon the tablet of my soul?

"Tell me again what you told me last night."

Pelagia was naked and gleaming. I was entranced by the movement of her hips as she leaned over to collect the spilling pots, the arc of her buttocks, the dimple at the small of her back as shallow as a kylix.

"I spoke to you of my father," she told me. "I want you to meet him." Her eyes were bright and innocent.

Nothing spoils so quickly as love.

———

Fathers and their daughters.

A man could write a book on the subject, and every page would be tragedy. Think of Oenomaus hearing his daughter's suitor was bound to slay him. Think of Antigone and her *pater*, blind now, stumbling toward his own death, and her by him always, the cursed child of his incest. I had made a habit of avoiding fathers, my own whenever possible, and certainly those of any of my acquaintances.

But some duties cannot be easily ignored. I had taken her, and she had stayed—not to mention that I was still in the first flush of what might be called love. It is as Homer himself claimed: love is magic to make the sanest man go mad.

As it turned out, they shared a dwelling in the upper reaches of the harbour. Both the house and her father were ancient. He was dressed in a robe of some sort, wool perhaps, but his body shook beneath it anyway. He had the look of an ancient king, too long-lived, strength fled, empire in ruins, left alone in the wilderness to be fed by birds or pulled apart by animals.

The house smelled faintly of licorice, and dust hung in the air like incense. Pelagia poured coffee for us—stuff thick enough I could have painted with it had I wanted to. The old man did not touch his, seemed barely to recognize her.

"Papa," she said in Greek, "this is the one I have told you about."

"Hrrm?" he mumbled.

"He has come to the museum."

A light came into him at that, almost physical so profound were the effects. I could see clearly that he was mad, or something like it, perhaps only old. I had seen professors like this before. The shears of Atropos dull in the face of tenure.

"Please," Pelagia said to me, pleading, "speak to him. Let him see what kind of a man you are." This had the predictable effect of stalling my tongue completely.

She stared at the two of us, one mad, one mute, and finally said, "Tell him what you know of beauty."

A harder question this, but some part of my Cambridge education sparked; I was used to being questioned in this way at least, inward examination being something avoided at all costs amongst those of privilege.

And so I spoke of beauty: I did not flatter, you understand, for I understood naturally she did not mean herself, but beauty beyond the particular. I spoke of its proportions, its limits—I spoke as Galen had spoken, I parroted Plato and Plotinus and all the others—I told them it represented a moral imperative. As I said these things, as I mimicked and recited, as if to an examiner, I felt something unspooling inside myself; the intimacy of his daughter had touched me profoundly. It was like a drug, and I began to speak

What was beauty to me? I had never told another living soul. It was . . . too truthful. Too revealing. I would have been scorned at Cambridge for the callowness of what I said; it lacked art, sophistication, restraint. It was too him I spoke now. Beauty justified all else in my life—wealth, privilege, intellect, ambition, these were meaningless. I had seen it as a child—the hidden face of humanity, all things crawling toward the grave—and yet something might be salvaged. Perfection was a ward, a salve, a shield.

But the old man turned away from me, crying, "No!"—and then again, "no! This is not *beauty*. Beauty is *strangeness*. It is not form but—" I saw a wild light in his eyes. He clutched at my hand, and pulled me along behind him with a hectic strength. This madness— I did not understand it—unless—had our tryst been discovered? Had Pelagia given me up? After all, I *had* deflowered her with all the vigour and abruptness of a set of garden shears. Perhaps, I thought, he intended to slay me—or worse, he would force me to marry. I tried to shake the him free, but his nails, thick and yellow as wax, had dug into my flesh.

The room beyond was badly lit, a hermit's cave, and about it were cast thousands of sketches. I recognized some of them: a bronze statue of Hera, imperious, sharp-breasted, with her faced caved in as if from a heavy blow; another recovered from a shipwreck with frilled, green growths pocking the skin; a third disfigured, attenuated by the heat of some vast conflagration. I knew these objects. We all knew them. They represented the pinnacle of that ancient civilization, their greatest achievements. All of them broken, bruised, disfigured.

And all of them . . . beautiful, taunting and inexplicable. It took my breath away. When the old man released his grip, I did not run. I could not. This was not a punishment, as I had feared, but something else: an education. I began to study the sketches more closely, fear dispelled, caught up only in the excitement of my intellect.

"Beauty is strangeness," he had said, and, yes, I believed him. Strangeness. That was what I saw. I traced the patterns: sketches of shards, reconstructions, but mad things filled with fanciful extensions, boneless limbs that stretched and circled, perverse bodies. Like nothing I had ever seen—and yet—like all that I had ever seen. I recognized the crow-footed writing making its way sideways across the skin of the page. Sometimes it was huddled. Other times it broke and ran, sprawled, stuttered, stilled.

I turned to the old man. Those bleak, staring eyes, I knew what they had seen: winged women and sphinxes, the curve of a falling blade, blood on the tiles, the pillars cracked, the colonnades fallen, and everywhere that sickening tension, the shadow falling between those vivid, discordant lines. "I know you," I tried to tell him, but that was not what I meant: I meant, I know what you have seen, I know what you have tried to show me, but it is broken, it is wrong . . .

"Good," he said in his throaty Greek. "I know you too." And it was clear to me that was not what he meant either: he meant, I know *you* are broken, I know you search for beauty but you cannot hold it in your hands for too long without destroying it, you are an idealist and you are wrecked. "It will be easier this way."

"What shall?" I demanded.

"You have been set a task of reconstruction?" he asked me. I scowled: nothing irks the old guard so much as their apparent heirs. But he waved his hand to dispel my doubts. "Of course, you have. An Englishman, no less! They would not choose another Greek, *could* not, who would touch the thing?"

"I am not so credulous as you would have me."

"Yes! *Credulous*—this is the very nature of the thing, *belief*." He plucked a page from the table. "What you see here—the ancient ones, *theoi*, masters of the market, the feast and the banquet, the altar and the tomb; they are the first forms; the unmoved movers."

"Figments," I told him. "Desire and terror pressed into the image of man—an abstraction of the chaotic, forced to serve the whim of philosophers and priests."

"And yet," he said, staring at me very closely.

I flinched. "And yet."

"They were beautiful once, but age has wrecked them. And there is something—*here*." He tapped at a hastily scrawled image, the

They stared out of the centre of the head, terrible. Hungry. "The perfection of art was the perfection of these figures. But they have been bent out of shape: the ocean devours the smoothness of their flesh, the grave eats its protector, fires rage and beauty sloughs off its skin. These . . . *representations*, they are as the hand is to the arm, the finger to the knuckle. The canker spreads, and the rot has set in unto the very root of the form. The pattern is corruptible!"

"I don't know what you mean," I tried to tell him, but I could not wrench my eyes from the paper he held. I remembered the fragments of bronze, and the patterns at which they hinted. Something beautiful or something monstrous. I knew what it should have been: a maiden straight-backed and glorious, the tilt of her chin, an imperious eye . . . but that was not how I saw it. I saw as *he* saw it, filtered through shadow and strangeness. It was as if my soul was at war with my intellect, and yet I knew if I had ever seen truly, it was in that moment.

"You know," he said, "I see that you know."

"It is a simply drawing," I insisted, "nothing more."

"It is truth."

"That is not how the artist shaped it. You know that, you *must* know that."

"The artist is dead! It is how the figure goes *now*," he snapped. "You have seen the stars, yes? Their figures? Yes, of course you have—the *theoi*, they watch us from the vault of heaven, their bodies twisted and deformed by what *we* have done to them. We have consigned them to rot and ruin. They cannot free themselves from those shapes we have created for them, for they are mould and wax both, the stone and the chisel!"

"You are too far gone," I told him, turning away. "This is madness, what would you have me do?"

"They wish to be seen as they are. Let the mould be broken, let the stone turn to dust!"

"I cannot," I cried. "Papadiliou will not have it!"

"You *see* as no one else does!" The old man's grin was mesmerizing. I felt myself coming under his power. The room was warm and dusty, the air dense, unbreathable. The figures around me seemed to shift and move as if the pages were stirred by some unknown breath, and, indeed, in that moment it felt the air began to chill as it did when a vast cloud interposed itself between the sun and the earth.

"It is—" but I could not say more. I cast my eyes wildly about the walls, but it was as if they had begun to recede, very slowly, away from me. The space curved: suddenly, they were not drawings, for no drawing could encompass so much *space*, no drawing could impose form upon such vastness, the chaos of heaven, and set among them in gossamer threads of light . . . what I could not say . . .

. . . except I saw the charnel grin of a woman, cut-out from the darkness, beautiful, perhaps the most beautiful woman I had ever seen but already her back had begun to stoop, her thighs run to ragged skin hanging, as a curtain does, upon a shuddering frame. From finger to knuckle, from wrist to elbow, she was perfect; but already her limbs were lengthening, her eyes wandering like errant planets, one grown large and the other squinted, then both empty as if someone had prised them loose from her skull . . .

"I cannot follow you!" I cried out, tearing at the papers he had drawn up, shredding them into a thousand irreconcilable pieces. And then it was as if the madness had passed. My lungs heaved, my pulse pounded, but the world was as I knew it to be: clothed in an impenetrable skin, flat, lacking depth, entirely knowable.

"Not even for my daughter?" he begged, and at this I felt a

strange tugging in my chest. I remembered Pelagia's scent, her curves, the fine grain of her hair. And more than that. I recalled how it had felt to know that she lay besides me, that she had shared my bed and chosen to stay. But already my memory of her was beginning to tarnish: the scent of her skin was as any woman's, her curve of her buttocks fine, perhaps, but no finer than a thousand other girls.

"I will not be so easily corrupted."

When he learned I was unmovable, he began to rock back and forth, biting at his knuckles. "You must, you must," he whimpered. "Please. Don't you understand? I—

should never have given them form!" And then quieter, pleading: "They will have me. They have promised it: *They shall set me amongst their ranks forever!*"

It is ever thus with the visionaries of our field; repudiation is never met with anything but hysteria.

I left the house as soon as I could.

I did not see Pelagia again, but, I confess, I did not seek her out either. I had never intended a long-term engagement, and I suspect she understood this in time. Most women sort it out for themselves sooner or later.

And by this time the local paper had printed a picture of my reconstruction. There was nothing revolutionary there, any of Cavanaugh's lot could have managed easily enough. The object had been a shield, I decided, not some votive offering as my predecessor had claimed. The decorations depicted straight-limbed soldiers, the glorious youths who would fall in battle, each of them a perfect figure of manliness and virility. I felt confident that the excavations of the remaining skeletons would bear that out in good time. Or perhaps I would be proven wrong—it did not matter so long as I had published; no scholarly opinion is eternal.

In the time that followed I was kept busy with a series of engagements designed to properly fleece the museum's patrons. It was at one such event that Papadiliou came upon me, disarmed by wine and uncharacteristically convivial. He clapped me on the shoulder, bellowing, "Well done, *old chap*, that's that then. Back to England, is it?" His hand was as heavy and unwanted as some massive limpet.

"Of course," I told him frostily. Now that my research was winding down, I had decided to accept an invitation to lecture at the Traveller's Club in London. This was only a minor find, but I had set upon it enough hyperbolic polish to impress those back home.

But as Papadiliou began to drift off, a sudden curiosity seized hold of me. "Wait!" I said, "My predecessor did not wish to join us? Some of the credit, surely, still belongs to him?"

"He died last week,." Papadiliou said, his eyes curiously misty, the Cambridge silk slipping away into something gruffer and more natural, as if he was moved by genuine emotion. "He was a *great* man. But his mind dulled in time, we could not keep him. We could not sponsor his . . . theories."

"I did not know," I told him.

"You would not," he continued. "But you may visit his grave, if you like. They buried him in the local cemetery."

But, of course, I never did.

And yet, despite my success abroad, when I returned home at last, I felt a profound weariness. The fashions had changed. London was abuzz with excitement. The Russians had launched an orb of polished metal into the heavens—Sputnik, they called it, the traveller. No longer did men of intelligence look to the earth, my father told me, no longer would they scrabble in the dirt after the lost legacy of those races that had come before and perished; it was to the heavens we must turn, to the future . . .

In his eyes I detected the familiar glint of fanaticism.

Perhaps my father was right. Perhaps I have failed to navigate the currents of progress, and, as a consequence, my contributions will be meager. My lecture was sparsely attended, conflicting as it did with a talk given by one of my colleagues at Trinity—a fellow called Hawking. But when I look into the night sky, I do not see what they see: an unspoiled frontier, so long denied to us, now graspable, conquerable. The idea of a lone figure, edged in starlight but untethered, surrounded by darkness, terrifies where it should inspire. I can well imagine the terror in his aspect, a twistedness in his face as if his jaw has come unhinged in some eternal howl. I remember too well the old man's words—the cosmos seem to me a haunted place, a graveyard.

In any case, another degree would not suit me at this point. One cannot spend one's time contemplating past failures; the road forks, a path is pursued or not, but always we must shuffle along, letting fall what will by the way. We should not bear so much upon our shoulders. And I am reasonably happy: I am awaiting news of a

to be expected—and there is a young woman of unusual good looks whom I have noticed frequents the corner of the quadrangle directly beneath my window. There are some advantages in keeping one's gaze close to the earth.

TWO BROTHERS

MALCOLM DEVLIN

THE DAY BEFORE WILLIAM FOUND THE BOY IN THE WOODS, A carriage arrived at Birchlands House.

While Miss Frith was writing names on the blackboard, *D'Artagnian, Louis, Philippe, Aramis*, William slipped out of his chair. He ran to the window of the schoolroom in time to see his father step from the carriage onto the gravel drive, which the night's snow had painted a thin and even white.

"Father's home," William said. Not to his governess who had joined him at the window, but to himself, as though spoken words might corroborate what his eyes doubted.

In previous years, before Stephen had left for the school, their father's visits to the house had been rare. He spent most of his time at his club in Mayfair, and visited the house only on occasional holidays or when the shooting season looked promising. He had not been home when Stephen had left for Greyhurst, nor had he returned during the subsequent four months, when William had been alone.

But now, the day before Stephen was due back for the winter holiday, the boys' father had come home. And there was something about his arrival which felt wrong to William in a way he could not articulate.

He ran to the door of the schoolroom and let himself out.

Miss Frith called after him, her voice rising to a wavering point: "Wait until you're called, William."

He ignored her. His father was a cold, unreachable figure and William disliked being in his presence. He had no intention of running to see him, but he was curious to know what had brought him home. He edged part way down the stairs until he could linger behind the uprights of the banisters, remaining mostly hidden from the hall below.

His father crossed the crimson tiles beneath him, beckoning for his man to follow. Briggs was a stocky fellow, buttoned tight in his uniform as though it would burst off him if he exhaled without care. He carried a heavy valise in each hand and William saw there was a long shaped parcel wrapped in brown paper hanging over his shoulder. Unlike his father, Briggs sensed William was watching. He glanced up to pinpoint him with dark eyes, and William shrank deeper into the shadows. Briggs turned away but remained a moment longer in the hall to exchange a few quiet words with the Jessie, the maid. When he turned again, William could just about make out the dark wooden stock of a shotgun wrapped neatly inside the package on his back.

His father didn't call for him that night, and William was content to be sent to bed early. He lay in his room, staring at the ceiling where shadows flickered from the ivy which fringed his window.

If Briggs had brought a gun, his father was expecting guests. He'd been known to host modest shooting parties in the fields and woodland to the north of the property. At this time of year, pheasants or partridges were likely game, but in the past few months William hadn't seen much activity around the gamekeeper's cottages, the presence of which, usually served as a reliable warning that a hunt was planned. On such occasions, the boys' freedoms about the house and its grounds would be curtailed. They would be expected to stay out of sight and out of earshot until all the guests had left.

Restless, William rolled over in his bed. If a shooting party was to happen, then it struck him as unjust. It meant Stephen would return to be ignored by father, to be shut up in the schoolroom with William. It was not the welcome home he deserved.

———

Stephen was a year older than William, but the way the two had grown up together, they may as well have been twins. Their mother had died when William had been six, and since then, the boys had been raised by the staff and Miss Frith, a slender, intense woman, who had shrank and shrivelled as the boys had grown older and stronger.

With their father absent, the boys were left to their own devices, free to explore every inch of the grounds of Birchlands and to make them their own. The house was an austere, angular building, hemmed in by an uneven mosaic of lawns and formal gardens, linked with a network of die-straight gravel pathways which the boys' imaginations refashioned into Roman roads, the Battle of Waterloo or elephant trails across the Alps.

Their father's one stipulation was that the brothers were forbidden from mixing with the children in the nearby village and it was a point on which the village children at least seemed content to respect.

With no-one else, the brothers became close allies, and if Stephen had not been told he was due to attend Greyhurst, they might have believed themselves inseparable.

The day before he'd left, Stephen had worn his brave face and it was a poor fit. His eyes were raw from where he'd scratched out the tears he didn't want the staff to see.

"If it were down to me," he said to William, "I wouldn't go at all."

It had not been down to Stephen. Greyhurst was not just a school, Greyhurst was a family duty. William would be sent there the following year, just as their father had attended when he'd been their age and their grandfather before him. There were photographs in the house which showed their father, their grand-father, their uncles and great-uncles looking sober in Greyhurst uniforms. There were long panoramic pictures of significant school years, regiments of pale-faced boys standing to attention. The family coat of arms, they were told, was embroidered on one of the score of pendants which decked the school's main hall. The brother's future there had never been in doubt, let alone questioned.

With Stephen gone, the days had ground on by with little incident. William was ill-equipped at being alone. He had rattled around the house, in search of distraction; wandering the grounds listless. He even come close to breaking his father's rule and considered crossing the southern field to reach the village, where the voices of the playing children rang like siren song; carried across the farmlands by the leading wind and leaving him only with a keener awareness of his isolation.

The days had dragged, and as they mounted up behind him, the anticipation of Stephen's return had grown into something

something competitive which had yet to bloom. He knew his brother would not have been idle over the past four months, he would come home full of stories about Greyhurst, his teachers, and his new friends, but William had nothing to say in return. He'd done almost nothing since Stephen had been away. Certainly nothing new; nothing that Stephen might find interesting, let alone be jealous of.

For the remaining weeks, this understanding galvanised William. He set about finding diversions for himself, if only so he would have something to tell Stephen about, to prove how he could cope on his own.

He took walks around the gardens, finding the longest path which did not cross itself; He asked the gardener, Mr Granville, for a patch of earth to work with and they had planted potatoes together in neat little rows. So that he might look brave, he slipped out before supper one evening and threw his uncle's leather-bound King James, spinning and flapping like a startled jackdaw, so it landed behind the crenelation over the south portico. So he might look agile, he clambered the vine, hand-over-hand, at the side of the door to retrieve it again.

At night, he would lie in bed imagining what more he could have done while left alone in the house, and by the time his father had arrived at Birchlands that afternoon, he'd fashioned a complex mythology of stories and anecdotes which never happened. It was a stockpile of cultivated lies to feed Stephen over the course of the holiday. He would ration them and use them to counter whatever true stories Stephen told. And in this way, Stephen would never know that William had been lonely at all.

The following morning, Jessie woke William early and busied herself spreading his freshly pressed Sunday suit across the dresser.

"Your father wants you to breakfast with him," she said, ushering him up and out of bed, clucking over him with an impatient frown. Jessie was from the village, she was young and inexperienced but keen and inexpensive. She had a round freckled face and stubborn ginger curls that would not all be pinned back no matter how she tried.

William had asked her once about the children in the village, and now she would talk about little else. She told him about how they played in the snow. They would wrap up warm, and gather amongst it, drawn to it like moths.

"The whole lawn out there is untouched," she said, nodding at the window. "If we was in the village, we wouldn't let all that lovely snow go to waste now. We'd have made a man of it, tall as you. Taller."

"I was saving it for Stephen," William said. It felt like a foolish reason when he said it out loud. He didn't look up at her. He imagined she didn't know what it was like to be left to play alone.

His father and Miss Frith were in the breakfast room when he arrived. Miss Frith looked pale, sitting upright and silent, more discomforted by his father than William was. His father was reading the newspaper and although he glanced up when his youngest son came in, he didn't say a word. William took his place at the table and waited.

Breakfast had been laid out and the three ate in silence, toasted bread and cold sliced meat. The newspaper held his father's attention. He ate around it, refolding it with great expansive flaps, which whomped and cracked like a fire under a clear flue.

When he was done, he folded the paper and set it aside. He looked at William directly.

"Your brother, Stephen, is due to return today on the 2:12 train," he said. "I propose we meet him at the station."

It wasn't a question but his eyes held William as though he was expecting an answer. Thoughts tumbled over each other in William's head but none lingered long enough to make any sense. His father didn't talk to him, his father didn't talk to Stephen. And yet—

"Yes," William said. "Of course."

the steam and smoke, the winter had taken a claim on it. The glass of the roof was muted by a mottled layer of snow and a barbed wind cut across the platforms picking at the coats of the porters.

Standing and waiting, the cold made William retreat inside himself, pulling his coat tight about him and ducking his head as far as he could beneath his raised collar. On any other occasion, Miss Frith would have subjected him to a stern lecture about the importance of posture, but the cold had got to her too. She had shrivelled within her heavy coat and her sensible shoes, and her breath came out in short little puffs which lingered about her like a veil.

Only William's father seemed unaffected. His own posture was good, the sort of thing Miss Frith would approve of with a curt nod and a pursed-lipped smile. He stood straight-backed and patient; his features, those solid, dependable lines and contours you often saw on the marble busts of well-bred Englishmen. He looked across the platform with a quiet confidence and a sense of expectancy which William thought misplaced. If anyone should be looking forward to Stephen's return, it should be the brother who had missed him so desperately and not the father who had barely acknowledged him for the first twelve years of his life.

When the train arrived, it appeared vast and monstrous to William's eyes, a black hole of iron and noise screaming as it slowed its speed. It hawked gouts of steam across the platform, making murky grey ghosts of the disembarking passengers and the railwaymen alike.

Stephen emerged from the hubbub surrounding him with the newly acquired air of one who understood his place in the world. He looked taller, more confident, unintimidated by the bitter cold.

He smiled when he saw them waiting for him, but it was not the lopsided grin which William remembered but a thin smile he didn't recognise, and it was not directed at him personally. When William turned, he saw the same smile reflected on his father's face. It was a cold expression; colder than the snow and the wind, and it was then William understood that while his brother had come home, he would remain alone.

The carriage brought them all back to the house, but during the journey, William found it hard to say anything to his brother. He tried to put it down to their father's presence but even once they were left alone back at the house, Stephen seemed distant. He regarded William's invitation to play with no more than a polite amusement. His attitude had cooled to something a little aloof, a little indifferent and William's plans for the afternoon were dismissed before they could be described.

"I don't think so," Stephen had said. "Besides, father and I are busy this afternoon."

It was only later that William discovered their father had invited Stephen to join him on an afternoon shooting expedition.

On seeing his face, Stephen had laughed.

"Nothing too grand," he said. "Not yet. Father bought me a 12-bore and thought I might try it on some rabbits or magpies. Something to practice on before a real hunt."

But it did sound too grand to William, it sounded far too adult to consider. The father he knew would never invite him on such a trip, he would never buy him a shotgun of his own. William had never wanted such a thing until that moment. It surprised him: a jealousy which made his hands curl into impotent fists. He retreated to his room, hoping his temper might cool, but in the garden outside, he could hear Stephen's voice as he passed under his window. He didn't hear what he was saying or who he was speaking to, but there was excitement and enthusiasm there which William felt desperately excluded from.

He lay on his bed and put his hands to his ears.

He waited until they were far gone before he got up again. Maybe he could run away? Maybe he could go for a walk. The house felt inexplicably crowded and he yearned for the quiet he had become accustomed to. He pulled on his coat and boots and ran downstairs.

As he passed the library, he saw someone inside. He saw immediately it was Miss Frith, but she seemed unaware of him standing, ~~watching her from the~~ ~~posture which was~~ strange to him. She faced the shelves, her back turned to him, her arms were outstretched and her hands were poised on the spines of the books. Her head was dipped and she simply stood there; silent and still except for a small convulsion of her shoulders as though she was expelling a sudden chill. For a moment, William thought she might be crying.

He edged away slowly and cut through the staff wing to the rear door.

The snow had not fallen with any great volume or consistency that winter, but a good inch had settled during the night, covering the front lawn evenly from corner-to-corner. Now that Stephen was home, its appeal had thawed and the snow remained pure and undisturbed through neglect rather than deliberation.

The far end of the lawn bordered a ragged copse where the boys had once played together. The trees had shed their leaves and the bare branches were spiked like fish bones. The season had diminished them following a decadent summer and now they were a mass of stark grey verticals, fading into a pale damp haze. Between them, the snow lay more thinly, with only disparate patches of white glistening amongst the layer of yellow-green mosses, made vivid by the winter.

A narrow trail led deeper into the trees. It followed the line of the culvert which marked the edge of the family's land but William followed it without paying attention. He'd walked this route so often, he needed no path to lead the way.

When they'd been younger, William and Stephen would play together in the culvert, lining their tin soldiers along its edge. Stephen's would always be the British, leaving William with either the French or the Boers, but William had never objected. He gave his French soldiers voices as they keeled over in the mud: Screams and wails; falsetto *mon dieus* which made his brother bend double with laughter.

They had played lengthy campaigns in those days. Neither had much of an eye for military strategy and when the charge was sounded, numbers on both sides would fall until only two remained standing, one on each side. The end game would stretch on and on. The two survivors would take off around the grounds, fencing, flying, ducking, weaving. They would scale trees and rocks. They would fall and miraculously recover, and only when the brothers would tire of the game would history prevail and Napoleon would fall to Wellington. The summer days stretched long and as the dusk began to gather, they would search through the mud for their fallen redcoats, gathering them in fistfuls and carrying them home.

William caught sight of something in the snow which snapped him back to the present. Alone at the edge of the path, there was the print of a bare human foot, toes clearly defined in the crisp, compacted snow left behind.

William stooped low to examine the find, then looked about him, searching for movement amongst the trees. But he could make no further sense of it than the fact it existed, pointing away from the house, deeper into the copse.

Now, for the first time, he looked at the track he'd been blindly following and saw he wasn't the first to walk it since the snow had fallen. A trail ran along it both ways, up to the border of the woods, and then back again; twin furrows etched in the snow, each erasing and confusing the other. The feet which made them had dragged in both directions, and the way the snow had softened in the vague afternoon sun gave no evidence that the same feet had left the print as well.

William kicked through the undergrowth until he uncovered a stick heavy enough to intimidate and light enough to wield. He struck it solidly a few times, scattering the dusting of snow it had acquired and—satisfied it was not rotten through—he hefted it in both hands like a club.

With that, William was on a hunt of his own. He didn't need his father. He certainly didn't need Stephen. He'd been patiently learning to occupy his time over the past four months and he was damned if he would allow himself to appear as upset and betrayed as he felt.

briefly only when the low wall which ran along the other side became exposed to the surrounding farmland. As William neared the southernmost boundary of the copse, he held his club out before him.

In the summer of the previous year, the boys had eavesdropped on the groundsmen's conversations about news of the peasant uprising against the Tsar in Russia. The boys had built a fortress at the far end of the culvert as the backdrop for an ill-considered attempt to re-enact the drama. They had not really understood what was happening or why, but both had agreed it sounded exciting. Even when their game had been discovered, and they each had received a sound thrashing for their troubles, they also agreed it had been worth it.

In the intervening year, the fortress had been slowly reclaimed by the untended woodland as though the peasants had breached its defences after all. The rot had set in, but its shape had weathered better than William had anticipated.

'Fortress' was a generous term for such a ramshackle construction: low woven walls plastered with wet mud and leaves; a poorly knitted grass roof and foundations augmented with piles of stones they had stolen from the culvert walls.

William could see the remains ahead of him: the stones had mostly toppled into piles, and the grass roof was gone entirely, but two of the woven walls still remained, propped against each other like a narrow tent. Cords of ivy climbed up through them, knitting them to the ground and lending them the air of something more permanent. They were not the walls the boys had built over a year ago, but walls which had been borne out of them.

And behind them, a shadow moved. The shadow of a figure, shredded through the twisted leaves.

Despite himself, William took a sharp intake of breath—a fine huntsman he would make, giving himself away like that. The figure froze at the sound. Its reply was a low, animal-like whimper.

Emboldened by what he took to be a display of weakness, William advanced.

"Come out," he said. "You can't hide in there. I can see you."

Closer, the figure appeared to be trying to prevent itself from moving, but the task was beyond it. It shivered uncontrollably in the cold, and the walls of the fortress shivered with it.

William slowed. This was no adversary. It was something far too wretched to fight back. Some hermit, maybe, or one of the children from the village who had become lost.

William lowered his branch and reached for the fortress wall with his hand.

"I won't hurt you," he said and immediately regretted how it sounded like a sign of weakness of his own.

But the figure didn't move as he pulled the wall aside. The mat of vines and branches gave easily, folding downwards to reveal what was hidden behind it as though it were concealed by nothing more substantial than a thin curtain.

It was a boy, or at the very least, the remains of one. He cowered in the ditch, shivering with the cold and his hands were held high, his forearms crossed, covering his face. His clothes were ragged and filthy; his feet were bare, the flesh shredded with angry sores. He stank as though he'd been living in a latrine and William gagged with revulsion and took a step back in surprise.

Startled by the sudden movement, the boy lowered his arms and looked up with wide, terrified eyes which William knew all too well.

It was Stephen. It was unmistakably Stephen. And it was not the Stephen who had returned, but the Stephen who had gone away.

The fear and anger which had haunted his eyes on the day before he left for Greyhurst were still there; they had grown over the months, become wilder: An expression of wordless horror carved onto ruined features.

William barely managed a breath. It was impossible, but it was too real to be anything other than true. And so, when he said Stephen's name, it was not a question.

Stephen's head bobbed up and down, the motion jerky and mechanical. Sounds came out but they were disconnected and senseless. William stared at the boy, his thoughts a confused clutter ... ping the branch in the path.

"Wait," Stephen managed. It was a torturous syllable. It sounded as though it had been coughed up from somewhere dark and hollow. William waited, but although Stephen was desperately trying to say something else, more words didn't come, only tears and further splintering breaths.

William looked back down the path as though there might be something, someone there capable of advising him. But he was alone with only the uniform ranks of pale winter trees standing silent and impassive around him, waiting his command.

He knew he had to do something. He had to get the boy somewhere warm, somewhere safe.

This understanding granted him resolve and he stumbled down the side of the culvert, his feet sinking into the brackish mud and loam which clogged its length. He tried to ignore the shock of cold as the black ditch water crept up around his shoes.

Closer, he could see Stephen was in a worse state than he'd first thought. His clothes were torn and mottled with grime. His skin was sallow, the whites of his eyes looked like red cracks in crusted yellow cream. A weak hand reached out and when it touched William's, the coldness of it came as a blow. William withdrew. He felt the chill more strongly himself, it burnt the tips of his ears and fingers; it gathered, heavy at his chest. For a selfish moment, he half-believed Stephen's touch had infected him.

"Please," Stephen said.

William swallowed hard, cementing a decision which had already been made. He stepped forward, crouching low. He held his breath tight and hated himself for it. The thinness and sharpness of his brother's shoulders appalled him and he felt Stephen spasm at his touch.

"Can you stand?"

Stephen didn't respond. His eyes were closed, his gaunt face tight with pain. William tugged at him, feeling the body give around the bones as though the two were barely connected. He found himself surprised by the weight of him. But it was a dead weight, like something pinned in the mud. Stephen's eyes opened wide and unfocussed, staring upwards at the wavering treetops circling above. His mouth opened wider still, a wordless, soundless exclamation which made William let go and stagger backwards.

"I'm sorry," he said. It didn't seem enough. "I'll get help."

It was cowardly, but the alternative seemed far worse, and he would be faster alone. He shrugged out of his coat and pressed it around his brother's skeletal shoulders.

"I'll come back soon," William promised, impatient not to waste any more time. "I'll bring back help, I promise I will."

Stephen's eyes found him again, they stared at him, feral and unblinking. He stammered something which didn't quite make sense and William backed away further, feeling wretched as he did so.

"I'll be as fast as I can," he said. He clambered up the bank of the culvert and ran.

It was as much as he'd planned. He knew he could not deal with this on his own. For Stephen's sake, it wouldn't be fair if he tried. He needed someone else. He needed someone like Briggs. Briggs could carry him, he thought. His father would get Briggs to help. He ran on, the tender, lifeless branches whipping at his face, snatching at his feet.

He broke out of the copse and into the garden. He didn't even stop for breath and ran headlong across the lawn, leaving a scuffed and slipshod trail through the perfect snow he'd been saving. He rounded the corner of the east wing and immediately collided with someone coming from the other direction. The surprise, rather than the impact, sent him sailing into a heap on the icy path.

Disorientated and shocked, panic overwhelmed reason and he yelled out.

A hand reached down and dragged him back to his feet.

"Watch where you're going, old man," Stephen said, more irritable than angry. He looked every inch the country gentlemen, all the way down to the pair of mournful looking rabbits strung together, hanging at his side.

William stared at him while Stephen patted the snow from his ~~shoulders~~ ~~~~~~~~~~~~~~~~~~~~~~~~~~~~~~~~~~~ muddy marks which streaked his shirt.

"Heavens, you look like you've been in the wars," Stephen said. "Does Frith know you're out without your coat? She'll give us both hell if she finds out."

The thought appeared to remind him of something that amused him and for a moment, his smile was genuine, unrehearsed.

"You're not still spending time in that ditch?" he said. "*Mon dieu.* I need to have words with Frith about the accent she's been teaching you. Yaxley, the French master at Greyhurst said I had it all wrong. Makes us sound like peasants, he said."

William said nothing. Having already seen and recognised the Stephen in the woods, he imagined the impostor—because this Stephen must surely be the wrong one—would be obviously monstrous in comparison. But both Stephens looked the same. The brother standing before him looked normal and reasonable. He looked healthier. His cheeks were pink with the smart of the cold, his eyes lit with a flat amusement. If he was alien to William, he was only made that way by experiences over the past few months which William had no part in.

"Something's eating you," Stephen said, studying him. "What is it?"

William remained silent, and for his efforts he felt his brother's hand tighten around his shoulder.

"Don't be childish," Stephen said. "What is it? What have you done?"

There was something in Stephen's tone which was familiar enough to make William doubt himself entirely.

"There's a boy in the woods," he said. "He's hurt."

It only sounded like a betrayal once he'd said it out loud. His throat felt sharp and sore as though something inside of him had torn loose.

Stephen stared at him.

"A boy?" he said. "Show me."

"No. Where's father? We should get Briggs and—"

"Don't be foolish; show me where the boy is."

For the second time that afternoon, William found himself backing away from his brother. But this time, he couldn't have explained why. Maybe he'd got it all wrong. He remembered the smile Stephen and their father had shared at the station. Would it make any difference if he insisted on speaking to his father alone? The outcome would be the same, he would only waste more time and the boy in the woods, whoever he was, didn't have time to squander.

Nevertheless, it was with considerable reluctance that William led the way back into the copse. The path he'd followed was still there, its clarity muddied by his own trail which criss-crossed it. He scuffed his feet as he walked, obscuring it further. He hoped looking petulant would distract Stephen from what he was doing.

For his part, Stephen remained quiet. He'd left his brace of rabbits hanging over a low branch at the garden-end of the copse and walked behind William, his footsteps precise and silent.

William tried to hide his nerves with noise. He started talking to cover himself and found he could not stop. Everything which had been building up within him for the past four months, everything he'd wanted to tell Stephen when he returned, it all came spilling out, uncontrolled.

Here were his precious anecdotes, polished and perfected. Here were his facts reimagined into fables. Tales of exploration and adventure that had never happened; gossip from the village he had never heard; friends he had never been permitted to make.

Here were the stories he'd practiced to himself in the hours and days he'd spent alone. He had been saving them, just as he'd been saving the freshly fallen snow on the lawn, but now Stephen was finally here, he cast them about him as they walked, his voice loud and clear to carry the further. They were no longer stories, no longer boasts or lies. They were distractions, they were warnings, they were lost to the mud and the snow.

The culvert was empty when they reached it, and while the disturbed snow could have been made by any creature in panic, there was nothing to suggest it had been made by anything so specific as the boy William had seen.

ruined fortress wall with his toe. He glanced back at William.

"Liar." He said it with half a smile as though he was still capable of playing along. "I might have known you'd make a scene."

He looked out to the edge of the copse where the adjoining field of grey fallow grass stretched upwards to the curve of the hillside.

Already he was tiring of the game. He turned on his heel and marched back the way they had come. When William didn't follow him immediately, Stephen stopped and looked back.

"Father's calling," he said.

William shook his head stubbornly. He'd not heard anything, but he followed anyway as he always did.

That evening, William's father did something he'd never done before. He came to visit his youngest son in his bedroom. Still wearing his hunting clothes, he brought the smell of smoke and sulphur into the narrow room on the second floor.

At first, neither of them spoke a word. William had already been in bed, and at the sound of the door opening, he'd swung out from under the covers to sit on the edge of the frame. A stripe of shadow hid his father's face, but William felt his eyes on him. Sharp and unwavering, they trapped him where he sat.

His father cleared his throat.

"You must be patient with your brother," he said. "Stephen is experiencing new things, a world away from this life you've both become used to. You need time. You both need time."

He turned to go and for a moment, William saw Stephen was waiting in the hallway outside. He too was dressed in his outdoor clothes. There was a lantern at his feet and something tall propped by his side which glinted brief and dull grey in the shaft of moonlight that fell through the window. William recognised the wooden stock had seen the day before, wrapped in cloth and hanging across Briggs' back.

His father turned back to William, blocking the view; his watch chain glinted in the hallway light like the flash of a smile.

"You mustn't be jealous of him," he said. "Next year you'll be at Greyhurst yourself. Next year, you'll understand."

He pulled the door to, and it was open barely a crack when he spoke again.

"Next year, William," he said, "it'll be you."

He closed the door. Somewhere outside, a dog barked. And once again, William was alone.

THE LAKE

DANIEL MILLS

August, 1997.

SAMUEL IS TWELVE. HE DESPISES HIMSELF: HIS THIN LIMBS, his hairless body. His friend Jason is thirteen but looks older. Jason is a Boy Scout and natural athlete, pitcher for the town's Little League team. The boys have known each other for years.

Samuel's house is less than a mile from the lake. Most evenings the boys ride bikes to the dam , but tonight they will walk, because Nick is coming with them.

They met Nick in July at church camp where Samuel's father was pastor. Nick lives with his father in the next town and attends a different middle school. He is pale, heavy, asthmatic. He wheezes when he runs, breasts bouncing in the shirts he wears to swim.

It is early evening, not yet suppertime. Samuel and Jason watch for Nick from the living room window. His father's truck pulls up short of the house. Its red body gleams, the hubcaps like silver sunbursts. The driver is visible through the windshield, the dark glasses that hide his eyes. His skin is shockingly pale, hands white where they grip the wheel.

Nick dismounts from the cabin and totters up the lawn. His father pulls out, the engine roaring as it gathers speed.

The boys pelt outside, anxious to swim. They meet Nick on the porch and set off with him, following the road along the lakeshore, its floating docks and ranks of summer cottages. Samuel and Jason go first, nearly running, while Nick trails behind, panting, pleading with them to slow down, to wait. They do not.

Eventually, they reach the dam. It is long disused: the sluices blocked with rust, the concrete chipped and pitted. The boys remove their shoes and socks. They scale the hemlock which overhangs the dam and lower themselves to the ledge.

Jason goes first, then Samuel, then Nick, who trembles as he releases his grip from the hemlock and stands unsupported on the dam. A motorboat passes, startling the gulls from a nearby thicket.

waves continue to move in its absence, spreading over the lake's surface like the cracks in a mirror.

The ledge is slick, wet with spray from the lake five feet below. Samuel, cautious, steps carefully over the dam, hooking his toes in the crumbling concrete. He goes from pockmark to crater, listening all the while for Nick's breath behind him: the catch in the other boy's throat, the occasional wheeze.

Jason is far ahead of them. Confident of his footing, he walks the ledge with an acrobat's grace, slowing only as he nears the center of the dam. Samuel has not been out so far, has never dared, but Nick is behind him and he does not want to appear afraid and so says nothing.

They reach the dam's center. The ledge is highest here. Behind them an old streambed runs downhill past a cottage shuttered for season's end then bends out of sight beyond a stand of hemlocks. The dark trees shimmer. The day's rain webs their foliage, hangs from branch and needle. The lake is calm, all waves dissipated. Samuel looks down at his reflection far below.

Jason strips off his shirt. The muscles show in his arms and shoulders as he raises his hands, joining them together over his head. He turns his wrists one against the other and stretches, bending himself from side to side.

Samuel asks: "What are you doing?"

"Limbering up."

"Why?"

"We're going to dive."

"Here? It's too high."

"Ten feet, maybe. No more than that. Same as the diving board at the *Y*."

"I don't know."

"Don't dive, then. I'll do it alone."

Jason drops to a squat. His legs tense. He straightens, readying himself for the jump.

Nick says: "Wait."

Samuel wheels around. He watches dumbly as Nick snorts from his inhaler and shuffles forward past him. The fat bunches at his elbows. His nipples show through his tee shirt.

He says: "I'll jump with you."

Jason grins. "Okay, then," he says.

Samuel reddens and retreats down the ledge. He turns his back on the others, faces the boarded-up cottage. The windows are shut, the doors padlocked.

Behind him Jason and Nick line up at the edge of the dam. He hears them, their breathing. Jason counting down from three. "One."

They jump. Samuel glances behind him, sees Jason fall with his back curved in upon itself and hands thrust out even as Nick steps forward timidly and drops from the ledge feet-first.

The air rushes up toward Nick, unbalancing him as he falls and flipping him onto his back. His tee shirt inflates, rides up, revealing his chest: the breasts like lumps of dough, the lines of yellow bruising near the waistband of his trunks. He strikes the water and plunges toward the bottom. Samuel's reflection unravels with the impact, shattered in the whorl of rising bubbles.

Jason breaches the water. He is some distance from the dam and making for the lake's center. His strokes are perfect: he cleaves the water with the ease of a boat's prow, his wake rippling behind him.

Samuel waits. Nick does not resurface.

The water re-knits itself, becoming smooth as glass. Samuel's face floats within it, a perfect image: the lines round his mouth, the lips wide as he yells for help. His throat yawns before him, black with the shadow from a dying eddy.

His voice is broken, shrill. It is enough. Jason hears him and turns round. He swims back toward the dam, shouting to Samuel as he draws near. He urges Samuel to jump in, to help, but Samuel cannot. His legs refuse to move, his eyes to close.

Jason dives, surfaces. There are weeds in his hair, water streaming down his face.

"Where is he?" he demands. "Can you see him?"

face, the tongue flapping uselessly against the dark of his throat. Jason swears and forces himself under again—longer this time though he comes up gasping, alone. He treads water briefly, breathing hard. Two deep breaths and he submerges himself for a third time, disappearing behind Samuel's reflection.

At last he resurfaces, Nick's head lolling on his shoulder. The other boy is limp in his arms, pressed close to his chest as he holds him up, kicking them both toward shore.

Samuel runs to meet them. He sheds his paralysis and sprints along the dam, forgetting his earlier caution. His bare feet sting as they slap the concrete.

Jason reaches the rocks near the end of the dam and pulls himself from the water. He drags himself forward with one hand then turns to hauls up Nick behind him.

There is blood in the boy's scalp and his tee shirt hangs loosely from his neck. His exposed chest appears soft, rubbery, white but for the bruises at his waist. They form a mottled line, purple and yellow, which disappears into his underwear.

Samuel sees them first, then Jason.

They look at each other, look away.

Jason takes Nick's wrist in hand and listens for the pulse. He cradles the boy's neck between his legs and leans forward, covering Nick's lips with his mouth.

He breathes in, out.

Nick startles and coughs. Jason exhales heavily, falling back. The strength drains from Samuel's legs, and he drops to his knees.

The coughing subsides. Nick's eyelids flutter and open.

His eyes are bulging, wild and white.

Samuel tells no one what happened that day. Jason, too, is silent but only because Samuel begs him not to tell. His fear still eats at him, his shame or something more.

Fall comes and with it school, the seventh grade. Nick disappears from their lives, and it is winter, January, when Samuel sees him again.

Early morning: sun coming up, gray smudges on thick cloud cover. Samuel sits in his mother's car at the end of the driveway, waiting for the school bus.

The morning is cold, below zero. The heat vents rattle. Samuel's head rests against the window, his breath misting on the pane.

Through that fog he watches the red pickup truck come barreling down the road, driving too quickly for the ice on the roads. Nick's father. Samuel recognizes the black glasses, the pale hands on the wheel, and then the truck is past them.

A face at the rear windshield: Nick. He is as pale as his father and his mouth is open, a black circle.

The years pass and Samuel is seventeen, a senior in high school. In the spring he gets his license and takes to driving the lake-roads at night, circling round and round the lake.

Most nights, Jason rides with him, the water-pipe in hand and the windows down, the night-air breaking like waves around them. Jason offers the pipe to Samuel but always he refuses, thinking of his father's disapproval, and weeks pass in this way before he caves.

Tonight they trade hits from Jason's water-pipe and park below the dam. "Leave the music on," Jason says, and Modest Mouse is playing as they climb out, slam the doors.

The car's headlights shine on the wall of the dam before them, the hemlock-branches through which they climb. They reach the dam and lower themselves down. Stand side-by-side on the ledge, their shadows stretching ahead of them into the water.

The night is clear. The stars are out, the bow of the Milky Way visible. It joins with its reflection on the water to form an ellipse, an open mouth.

"Well, shit," says Jason. "That's really something."

Samuel is slow to respond. When he does he says it is like the future that waits for them, ready to swallow them whole. He is ~~thinking of the coming~~

but Jason, laughing, tells him he is stoned.

So they talk of other things: Boy Scouts and church camp and summers spent swimming at the dam. One morning in particular when they donned goggles and snorkels and swam out to the center of the lake which marked the boundary between two towns. They crossed the border, Samuel remembers, then turned round and swam back to shore.

Jason asks: "You think you still have those snorkels?"

"Sure. Back at the house."

"What do you say we try them out?"

"Tonight?"

"Yeah."

"Alright."

It is after midnight. They walk back to the house and let themselves into the mudroom. The snorkels are in the closet along with two sets of goggles, the lenses gray with dust and spider silk. Samuel hands one set to Jason and takes the other for himself.

Silently, then, they slip outside, drawing the door shut behind them. Returning to the dam, they strip to their boxer shorts and climb the hemlock. Jason squats and leans forward to rinse his snorkel in the lake-water. Samuel follows suit then takes the mouthpiece between his lips. He gags at the taste: mud, mildew, puddled snowmelt.

Jason laughs, his face hidden behind his goggles. Samuel turns from him and looks out toward the lake, its center. His breath moans in the snorkel.

The moon is waning. The stars cut brighter for the ranks of darkened cottages all around, and the Milky Way is on the water, rippling, opening from itself to receive them as they step forward and drop from the edge.

Samuel hits the water. The lake closes over him, colder than he expected. It sloshes over the snorkel-top and fills his mouth so that he comes up coughing, blind where the lake has seeped into his goggles.

He treads water. "Jason?" he manages.

A voice drifts back to him. "Yeah?"

Jason is ten feet away, nearer the shore, where the lake is shallow enough for him to stand. His bare chest is visible where it thrusts from the water, a web of stars.

Samuel says: "Nothing."

Jason leans forward and submerges his head. He wades along the shore, parting the water before him with his hands.

Samuel empties his goggles and snorkel and begins to swim. The lake-bottom rises out of the blackness as he nears the shallows, the shore.

His toes touch mud and he continues at a walk, wading as Jason did with his goggles submerged in the water. Beyond the glass the lake-bottom appears as a moonscape, lit by stars and cratered where his feet break through it, raising plumes of muddy debris.

He rotates his head toward the lake's center, the line dividing his town from Nick's. The water is deepest there, he knows, and before him the darkness draws itself into thin bands interspersed with beams of light, stars shining through from above.

All is quiet. Samuel is conscious of no sound save the whistle of air in the snorkel, the slow and even lapping of the lake. The weeds ripple beyond his goggles, the mud blossoming before him at each step. He spreads his arms and brings his hands together, dividing stars from darkness from whirling mud.

The silence is broken.

Samuel hears a heavy splash behind him, as though someone else has fallen from the dam. Panting, grunting. The sounds of frantic swimming.

He spins round, startled. He tears the goggles from his head.

Jason is halfway out of the water, running. He reaches the rocks and scrambles up them, and he must have lost his boxers somehow, because Samuel sees that he is naked, his buttocks showing, white and wiry. He vanishes over the lip of the dam.

Samuel goes after him. He thrashes a path through the shallows and bolts up the wet rocks. He falls once, twice, cutting open his foot. He reaches the top ~~~~~~~~~~~~~~~ swinging himself down from the hemlock.

Jason is in the car. The passenger-side door is open and he has draped himself in a red gingham picnic blanket. He holds the pipe between his teeth with the lighter in one hand and the other hand cupped round, trying to coax a spark.

"It's nothing," he says, mumbling. "Freaked myself out, that's all."

"All? You scared me."

"Thought I saw something. In the water."

"What did you see?"

Jason shakes his head, will say nothing more.

Samuel retrieves their clothes from the dam. When he returns to the car, he finds Jason seated with eyes closed and pipe lit, smoke curling up from his open mouth.

Samuel starts the car, pulls out. Jason dresses himself in the dark while Samuel averts his gaze, watching the road unfold in the glare of the high-beams.

Jason's breathing is unnaturally loud. Samuel turns on the radio.

Jason's house. Jason crosses the lawn with his hands in his pockets and mounts the steps to the screened-in porch. Samuel watches. The headlights strike through the screens, making shadows like nets which close over him, catching Jason as he turns, waves, disappears inside.

The separation happens slowly, by degrees. On Friday, Samuel calls

Jason's house and speaks to his mother. She tells him Jason is out. "Lauren came by and picked him up."

Lauren? The name means nothing to him. Samuel spends the night in bed with his headphones on and his face to the ceiling, the fan-blades going around.

The weekend passes with no word from Jason. Sunday night, Samuel goes out walking. His footfalls carry him up hill to the lake, the dam—and that is where he sees them, seated together on the ledge. Jason with his back bent forward, his head in his hands. The girl beside him with her arm extended, hand spread across his back. She is speaking to him softly, almost whispering. Jason's shoulders shake.

Samuel skulks back to the house, says nothing of what he saw. In school the boys continue to greet each other, passing in the hallway, but Jason takes to spending the weekends with Lauren and week-nights, too, once summer arrives.

In the autumn Jason leaves for college on a baseball scholarship and Samuel goes to work for his uncle, who owns a contracting business. He sees Jason around the holidays, but only then, and soon they lose touch altogether.

Samuel is twenty-one, twenty-two. Sometimes, at night, he remembers the lake as it was on that night in May with the stars in its folds and the Milky Way on its surface, yawning, joining its reflection to receive him as he fell.

In dreams he stands on the dam, cold concrete between his toes. He hears his own breathing, strained and whistling, and Nick's face is in the water below. It shimmers in place, floating on the dark that whirls up from beneath.

The image stays with him on waking, a trapped melody. One night, late, he staggers out of bed and tiptoes downstairs to his father's office. He digs the address book out of the desk and flips through it until he finds Nick's number.

He takes down the phone from the wall and dials the number. He raises the receiver to his ear, waits for a ringing from the other side. He has no idea what he will say, how he will begin.

Four beeps in sequence. A woman's recorded voice.

The number has been disconnected.

2012. Samuel is a manager in his uncle's contracting business, a youth pastor in his father's church. He teaches Sunday school, arranges field trips to the lake in summertime. He lives alone. His apartment is in the next town but he drives up to the lake on Sundays for dinner with his parents. From them he learns that Jason is engaged. His mother says: "He's coming home for the wedding. They're getting married at the lake."

on the night of the wedding he cruises round the lake at twenty miles per hour, watching for signs. He spies one, slows. *Jason + Amanda*, it says, the words in green letters on a yellow background. An arrow points up a driveway to a big house overlooking the water. Rented for the occasion, he thinks.

A tent has been erected on the lawn, tables laid with champagne flutes and electric candles. The wedding, it seems, is over, but the dancing continues, men and women whirling together beneath strings of Christmas lights. They are beautiful, achingly so, wearing their best clothes and dancing, pairing off to music he can't hear and always the lake behind them, its awful stillness. The water is calm, un-rippled. Purple with the reflection of a sky that isn't there, not really, and he thinks of his childhood, the years since high school. The surface of his life and the memories it hides. The bruises at Nick's waist. His father's black glasses.

Jason's voice. *Thought I saw something. In the water.*

Samuel backs out into the road. He straightens the wheel and depresses the gas pedal, anxious to be away. Thirty-five, forty. He rounds the northwest corner of the lake just as a pickup truck pulls out from a side-street, cutting him off.

He slams the brakes. Taps the horn as he approaches, but the truck does not increase its speed. Twenty miles per hour. He is ten feet from the other vehicle, less. The tailgate flaps up, down— groaning, broken—and the truck itself is filthy, half-decrepit.

Samuel strains his eyes. He leans into the glow of his headlights but cannot discern the color of the pickup for the layers of rust and mud. The license plate is similarly indistinct, a gray rectangle, while the truck's rear windshield is fogged over, opaque but for a swath where someone has wiped it clear from inside.

Samuel glimpses movement in the cabin, the flutter of something white. He flashes his high-beams. Glimpses a face at the window, a boy.

The child's eyes are black, or appear so, as is the mouth that drops open, crying out, screaming for help while the tailgate bangs up and down.

Samuel brakes, hard. His car shudders, screeches. Stops.

The truck drives away.

Samuel's mouth is dry. His hands shake as he fumbles for the stick-switch, his brights. He sees it again: that face at the window, an open mouth. Screaming even as the truck vanishes beyond the cone of his headlights, leaving the empty road, the windblown trees. The leaves and the patterns they make like ripples in water.

He stomps down on the accelerator. The engine responds, pushing up toward forty. The lake drops away to his left, the north shore visible through a lattice of birch-branch and pine, and again the pickup is before him.

The tailgate falls open, releasing a cloud of dust from the truck-bed. It rears up before him, white and fine where his headlights strike through, illuminating the interior of the cabin. The driver's head is visible, a shimmering in the truck's rear-view, but only for a moment before it is gone, eclipsed by a hand at the back windshield: a child's hand, the fingers spread.

Samuel slows, his bumper five feet from the truck's tailgate.

He turns on his high-beams, flooding the pickup's interior, revealing the dark stains on the dashboard and headrests, the mold sprouting from the upholstery. The cabin swims with damp, trapped breath whirling like smoke before the light.

The hand vanishes, reappears.

It thumps feebly the glass.

The truck accelerates. The chassis shakes as the driver up-shifts, shedding flecks of paint or rust which spatter Samuel's windshield and skitter away into the night.

Samuel speeds up to maintain his distance, punching his horn all the while. He flashes his brights, but the truck will not slow, will not pull over, and together they follow the road as it curves to the south, away from the lake, dark trees yielding to farm-fields, fence-posts.

He presses down the gas pedal. The speedometer jumps to fifty-five, sixty, bringing him within two car-lengths of the truck. The road ahead of them is clear. He jerks the wheel sharply to the left

level with the cabin.

The driver-side door is rusted out, sealed over. The window is misted with breath, smeared with fingerprints. The windshield, too, is completely obscured, though the truck continues to accelerate, pushing seventy as they approach the straightaway.

Samuel rolls down his window. He shouts across the seat, but the other driver pays no heed. With the window down, Samuel hears a thudding from the truck and sees the boy's face at the window. There are bruises about the mouth and neck but the features are familiar, somehow, the eyes, though in this moment, he cannot be sure if it is Nick's face, or Jason's, or his own—and then the road is sliding out from under him.

He hits the ditch. Flips, keeps rolling. Tumbles end-over-end through the hay-fields. The airbag explodes from the steering column and he hears a sound like waters churning, sees the stars come rushing toward him: the Milky Way, its open jaws.

He survives. A young woman, driving behind him, witnesses the accident and phones for help from her car. Later, in her statement, she says that he was driving erratically: changing lanes, shouting out his window. She makes no mention of a second vehicle.

He is in the hospital. The days pass and he is discharged, sent home to recover. Home: his parents' house, where he is treated as a sickly child. His mother hovers by the bedside, reading passages aloud from the Bible or *Reader's Digest*. His father kneels by the bed with his hand folded round Samuel's, offering up prayers for his recovery.

Some of his Sunday School students come to visit, three boys in tee shirts and swimsuits. They linger in the doorway, their limbs white and hairless. One boy is heavier than the others, the fat forming dimples where it overhangs his knees. They sing songs from church, their faces like masks showing nothing, and afterward, the fat boy says they are going swimming.

"Off to the beach, then?" Samuel's father asks.

"No," the boy says. "We'll probably just go up to the dam."

The final song is sung—*let the lower lights be burning, send a gleam across the wave*—and his father ushers them from the room. Samuel listens for their voices as they retreat downstairs, the door closing behind them.

The boys are gone.

He heaves himself onto his side, turns his face to the wall.

A CHANGE OF SCENE

NINA ALLAN

"**D**O SAY YOU'LL COME," PHRYNNE SAID. "I FANCY A CHANGE of scene."

I'm telling you from the beginning, because it seemed to me even then, before anything had really happened and we were still sitting in Phrynne's elegant drawing room in Muswell Hill, that there was something odd in her behaviour, something not quite right. There was a hectic red spot at the centre of each cheek, and Phrynne herself seemed full of an unnatural energy, buzzing with it almost, the way a child will, just before it throws a tantrum or bursts into tears.

I had seen grief before, but not like this. Grief seems mostly to exert a stupefying effect, slowing its victims down, paralysing them with lassitude. Gerald had been dead less than a fortnight, yet Phrynne seemed restless, malcontent, antic. Tension surrounded her, like barbed wire. I was on edge right through the funeral tea, afraid I suppose that Phrynne might do something outrageous, though what that something might be I could not have said.

As soon as the last guest had departed she whooped with what could only be called delight, poured us each a large sherry from the decanter on the sideboard and asked me—begged me, it seemed like—to go away with her, just for a little while, to take a short holiday.

What could I say? Phrynne and I had been friends since school. Even if we had inevitably grown apart with the years—her marriage, my marriage, my son, her divorce—I could not forget that there

197

had once been a time when we shared everything. We were closer than sisters, closer in some ways even than lovers. A friendship of that kind is a rare thing. I felt I owed it to her, not just to Phrynne as she was now but to the Phrynne who once swore to me that there was nothing more important to her than our togetherness.

I felt I owed it to *us*, in other words. To the idealistic and passionate young people we once had been. I suppose I even hoped that now that we were both widows and free to do as we pleased, some of the old excitement of our friendship might be rekindled. I had other friends, of course, but none like Phrynne.

If I am honest, I think I harboured a superstitious belief that if I held true to Phrynne now, I might finally, as I had always secretly wanted to, become more like her.

It wasn't as if I was short of time, either. People had been insisting I should take a holiday ever since Freddy died.

"There's nowhere I want to go," I would laugh, reassuring them that I was all right, that I was really all right, that my new life without a husband was bearable and my sanity sound.

"Of course I'll come," I said to Phrynne. "It'll do me good to get away from things for a bit."

Phrynne leaned towards me and grabbed my hands, her preoccupied expression dissolving into a smile so radiant and so natural that I felt an immediate rush of satisfaction at being the cause of it. I couldn't help but recall all the times in our youth when Phrynne had chided me for not being the spontaneous and carefree spirit she seemed honestly to believe I secretly was.

"You should let your guard down more, Iris," she would say. "What's the worst that can happen?"

At least on this occasion I had not disappointed her.

Our sabbatical was set to begin the following Friday. Phrynne telephoned me on the Wednesday to arrange our rendezvous, at a coffee stand on the concourse of Liverpool Street station. She had told me not to worry about the travel arrangements, that I should leave the practical details to her.

"I want it to be a surprise," she said. "Anyway, it'll give me something to do. You're always telling me I should be more organised."

I could not remember saying anything of the kind, either recently or in the past. Indeed I had always privately ascribed to Phrynne—who prized her casualness as a virtue—a preternatural talent for organising things and people exactly as she wanted them.

"But how will I know what to pack if you won't tell me where we're going?" I protested.

"Don't be so boring. This is supposed to be an adventure."

I knew from experience that there was no point in arguing with Phrynne once she made up her mind about a thing, and in truth I was happy to fall in with her plans. I could not think of a single occasion on which I had set out on a journey without knowing where I was headed, and the thought of doing so now seemed strange and daring and frivolous all at once.

"Darling," Phrynne exclaimed as I moved towards her through the crowd. "We have to hurry. Our train leaves in less than ten minutes. Take these." She pressed a packet of Danish pastries into my hands then whisked away across the concourse, returning seconds later with a luggage trolley. Laughing, we loaded it up then guided it through the barrier and on to the platform. The train was not too crowded, and we ended up with a compartment to ourselves.

As the train pulled away from the station I realised I had forgotten to check the departures board for our destination.

"Where are we going?" I said to Phrynne. "Cambridge?"

Cambridge seemed likely, now that I thought of it. Gerald had been a Cambridge man. I seemed to remember he had once tried to persuade Phrynne that they should move there. And Cambridge is particularly beautiful on summer evenings.

"Good Lord, no. All those ghastly colleges stuffed with mummified old men. What would we want to go there for? I can't think what Gerald saw in the place. We're off to the seaside."

"It sounds like heaven." I laughed, gazing out of the window as we groaned through London Fields. Phrynne's mention of Gerald—so soon—had taken me aback rather. Now that Gerald Banstead was safely dead I found it easier to admit to myself what I had always known: Phrynne had never loved her second husband, not even for a day.

We changed trains at Ipswich, and then again at Norwich. Once we had settled into our new compartment, Phrynne began to rummage in one of the two enormous carpet bags she had brought with her as baggage and produced a bottle of champagne and two crystal goblets.

"Practice, my dear Iris." She set the glasses on the fold-down table and then drew the cork. There was nothing to stop us, no one to see, and after my initial surprise I found myself entering wholeheartedly into the spirit of the occasion. By the time we reached Salhouse, I was beginning to feel quite lightheaded. London seemed far away, not just in terms of distance but in terms of philosophy. It was as if, somewhere between Norwich and Diss, we had jumped the tracks from one universe into another.

The landscape through the carriage window was so flat it seemed featureless, until the moment I realised that if I stared at it for long enough its very featurelessness exerted a hypnotic effect. Instead of retreating into the sameness, specific details—a tithe barn, a lone elm tree, a bridge, curved like a sickle, arcing above a river—seemed to leap forward, impressing themselves insistently upon my sight almost like the gem-hued, furiously bright objects in an exhibition of Technicolor photographs I had seen once in a gallery on the outskirts of Tokyo.

In the end I was forced to stop looking. I turned instead to Phrynne, who was scrutinizing me quizzically, twirling her almost-empty champagne flute between her thumb and forefinger.

"Have you been to North Norfolk before?" she asked.

"Once, years ago. Freddy knew some people in Sheringham. We came up for the weekend." If Phrynne had not put her question I would most likely not have remembered our visit to the Carmichaels. It had occurred at an unhappy time in our marriage, and I suppose I had done my best to mentally erase all trace of it. Had it not been for the champagne, I would probably not have mentioned the trip at all.

"Oh, *Freddy*," Phrynne said. She settled herself more comfortably, resting her head against the seat back and closing her eyes. Her eyelids were coated in a silky-textured, lavender-coloured eye shadow, a modern shade I liked the look of but would never dare try.

Freddy always hated me to wear makeup.

"What do you mean, 'oh Freddy,'" I said.

"Nothing." She poured the dregs of the champagne into her glass. "But don't you find it a relief? To be free of them, I mean. A little bit, anyway."

"Free of them?"

"The men." She gulped at her drink, her still-narrow throat expanding and contracting like the vocal apparatus of a lithe and exquisitely marked tree frog. I sat silently, watching her and thinking about Freddy. Freddy and I had been married for almost thirty years. We had a son together—Ian—whom we both adored. I knew friends of ours who would have characterised our marriage as ideal. I never sought to deny this, even though I sometimes wondered if our seeming compatibility had more to do with our separateness—our unspoken agreement never to make undue demands on the other's privacy—than with what our acquaintances referred to idealistically as true love.

Not that I didn't love Freddy—of course I did. But now that he was gone, my life seemed to be carrying on equally well without him. Aside from a few short weeks immediately before our wedding, I can honestly say that Freddy never caused me a day's pain in his life.

Even then, during that awful month when I seriously considered calling off our engagement, the doubts were mine, not Freddy's. It was always a consolation to me, later, that Freddy never had a clue about what I went through. As always at that time, the person I confided in was Phrynne. Phrynne had been against Freddy from the start.

"You can't marry him," she insisted. "It would be like marrying your own father. And the man has a face like a toad. I'd die of repulsion, if it were me. If boredom didn't kill me first, that is."

"He's a nice man," I wailed.

"*Nice?*" Phrynne flung the word back at me like a soiled tea towel. "Is that really all you want from life, Iris? For it to be nice?"

Apparently it was, because three weeks later Friedrich Gutheim and I were married by the registrar at the civic offices of West Hampstead. Phrynne had recently become acquainted with the young diplomat, Arthur Wing, who was destined to become her

and lean, with eyes of such a penetrating blue that you could not help staring at them. He also turned out to have a powerful opium addiction. Whether Phrynne knew this at the time of her marriage she never told me.

They were married at the Church of All Saints, Spitalfields. The couple became divorced in the late summer of 1969, almost exactly three years to the day.

Now, as the sluggish little train eased itself through the pallid sunlight towards West Runton, I remembered Phrynne's first meeting with Gerald Banstead, in the sitting room of our house in Highgate. Phrynne had arrived with someone else—a television actor, as I recall—but she seemed to set her sights on Gerald from the moment she saw him.

Her determination was a mystery to me, even at the time. Gerald was Freddy's colleague, and of a similar age. He was precisely the type of man Phrynne would normally have labelled dull at twenty paces. I would have judged the chances of any attraction between them as non-existent, at least from Phrynne's side.

"I've often wondered what made you fall for Gerald," I said to Phrynne. "He was never exactly your type, was he?"

"Fall for Gerald? Ha!" She laughed, a short, sharp report, like a gun going off. "Gerald wasn't the type you fall for so much as settle for. Hardly a dynamo, in any sense, I'm sure you'd agree." She raised her glass to her lips, seeming to forget that it was empty.

"That's not fair," I said quietly. I felt sick to my stomach. It's the drink, I told myself. Just the drink. She's been under such a strain, what with the funeral and everything. This was bound to happen.

Phrynne threw me a look. "But I'm not fair, Iris, you should know that by now. I don't mean anything by it. Buck up." Her voice was softer than before, as if whatever demon had been goading her was now assuaged, at least for the moment. She wiped the rims of both glasses with a tissue then stowed them back in her carpet bag. "We've arrived."

It was true. Even as she spoke, the train was juddering to a halt. I looked out upon a square red station building, with even, well kept flower beds to either side. A second building housed a cafe and public conveniences. The platform sign said Holyhaven. So far as I could remember I had never heard of it. A number of passengers stood waiting at the platform edge.

"What is this place?" I said.

"It's the quaintest little town, you're going to love it. Gerald and I came here on our honeymoon."

As we hurried to shift our luggage from the compartment and on to the platform, I asked myself repeatedly what on Earth could have persuaded Phrynne to return here. If there was one thing Phrynne detested it was backwaters like this.

It can only be because of Gerald, I thought. Gerald and me. She's brought me here to be humiliated.

I immediately dismissed the idea as ludicrous.

Phrynne had booked us rooms at a pub called The Bell. Driving through the streets of Holyhaven in the station taxi I could not help noticing that there were other, somewhat grander accommodations available in the town—*classier*, Freddy would have said, a word I hated. A seafront hotel called The Esplanade in particular, boasting a Michelin-starred restaurant and 'all rooms ensuite', seemed much more Phrynne's kind of place, but when I mentioned to her that they were advertising vacancies she shook her head decisively and proclaimed that The Esplanade was guilty of inferior service.

"They don't have time for you any more, these big places," she said. "The Bell is completely different—a real find. They'll light a fire in your room of an evening if you want one, and the food is superb—the best kind of home cooking. None of this stingy nouvelle cuisine horror. You'll see exactly what I mean from the moment we get there."

My own experience of staying in public houses—travelling around for Freddy's work, mainly—told me they were cramped, noisy places where the comfort of the overnight guests invariably came a poor second to the demands of the regular drinkers. I had the uneasy feeling that Phrynne's fond memories of The Bell at H~~elch~~ had been on her honeymoon, after all, when she had last stayed there. How could our game middle-aged widows' enterprise possibly compare with that?

I was pleasantly surprised by the exterior of the pub, however, a sprawling cob-and-thatch, bright with new whitewash, the freshly blackened porch steps flanked by a retinue of stone and terracotta planters packed with wallflowers and geraniums. The taxi man deposited our bags at the kerb then tugged on the bell pull to summon attention. The door was opened by a youngish, fresh-faced woman with her dark hair gathered in a loose ponytail.

"Mrs Banstead and Mrs Gutheim," she said. "Welcome." Her voice was clear and confident, with just a trace of the local accent. She bent down, grabbing my weekend holdall and the larger of Phrynne's two carpet bags and lifting them off the ground with apparent ease. "You can leave the rest of your things just inside the door there. Robbie will bring them up for you in a moment. I'm Danuta, by the way."

"Danuta," Phrynne said. "What an unusual name."

"My dad was Polish. Came over to fight with the RAF. He died last year."

"I'm sorry to hear that."

"No need. He had the life he wanted. He loved this place."

"You're new here, aren't you?"

The woman—Danuta—looked confused for a second, then nodded and smiled. "You mean the pub? Depends what you call new. Robbie and I, we took the place over about ten year ago now. It was in a horrible state when we bought it, I don't mind telling you. But we're pleased we stuck with it."

She shouldered her way through a doorway leading off the main saloon, leading us up the stairs to the floor above. The staircase was narrow and creaky, obviously ancient. There was a pleasant smell of cigar smoke and wood polish.

"I've put you in the two rooms at the back," Danuta said. "You'll find it's quieter. And one of you will have a view of the sea."

"Oh, Iris must have the view," Phrynne responded immediately. "I insist on it. I want her to see the town at its absolute best."

"Well, let's hope we can give you the weather to go with it, then," Danuta was saying. I was aware of their conversation, but distantly, as if it were going on in another room. My mind kept circling back to something Danuta had said earlier—about The Bell being in a bad state of repair when she and her husband Robbie became the proprietors. Something about her words didn't make sense, and after a moment or so I realised what it was. Gerald and Phrynne had been married twelve years—twelve years and six months, to be precise. That meant they would have come to Holyhaven at least two years before Robbie and Danuta took over The Bell.

Phrynne had said nothing about the pub being run down when she was here. Quite the opposite. Could we be in the wrong pub? I thought it at least possible that Danuta had her dates mixed up, although that hardly seemed likely. What did it matter anyway? We were here now, and Phrynne seemed happy. I decided to leave it at that.

"Wouldn't you, Iris?" Phrynne said. I jumped, startled. Phrynne was looking at me expectantly, and I realised belatedly that she had asked me a question that required an answer.

"I'm sorry?" I said.

"You were miles away! I was just saying to Danuta that we would probably like to eat dinner here this evening, if that's all right with you? Seeing as we've been travelling for most of the day?"

"Yes, of course, that would be lovely." Danuta was eyeing me with what looked like concern. I smiled in what I hoped was a reassuring manner. "Phrynne's right. We've been on the train so long I can still feel the motion."

Our rooms were at the end of the first floor landing, the two doors abutting one another at right angles. In the confined space of the low-ceilinged corridor there was barely enough space for the three of us to stand together without colliding. I was beginning to feel uncomfortable, not simply on account of my own small lapse in concentration but because of Phrynne. She seemed excited, nerved up, the same as she had been after the funeral. Whether this was the result of being cooped up in train carriages for so long or ~~for some other reason I didn't know, but she was in one of those~~ moods where she was liable to do or say anything.

I didn't want her to embarrass herself in front of Danuta, who I thought seemed nice.

"I think I'll have a rest in my room, if you don't mind," I said. "It'll give me a chance to unpack."

"Let's both do that," Phrynne said, seeming to seize on the idea. "We can have a drink in the bar later. A celebration." She smiled at Danuta, one of what Freddy always used to call her winning smiles. Like sunlight at the top of a volcano.

"Robbie'll bring the rest of your things up," Danuta repeated. "The bathroom's at the end of the hall." She pointed towards a doorway at the opposite end of the landing then retreated downstairs. Phrynne watched her go. The unnatural brightness that had animated her face just a few moments previously seemed to have ebbed away entirely. A smile still flickered about the corners of her mouth, but it seemed empty somehow, just a residue, like the encrustation of mud that gets left behind on kerbstones in the wake of receding flood waters.

"What a pleasant woman," I said. "Were she and her husband managing the pub before, when you came to stay here?"

"Goodness knows. Why on Earth would I remember something like that?" Phrynne spoke without looking at me, still gazing off down the empty hallway as if she were expecting someone to appear there at any second. "Not much of a place, is it? I'd forgotten how poky it is up here."

"Oh, nonsense. I think it's lovely. Deliciously quaint, just as you said, and so much cosier than one of those white elephants down on the sea front. You're tired, that's all." I placed a hand on her shoulder. "We'll both feel a lot livelier once we've had a sit down."

"You're right, as always." Phrynne yawned. "And I suppose we really should unpack." She lifted the carpet bag across the threshold of her room and then closed the door. I felt aggravated but not surprised by the change in her mood. Phrynne had always been like a child in that way—brimming with enthusiasm one minute then grumpy with boredom or impatience the next. I considered knocking on her door and asking if she would like the room with the sea view after all, but decided against it. She was probably best left to herself for a while.

As it turned out, the sea room was large, occupying one whole corner of the building and with pale gold afternoon sunlight spilling in from both sides across the polished floorboards. A large four-poster bed, piled high with starched white pillows and covered with a hand-sewn patchwork counterpane, stood at the centre. There was a wash hand basin in a curtained alcove, and a selection of tourist information leaflets had been neatly arranged on a low table before the fireplace. It was indeed a lovely room, and for the first time since stepping into the taxi I felt a rush of genuine gladness at our arrival.

I unpacked my holdall, hanging my clothes in the small built-in wardrobe and placing my two library books—a biography of Rosamund Lehmann and the new Patricia Highsmith—on the night stand beside the framed photograph of my son Ian that I always carried with me whenever I travelled. The photo showed Ian at the age of sixteen, just before he won the scholarship to Beeston and while he was still living at home in Highgate with Freddy and me.

There was a transparent, otherworldly look about him at that age that still breaks my heart. It was as if he had not yet joined the world, not properly. Of course age has altered him, as it changes us all.

"Gorgeous, wasn't he?" Phrynne said when she first saw that photo. Her use of the past tense hurt me, especially the subtext—*Ian looks just like his father now*—although naturally I never said so.

It is strange, but whenever I look at that picture of Ian I cannot help but think of Phrynne at the same age, although Ian and Phrynne are not even remotely alike.

One of the room's two windows looked down upon the pub's back garden. The other—the side window—overlooked the narrow lane that led down the hill into the town. The last of the sun's rays glanced off cottage rooftops, turning their dove-coloured slates like a swathe of grey-green taffeta, lay plainly in sight.

I rested my elbows upon the window ledge and gazed out. It was not quite warm enough to have the window open, but I found I could easily imagine the brisk cries of gulls, the refreshing aroma of sea salt and tamarisk. I forgot about being tired, and I forgot about Phrynne. I breathed deeply of the phantom scents, imagining myself once again a young woman, unmarried, with a world of choices ahead of me and only insignificant mistakes behind.

No Phrynne, no Freddy, no Gerald. For the first time in a long time I felt completely happy.

"Do you fancy a walk?" Phrynne said. "Just down to the sea and back—there's still time before dinner."

Phrynne after an hour's rest seemed a different person, restored to the mood of optimism and excitement in which she had greeted me that morning at Liverpool Street. More, she seemed touchingly eager to spend time with me, and I was reminded of the day we first met, as thirteen-year-old schoolgirls in our form room at Queen Charlotte's. I noticed Phrynne at once, because she looked so confident, so imperious, like the *infanta* in that famous painting by Velasquez. Even the dowdy Queen Charlotte's uniform, with its frumpy knee-length skirt and boxy blazer, did nothing to diminish the glamorous impression she made. I watched her and waited, expecting her to be taken up more or less instantaneously by the

Dawson twins and Corinne Montagu. Like Phrynne I was new at Queen Charlotte's, but you only had to be there five minutes to understand that the Dawson twins and their chosen cohorts held the form room and our end of the school yard to ransom with their sartorial superiority and ironclad sarcasm. But it was my desk Phrynne wanted to sit at, me she wished to confide in, right from the start. This seemed so unlikely and so inexplicable that for a while I even wondered if she was playing a trick on me, luring me into her confidence so she could spill all my most fiercely guarded secrets to the Dawson twins at some later date. When a term and a half passed and nothing of this sort had happened I was forced to concede that Phrynne genuinely wanted to be my friend.

I never was able to decide why she had chosen me.

"She's using you, you know," Freddy said to me once. This was early on in our marriage, when we were living just off the Archway Road and Phrynne was still married to Arthur Wing. "Women like that, they can't stand not to be the brightest light in the room. They need a backcloth to shine against. Don't tell me you've never realised?"

That was quite a speech, coming from Freddy. I supposed there might be some truth in what he said, but then Freddy never did like Phrynne much. I thought it just as likely that he was jealous.

"A walk would be perfect," I said to Phrynne. "You can show me the town."

"Hardly a town," Phrynne said with a smile. "About the most exciting thing you can do here is post a letter."

"Then I for one intend to post lots," I retorted. "Let's go."

We set off down the hill, proceeding along the same cobbled lane that I could see from my bedroom window. At ground level the lane seemed narrower and rather dank, the cottages more bunched together and less picturesque. It was the dusk, I supposed, that made them seem that way. Big cities come alive at night. Small towns and villages—especially the more secluded kind—tend to fold in on themselves. The biggest disappointment was the sea. The tide was going out, and instead of the opalescent turquoise banner I had glimpsed from my window we were confronted instead by a murky vista of claggy sand. What I could see of the water was the colour of clay.

What a dismal little place, I thought. And then, the oddest thought: we should never have come here.

I shivered inside my jacket. "Perhaps we should think about heading back," I said. "It's getting cold."

I thought she would agree at once—if there is one thing Phrynne won't tolerate it is physical discomfort—but she turned to me with bright eyes and the same exuberant smile she had used on me when she suggested we should go for a walk in the first place.

"Not yet, surely? I'm enjoying the fresh air. All those hours cooped up on trains."

"All right," I agreed reluctantly. "Let's go this way." I pointed along the front. I could see lights, and as we set off towards them a woman's laughter rippled across the terrace of a tall, whitish building I recognised as The Esplanade hotel. Quite suddenly and for no reason I found myself craving the company of that unknown woman. I wanted to learn her name, to discover the source of her laughter. She sounded so carefree, somehow, so full of life.

I pressed my hands deep into my pockets.

"Did Gerald like it here?" I asked Phrynne. I said it more for something to say than anything else. I did not particularly want to know what Gerald had thought of his stay at The Bell, the dingy seafront parade, his honeymoon with Phrynne. I remembered the way Phrynne had laughed when she told me that she and Gerald were getting married. The way I'd exclaimed and hugged her and kissed her cheek.

"Apparently. It was Gerald who insisted we come here, anyway. I wanted to go to Marbella." She linked her arm through mine. "I'm sorry, Iris. I should have said sorry years ago."

"What on Earth for?"

"You know." She glanced at me quickly and then looked away. "Gerald was a good sort, but I was never in love with him. We should never have married. It was a disaster for both of us, but that was my fault, not his. I just hope I didn't make life too awful for him."

"Gerald loved you."

"I suppose he thought he did, for a while, anyway. But what he loved was an image, the person he wanted me to be. Not me at all."

I was about to protest, to tell her she was wrong, that of course Gerald had cared for her. But then Phrynne suddenly came to a standstill. She took hold of my hands, gripping them tightly and almost painfully in both of hers. "Listen, Iris, I've never told anyone this, but there was someone else, another man I was going to marry. After Arthur, I mean, and a long time before I met Gerald. I met him in Naples when I was there with Arthur that time. God, I hated Naples. The heat, and the filth in the streets. I can't stand the place, but that was where I met Alec, and where I fell in love properly for the first time in my life, isn't that strange? I know what you think— that I'm not capable of love, at least not in the way you understand it. But Alec changed something in me. You could say he woke me up, and I think it might really have worked. He made me feel there was—I don't know, a point to things, something to live for other than myself."

"What happened, then? You're not telling me you left him for Gerald?"

"No, Iris, I'm telling you he killed himself. Whatever I was to him, it turned out it wasn't enough."

We walked on in silence towards The Esplanade. Phrynne was holding my arm again, and when I turned towards her the lights from the terrace outlined her in silver. Her hair seemed to stand out in a nimbus about her head, and her eyes, half-closed against the chill, glinted metallically. She had that film star look about her, that combination of arch worldliness and fragility, and I felt myself consumed by the urge to kiss her, to take her face between my hands and press my mouth to hers until her lips parted and granted me admittance. I started back from her, confused and repulsed, yet unable to dispel the image of her tongue, sliding over her teeth like a live pink mollusc.

"Phrynne, I'm so sorry," I managed to say.

"It's a long time ago now," Phrynne said. "Come on, let's go back. I don't know about you, but I could do with a drink."

We returned to the pub, not along the front this time but through the streets of the town. There was not much to the place really, Phrynne was right, and if not for the tourist shops and eating places in the cluster of interconnected alleyways just south of the harbour, there would have been even less.

Plenty of churches, though. I counted five of them.

"Do you suppose that's how the town got its name?" I wondered aloud. "Holy h——?"

"I honestly don't know," Phrynne said. "It was Gerald who was interested in history, you know that as well as I do. That was probably why he wanted to come here. Always poking around inside old buildings, Gerald. The one thing I do remember is that they were having a bell-ringing practice the night we arrived. You wouldn't believe the racket, once they all got going. The din seemed to go on half the night."

"Things seem quiet enough now."

"They've passed an anti-ringing statute, probably. Or lopped a couple of heads off. You know what people are like in the country."

We both laughed then, and things seemed all right again. The lane leading up to The Bell was steeper than it had seemed going down, and we arrived at the pub out of breath but in good spirits. In the saloon bar a sturdily built, florid-faced man and two younger men who were clearly his sons sat hunched over one of the window tables engaged in a noisy discussion about football. All three had partially drained pint glasses in front of them and aside from a brief glance from one of the younger men they paid us no notice. A fourth, much older man sat in the far corner reading a newspaper. A pipe and a tin of tobacco lay, as yet untouched, on the table beside him. He had silvery, close-clipped hair and the kind of upright, straight-backed posture that reminded me of certain characters in the drawings by that comic book artist Freddy admired—Garrick Greer, his name was—who did all those satirical sketches about life in the army.

Old codgers lounging in front of the fire at the officers' club, reminiscing about how grand life had been when they were in charge of India.

Freddy found them tearingly funny but they left me cold.

Phrynne looked around the room, still smiling.

"It's lovely and warm in here, isn't it?" she said. When her eyes fell upon the man in the corner the colour drained from her face in less than a second.

"Colonel?" she whispered. She moved towards him, almost tripping over the corner of one of the deep-pile rugs that were scattered about. The man continued to read his paper, seemingly unaware that he had been spoken to. Only when Phrynne stood less than three paces from his chair did he finally look up.

"My apologies," he said. He folded the newspaper over his knee. "Were you needing to speak with me?" He did not sound at all as I had expected. He spoke with an accent, French, or maybe Russian, I wasn't sure. I remembered Danuta telling us her father was Polish, but had she not also mentioned that her father had died? This could not be him, surely?

Phrynne took a rapid step backwards.

"I'm most terribly sorry," she said. "I've mistaken you for someone else."

"I don't mind being mistaken," said the man, smiling at Phrynne in a way that made me feel distinctly uncomfortable. Phrynne must not have liked it either, because she made no attempt to prolong the conversation.

"I'm sorry for disturbing you," she repeated. She nodded curtly then turned away, scooting back towards me at a near-run.

"I'm such an idiot," she said, then giggled. Her cheeks were bright red.

"Who on Earth was that?" I darted a glance towards the man in his corner and saw he had gone back to reading the newspaper.

"Goodness only knows. I thought for a moment he was someone I knew, a Colonel Shotcroft—he was here when Gerald and I were here. Lovely chap, a real gentleman. But of course it couldn't be— the Colonel was old, even then. He—"

She left the sentence hanging in midair, and I supposed she didn't want to say what I had guessed anyway: *the Colonel would be dead by now, he would have to be.*

"You were bound to think of him though, weren't you, coming back here after so long?" I spoke in what I hoped was the voice of reason. "Anyway, there's no harm done. I'm always seeing people in the street and thinking I know them from somewhere."

"Well you would, Iris. Head in the clouds, that's you. Let me buy you a drink before they throw us out on grounds on insanity."

She seemed fully in control of herself again and as so often in the

confidence. I had never been into a pub by myself, and the idea of ordering drinks at the bar made me nervous, even though I knew the transaction was essentially no different from asking for a shoulder of lamb at the butchery counter.

Phrynne sauntered up to the bar as if she ordered alcohol in pubs every day of her life.

"We'll have two whisky sodas, please," she said. Her winning smile was back. I had rather expected to see Danuta serving behind the bar. A man was there instead. He was tall, with tanned bare forearms and a heavy gold signet ring on his right index finger. He wore his hair long, tied behind his head with what looked like an old shoelace. Freddy would have called him a layabout, but I thought the style suited him.

He looks like a merman, I thought. I could feel myself blushing.

"Coming right up." He spoke with the local accent, like Danuta. I wondered if he was Danuta's husband, the mysterious Robbie, or just someone who worked here. "Everything all right for you two ladies? Anything else I can get you?"

"I can think of one thing," Phrynne said. She leaned forward across the bar, still smiling her winning smile. She tapped her fingers against the wood, placing her hand close to where the merman's hand was resting. I realised to my horror that she was attempting to flirt with him.

"You must be Robbie," I said quickly. "Thank you for bringing up our luggage." About half an hour after our arrival I had left my room to go to the bathroom, and discovered my own small haversack and Phrynne's second carpet bag lined up neatly in the corridor outside. Observing Robbie now, I found it surprising that such a solidly built man could come and go so silently.

"We aim to please." I could not help noticing that it was Phrynne he looked at as he said this, and not me. "And two whisky sodas." He turned away to prepare the drinks. Phrynne compressed her lips in a silent smirk, slowly raising one eyebrow in a gesture that took me back so instantaneously to our schooldays that the urge to laugh aloud was almost irresistible.

Phrynne saw the look on my face and raised a hand to her forehead in a mock salute.

You beast, I mouthed.

"We aim to please," Phrynne murmured, timing her speech to coincide exactly with the gaseous exhale of the soda siphon. "I think we'll take these over by the fire," she said in a normal voice to Robbie as he placed the two filled glasses on the bar. "Is it all right to add our drinks to our bill?"

"No problem at all. I'll set up a tab for you, shall I?"

"That would be lovely." She paused. "May I ask you a question?"

"Ask away."

"Do you happen to know of a Colonel Shotcroft? Mike Shotcroft? He lived here for some years. At The Bell, I mean. I was wondering if you might have an address for him."

Robbie shook his head. "Before my time, I'm afraid. Danny and I don't take long-stay guests, never have done. You should have a word with Danny, though. She was in contact with the people who had this place before us. For a while she was, anyway. She might know something."

"The Pascoes?"

"Is that what they were called? I think you're right. But you're best to ask Danny."

"Thank you, I will."

We carried our drinks over to the second window alcove. I was surprised that Phrynne had returned so readily to the subject of this Colonel Shotcroft. Her mention of the couple who ran The Bell

previously—the Pascoes?—was also confusing. When I had asked
her about them before, she claimed not to remember them.

"Was Colonel Shotcroft a friend of Gerald's, then?" I asked her
as we sat down.

"Not at all. Mike Shotcroft was my friend." She took a gulp of
her drink and then closed her eyes. "It's honestly not important.
We hardly knew him, really. But he was good to me once, and I've
never forgotten. I'd like to know what happened to him, that's all."

"He's probably moved away. People do, you know."

"Probably." She swirled the whisky around in her glass. "Are you
glad we came?"

"Of course I am. It's wonderful to be away from London. From
everything, really. We should have done something like this years
ago."

"You're right, we should. I'm sorry I've been so useless to you."

"That's rubbish. You're my closest friend, Phrynne, you always
have been."

"Well, if that's true then I'm lucky to have you. Most people
would have given up on me years ago. Decades."

She continued to play with her drink, gazing down at the square,
shiny facets of the ice cubes as if expecting to see the future in them.
A better future. I felt suddenly overwhelmed with tenderness for
her. Of course it was true that she could be thoughtless, selfish even.
But I had known her all my life, and that counted for a lot. In
showing her lack of willingness to compromise, or be compromised,
her selfishness was something I valued, even. She was still the same
Phrynne. I thought of what she had told me down on the sea front,
about the man she had loved, and who had killed himself in spite of
that love. A tragedy like that would have destroyed most people.
But it was impossible to believe that Phrynne would ever give up
on life, no matter what happened to her.

Most other people I knew were dead by comparison.

"Now you listen to me," I said to her. "There's to be no more talk
of this kind. You're a good person, Phrynne. I know you don't
believe that, but you are. This is supposed to be a new start,
remember? That goes for both of us."

"You're marvellous, do you know that?" She raised her glass. "Here's to new beginnings."

We clinked glasses, and I took a first long sip of my drink. I hadn't drunk whisky for years, not since Freddy died. I was surprised to find I still had a taste for it.

"This takes me back," Phrynne said.

"Takes you back how?"

"Do you remember the time we found all those empty whisky bottles in Harriet Wrongfoot's supply cupboard?"

"Oh God, Phrynne. Trust you to bring that up. Of course I remember." Harriet Wrightfoot was our Art mistress at Queen Charlotte's. Phrynne always used to refer to her as Harriet Wrong-foot, or Leftfoot, or just plain Sinister. The incident with the whisky bottles had landed us in a great deal of trouble and for a time I seriously believed we would be expelled. Naturally Phrynne thought that was a hoot, too.

You know what it's like when you begin to reminisce about the past? It's as if the present, with its ambiguities, melts away. In the past all allegiances are cancelled, all outcomes are known, all time is forever. That's how it feels, at least. Phrynne and I hadn't talked about Queen Charlotte's in years. Not since Phrynne married Gerald, anyway.

We swapped school stories all through dinner. Several times I found myself laughing so hard I could barely breathe. We retired to our rooms at around ten-thirty. We agreed it had been a long day. Both of us felt the need of an early night.

"Thank you for being here," Phrynne said as we climbed the stairs to the upper landing. "I never thought I could be this happy again."

I washed my arms and face and got into bed. I had planned to make a start on the Patricia Highsmith, but found I was too tired to concentrate. Just before I fell asleep I thought of Phrynne, what she had said about being happy.

I thought perhaps the pain of the past could be buried, after all.

———

If I am to tell this honestly, and there would be no point in telling it otherwise, then I am bound to admit to you that I was in love with Gerald Banstead, and although we never discussed the matter openly I knew that Gerald was in love with me, too.

There was never any question of us doing anything to alter our situation. Gerald was Freddy's oldest friend—they had known one another since forever. Gerald couldn't bear the idea of betraying that friendship, and neither could I. Freddy was a good man, he didn't deserve that. Besides, there was Ian to think of. To act would be to destroy everything. We both knew that things were best left as they were, for everyone's sake.

And in spite of the circumstances, our love always brought us more joy than it caused us anguish. It began slowly, as the deepest and most abiding affections often do. Gerald had never married—Freddy once hinted to me that he had been let down badly as a young man, an emotional jolt from which he had never fully recovered—and he was often at our house, both the Leighton Road house and later, in Highgate. In the beginning I saw him simply as Freddy's friend. It was only as we came to know one another better that we realised how much we had in common. We both loved music, and often attended concerts together. Gerald had a passion for art, and even collected in a small way. Some of our happiest times together were spent on trains, heading out to obscure sale rooms in the suburbs on the trail of some minor painter whom Gerald stood convinced was an unrecognised genius.

Freddy never minded these excursions. In fact he encouraged them. He didn't care for music at all, and the art world bored him. He had his whist drives and his chess club. He often used to remark on what pleasure it gave him, to see us enjoying each other's company as we did.

When Gerald met Phrynne, everything changed. It never occurred to me even for a second that there was any danger. Gerald was twenty years older than Phrynne and not even remotely the kind of man she would glance at twice. As for Gerald, he never seemed to notice other women at all.

On the evening they first came together my only concern was

that Phrynne would be so bored she would end up overdoing things in the drinks department. Freddy hated seeing anyone drunk, women especially.

Of course at the time I knew nothing of Phrynne's recent tragedy, of her lover's suicide. If I had done, I might have been more cautious in introducing them. Gerald Banstead must have seemed to offer everything—stability and security, common sense—her dead lover had not. As for Gerald, did he simply decide that it was time for him to marry, to seek some security of his own? If that was so then I was hardly in a position to criticise, although this still did not explain his decision to throw himself at a woman who was bound by her very nature to bring him nothing but heartache.

Because Gerald did throw himself at Phrynne. Almost from the moment he saw her, he was like a man in a delirium.

Suddenly there were no more phone calls, no more impromptu outings to Amersham or Staines. Suddenly I was just Freddy's wife. It was like a bereavement, but a bereavement I was to suffer alone, without the comfort or even the knowledge of family or friends.

When Phrynne asked me to be her maid of honour, of course I had to say yes.

"You are an angel," Phrynne said. "If you only knew how much this means to me."

For the whole of that summer and the following winter I felt I was in hell. As winter passed into spring I forced myself, at first unwillingly and then with growing enthusiasm, to take up new interests. I even revived a much-cherished ambition to research and write a history of our house in Highgate. I had discussed this idea with Gerald but never pursued it, or at least not properly. Now it became my main focus of attention.

The more time passed, and with the deaths of first Freddy and later Gerald, the more I wondered if I had been lucky after all, to exchange love for freedom.

I still missed Gerald, though. I missed our outings. I missed the little secrets we held together, harmless tokens of intimacy but treasured ones, nonetheless.

The scars of some betrayals do not fade.

"I've been looking at some of those tourist leaflets," Phrynne said over breakfast. It was a good breakfast—scrambled eggs, with locally cured bacon and coffee so strong and so hot it reminded me of the various trips Freddy and I had made to Paris over the years, the small cafe close to Montmartre that we thought of as ours. I had not slept well, and so drank more of the coffee than I might have done normally. "There's a walk we can do, along the coast path. The views are supposed to be wonderful. And there's a church with some famous murals . . . .

"I thought you weren't keen on churches."

"We might as well though, seeing as it's there. If you really don't fancy it we can always go into Sheringham on the train."

"No," I said. "We can do Sheringham tomorrow. I'd rather see the murals."

I did not particularly want to see the murals, or at least not with Phrynne, who I knew was only interested because a tourist leaflet had told her that she should be. Still, we had to fill the day up with something. When we returned briefly to our rooms after breakfast to put on outdoor clothing I looked for and found the leaflet Phrynne had been talking about. It included a simplified map, showing how the coastal path branched off from the end of the promenade and then, after about two miles or so, intersected with another footpath that led back inland. The church of St Barnabus, where the murals were, stood at the juncture of the two footpaths, overlooking the sea. The leaflet described St Barnabus as 'a gem of early Norman church architecture' and 'uniquely situated'. The murals, created in the early eighteen-twenties by a local artist named Jeb Sudworth, were said to depict the town of Holyhaven and its seasonal customs in 'scintillating detail'.

I was immediately fascinated, and felt bad for accepting Phrynne's perfectly fine suggestion with such ill grace. I put my bad night down to sleeping in a strange bed. I had awoken suddenly at around two in the morning, convinced I could hear church bells ringing. Only once I was properly awake was I able to understand that the pub and the street outside were completely silent. Although I fell asleep again quite quickly I still had that muzzy-headed feeling, as if I had lain awake for most of the night. None of this was Phrynne's fault, and I resolved to make it up to her during our walk.

I swapped my ordinary outdoor shoes for walking boots, and transferred my purse and my reading glasses from my handbag to the small backpack I had brought with me for precisely this kind of outing. I put the tourist leaflet in too—I thought it might be useful to have a copy of the map.

I joined Phrynne outside in the lane. She had changed into corduroys and an expensive-looking pair of brogues. We set off down the hill towards the town. Ten minutes later we were on the cliff path. The sun was out, but there was a stiff breeze blowing, and I felt glad of my fleece-lined walking jacket. I glanced at Phrynne. Her camel-coloured belted mackintosh appeared more suitable for Richmond Park than the North Norfolk coast, but if she was feeling the cold at all she gave no sign of it.

"Isn't this splendid?" she said. "I feel I could walk for miles."

I would never have put Phrynne down as an outdoor type, but the wind had brought a bloom to her cheeks and with her hair blown back off her face she looked not just younger but more alive, radiating good health and high spirits in a way—I realised this now—that she had not done for some years.

As so often in the past, I felt stodgy and dour by comparison.

Was it any wonder, in the end, that Gerald had preferred Phrynne to me?

I brushed the thought aside. It was all so long ago now. What could it matter?

"Did you visit this church when you were here before?" I said, meaning St Barnabus.

"I really don't remember. You know how it is with churches, they all blend into one." She paused. "I think it's this way." She waved a hand to where a muddy-looking path cut a course across fields on its way inland. A cluster of greyish farm buildings jutted out from the horizon.

"Are you sure? The map says we should follow the cliff path."

"This must be a short cut, then. Look." Phrynne pointed to something at the head of the path, a knee-high triangle of grey granite, roughly carved with a cross and beside it three capital letters: STB.

We struck out across the field. Away from the cliff top the wind dropped almost immediately. The air felt almost unnaturally still, clammy with the scents of wet grass and cow manure. As we drew closer to the farm buildings I realised with a shock that most of them—three large barns, a row of loose boxes, a long, low building I thought was probably a pigsty—were derelict, their gaunt skele-tons outlined against the darkening sky. Only the farmhouse itself seemed in any way cared for.

An ancient Morris stood aslant in the drive. A faded curtain billowed from an upstairs window.

"Talk about bleak," Phrynne said. The path led us directly across the entrance to the farmyard before widening into a rutted lane. To me, the derelict farm seemed more than just bleak, it seemed sinister, the bricks and mortar embodiment of a life that had failed. I remembered a film I had seen once—alone, not with Freddy—in which a woman turns the pages of an old photograph album and suddenly comes upon a picture of her sister, taken on the evening before she died. The sight of those rotting buildings made me feel as I imagined the woman in the film might have felt. I know how foolish that sounds, but that's how it was.

After skirting the farm, the lane pottered gently downhill past a trio of whitewashed cottages. The cottages appeared more pros-perous than the farm, more welcoming, certainly. A young-ish woman, her hair covered by a striped kerchief, was hanging washing on a line in one of the gardens. She waved to us as we passed, and I wondered about asking her if we were heading in the right direction for St Barnabus, but then Phrynne, who was walking ahead of me, called back over her shoulder that she could see the church.

"Hurry up," she said. "The view is incredible."

I hastened my step, glancing back only briefly at the woman in the striped kerchief, who had gone back to hanging out her washing. A child's things, I noticed—a miniature pair of denim dungarees, some little cotton shirts. Did the woman and the child live here alone, I wondered, or was there a husband and father somewhere about?

I could not imagine how I might have coped, bringing up Ian by myself in a place like this.

I wondered if Phrynne had ever thought of having children. The idea was ludicrous somehow, almost mad. Perhaps she'd been unable to have any. Certainly it was not something she had expressed regret about.

The road plunged into the undergrowth, narrowing until the branches of the trees—some rather windblown-looking pines—became intertwined into a single dark mass overhead. Then, so suddenly it was like falling, the path erupted into the daylight. We found ourselves on a sandy outcrop of land, high above the water and with the waves churning away at its base like a pack of wild dogs.

It was as if the land were sticking its tongue out at the sea. At the farthest end of the spit, ringed about by beach stones and yellowed grass, stood the church of St Barnabus.

As Phrynne had said, the view was incredible. I was just uncertain whether, in its stark severity, it was a view that anyone would want to look at for very long.

"I suppose we'd better go in, seeing as we're here" Phrynne said. She drew her mackintosh around her, as if it had only now occurred to her that the garment really was too insubstantial for the Norfolk climate. She walked towards the church, and as I moved to join her I couldn't help feeling relieved that we had, after all, ignored the map's directions and chosen the short cut past the farm instead. The cliff path still existed, but I could see now that parts of it had become eroded, leaving only a thin strip of solid ground between the brambly undergrowth on one side and the near-vertical drop to the sea on the other.

The church itself was long and low, with the tall square tower so typical of many of the churches in East Anglia. Like a pointing, accusatory finger, it seemed to berate the sky.

"They don't still hold services here, surely?" Phrynne said. "The place must freeze solid in winter."

Similar thoughts had occurred to me, and I was half expecting to find the church shut up, the famous murals, if they existed, under lock and key. In fact the door opened easily. Phrynne took a step backwards, as if in surprise.

"God," she said. "I hope it's safe."

There were no pews, no pulpit or altar either. Instead, rows of ~~wooden chairs faced~~ ~~~~ getting the ~~~~ phere of a schoolroom from which both teacher and pupils had been mysteriously spirited away. Otherwise it was as if the interior of the church had been systematically stripped, wiped clean of anything that might draw attention away from the hordes of painted images that lined the walls.

I had expected the frescoes to be faded: delicate, subtly tinted antiquities of the kind you see in museums, the Renaissance nativities and epiphanies that Gerald would stand before for hours in the National Gallery. In fact, Sudworth's murals were a cacophony of colour, a maelstrom of brightness that was close to shocking in its intensity. Beneath the artfully positioned alcove lighting and the two vast skylights, the ochres and greens, the ultramarines and vermilions jostled and jousted for prominence as fiercely and with as much abandon as if they had been laid down merely months ago instead of centuries.

Just inside the church door, a laminated square of text had been fixed to the wall.

The Sudworth Murals

A cycle of visionary works by the artist Jeb Sudworth, depicting the ancient ceremonial performed annually in the town of Holyhaven to celebrate the Feast of All Hallows. The bells of the seven churches were rung throughout the hours of darkness in order to enliven and propitiate the dead. A re-

enactment of this service is still performed each year on
October 31st by the town's bell ringers. Jeb Sudworth was born
in Holyhaven in 1796. He underwent no formal training as
an artist, and was entirely self-taught. Some have compared
his talent and later insanity to that of the 'peasant poet' John
Clare.

For some moments I stood immobile, trying to concentrate on
the words yet finding my eyes constantly drawn back, with an
almost physical compunction, to the capering, leaping hordes that
seemed the sole and rightful occupants of St Barnabus church.

There were nine tableaux in all. Each showed a different view of
the town—the promenade was there of course, also the squashed-
together fishermen's cottages in the alleyways behind the harbour,
the long walk uphill past the twin churches of Mary Magdalene
and St Oliphant. I was even able to make out The Bell, in its familiar
setting halfway up Wrack Lane. Beside it stood some kind of barn,
a sagging, timber-framed building that no longer existed. I
supposed it must have been demolished sometime in the last
century.

And the streets of this painted town were filled with people. At
first sight, it looked as if a festival was in progress—the sheer
number of participants, and the brightness of their apparel, made
this seem obvious. It was only as I examined the panels more
closely—my eyes mere inches from the painted plasterwork,
drinking in the detail—that I realised that the clothes of the dancers
and revellers—men, women and children—were torn to tatters.
Shreds of bright cloth flapped in an imaginary wind. Wildly expansive hand gestures ripped waistcoats and bodices wide open.
Writhing bodies and pumping feet trampled shoes and jerkins and
dresses into the dust.

It was not a festival at all, but a *bacchanal*, an unholy feast, a
Dionysian orgy. I recoiled from what I saw, not so much from what
could only be described as the lewd vigour of the cavorting towns-
people as from the fact that I had not understood sooner what the
murals depicted.

I had imagined a pastoral by Rubens or Claude. What filled my eyes instead was a scene that more properly belonged inside the mind of Goya or Hieronymus Bosch.

I turned away, dismayed. It was only then that I remembered Phrynne. In my strange dalliance with Sudworth's paintings I had forgotten a creature called Phrynne even existed. Now I became aware that she was spinning in circles—dancing, really—beneath one of the skylights, the contours of her upturned face softened and blurred by the mist-coloured light of the outside. Her mackintosh had come open. Its loosened belt whipped like a strand of mud-coloured seaweed through the air.

"They're all dead, Iris," she crooned. "Can't you see that? Can't you *see*?"

She darted forward, seizing my wrists and swinging me around, laughing in a high, unearthly voice as she tried—or so it seemed to encourage *me* to dance, to join with her in whatever perverted ecstasy she was experiencing.

And the terrible thing is, I wanted to. Join her, I mean. For more than a moment and through our linked hands I felt or imagined I felt a shadowy, threadlike echo of the rhythm she was feeling, that they were all feeling, the beat of the drum that called them, that said on! *On*! A fusillade of satanic timpani, a threnody of mischief, a marmoreal rat-tat-tat of encroaching doom.

But then she flung my hands away as if they repulsed her, as if they were toads. She grabbed me fiercely by the hair, forcing my head around so that I once more faced Sudworth's paintings, the long, central tableau that showed the clock tower of St Agnes, the gleaming, tooth-like houses, running away down the street to either side.

"Look, *look*," Phrynne commanded, groaned really, as if she were in the grip of a sexual release so powerful it threatened to break her. I had to look—with my face pressed almost into the plasterwork how could I do otherwise?—and then at last I comprehended what Sudworth had painted.

The dancers were corpses. The creeping, sagging discolorations of their rotting flesh had been represented by the artist's brush as a jester's motley, the teeth rattling in the caves of their skulls as agates and pearls.

And could the woman in the red hat—a balding, raddled fish-wife, her dead child still clamped to her breast—really be Phrynne? How was it possible that in the humpbacked, grovelling figure of the grocer outside his shop I recognised my husband Freddy? In the embittered wraith of a schoolmaster my beloved Gerald?

My human mind, the wise companion that greets me when I wake and counts me down through the sometimes-anxious moments that precede sleep, insisted it could not be so, that what I saw was a fantasy, brought on by my restless night and my friend's strange behaviour. Yet another part of me—the impassioned dae-mon that had answered the drum—leapt up again to dance, whis-pering to me that Phrynne's wedding night here in Holyhaven had been an awakening to much more than love, that she had passed beyond the realm of the known and into the abyss.

I wanted to run, then. To leave the church without looking back and never return.

I could not do it, though. Phrynne was my closest friend, and I could not forsake her.

I wrenched myself from her grasp. "Phrynne!" I cried. "We've seen enough. Let's go."

I reached out to take her hand. Her brittle fingers gripped mine. They were icy cold.

"Don't you like them?" she said. "Don't you like the pictures?" She spoke more slowly than usual, as if she had been drugged, or had just awoken from a deep sleep.

"No, I don't," I said. I tugged at her hand, encouraging her to follow me, and in the end she did, the belt of her loosened mackin-tosh trailing after her across the flagstones. Her eyes were big and shiny, like glass marbles. I leaned my shoulder against the church door and heaved it open, still clutching on to Phrynne with my other hand. It was only as we emerged into the open air that she seemed to come properly awake. She shook her head and looked about herself. She seemed confused, as if she had forgotten for a moment where we were.

"It was close in there, wasn't it?" she said. "Really muggy. I thought I was going to faint."

"Are you all right, Phrynne?" I said. I felt dazed, overwhelmed by the sense that something terrible had happened, or almost happened, but without the words or the experience to know what it was. All I knew was that I had glimpsed something—the corner of a world—that bore little or no relation to the world I was accustomed to living in.

Had Sudworth's murals even been real? Was it possible to dream while you were awake? I had heard of such things, read of them, perhaps, but never with such ———————————— my mind was filled with such questions, buzzing around my head like pernicious insects. I wanted to take Phrynne by the shoulders and shake her, to demand that she tell me what she had seen and felt, above all *what she knew.*

I didn't, though. I remained what I now saw I had been my whole life: a coward.

Phrynne blinked at me sleepily, then grinned.

"You know it's our bed you're sleeping in, don't you?" she said. "Mine and Gerald's? That awful four-poster? The bed where we *fucked?*"

She gave me a sidelong look, an awful look, like a scientist gauging the outcome of a risky experiment. "Don't tell me—you'd rather not know. That's the thing with you though, isn't it, Iris? You'd always rather not know. You asked me on the train how I came to fall for Gerald, but even then you didn't want to know, not really. I fell for him, dear Iris, because I could see from the moment I walked into your living room that you were itching to fuck him, and he you. I couldn't understand why you didn't just get on with it, to be honest. Freddy wouldn't have divorced you even if he'd found out, which he wouldn't have. About as perceptive as a block of wood, our Freddy. But of course you and Gerald were both insisting on playing out some kind of low-rent Greek tragedy, and I was turned on by the thought of ruining your little romance, I suppose, God knows why. Gerald Banstead turned out to be as boring in bed as Freddy was in conversation." She smiled. "You really weren't missing much. Do you honestly think a real man would have put up with all that lady in the tower stuff? He was probably more interested in Freddy than he was in you." She paused. "Or Ian. Ian was beautiful when he was younger, wasn't he? Quite the Ganymede."

I gaped at her, appalled. She had to be mad. My mind filled with confusion—was it possible for someone to be driven insane simply by looking at a picture?—and then I screamed at her, really screamed, as I had not done since my girlhood, when all things seemed possible, at least for a while. Even rage.

"You bitch!"

"Not dead yet after all? Bravo."

"You're a monster. I can't bear you near me." I began to sob. I ran at Phrynne, who seemed to be blocking my path, although she was probably not doing so deliberately. She drew aside, still smiling, and I found myself hurtling down the path—not the path that we had come by but the partially eroded path along the cliff tops. I realised immediately that I had no choice but to keep going. The alternative—turning around and facing her—was too awful.

How could I have believed this banshee, this gorgon, this *alien* to be my friend? How could she have changed so? I wondered, before realising I was bound to admit that she might *not* have changed, that it was more likely she had been hiding her true self all along. That the Phrynne I thought I knew was always a lie..

How little we know one another, really. In the midst of my grief and fury and terror I did not think to ask myself how I seemed to her.

I flung myself along the path, doing my best not to trip on the stones and chunks of loose rock that littered the ground. I did not look down. I did not look back. After a breathless ten minutes or so I came to the point where the cliff path began its descent towards the town. As the going became easier and safer my heart rate slowed. I sat down on one of the stone benches that had been placed at intervals for walkers to rest and enjoy the view. I stared out at the sea for some minutes—the tide was coming in, a white triangular sail marked the horizon—and then finally looked back along the path the way I had come.

There was no sign of Phrynne. I told myself she must be returning via the other path—the safer path—but for those moments at least some base part of me did not care much, either way.

I could not face going back to The Bell, at least not yet. I walked along the promenade until I came to The Esplanade hotel. I sat down at one of the tables on the terrace and when one of the waiting staff approached me I informed him that I would like to take lunch.

"Certainly, madam," he said. "I'll bring you a menu."

I ordered the grilled sea bass with new potatoes and a glass of white wine. No doubt you will think it pathetic, but I felt elated. I had never done such a thing before, you see—ordered lunch for myself, on my own, in a restaurant—and it had never occurred to me that it could be that simple, that natural.

It was as if, for the time I sat there, the world was mine.

I walked back up the hill to the pub. It was five o'clock by then, still an hour before The Bell opened for business. I hoped I would be able to get to my room without having to speak to anyone. I did not want to talk about Phrynne, or ask about her, or be forced to invent a plausible reason for her absence.

In fact there was no one about. I went upstairs. Phrynne's door stood firmly shut, and no sound came from her room. I closed my own door and lay down on the bed. I felt utterly exhausted. I remembered what Phrynne had said about this being the same bed she had shared with Gerald, but the idea seemed to have lost all potency.

So bloody what? I thought. It was as if my life before the present moment had been leached of colour. The past, and all it contained, no longer mattered.

I picked up my book—not the Highsmith this time but the Lehmann biography—but fell asleep before I reached the bottom of the page. When I woke it was gone six, and getting dark. I could hear—very faintly—noises from the saloon bar below. I got up and drew the curtains, then went out on to the landing and knocked softly on Phrynne's door. I felt certain she must be back by now. When there was no reply I knocked again, this time more boldly, but there was still no answer.

"Phrynne?" I said, putting my eye to the keyhole. "Phrynne?" My insistent utterances of her name were beginning to take on a hopeless, hollow tone. What if she never comes back? I thought. What then?

I put on my shoes and went downstairs. Danuta was behind the bar, serving three youngsters decked out in beach gear. One of them—a young man still in his teens—smiled at me as I entered, his smooth, unworried face beaming with good humour. Such a lovely smile, I thought. For a moment he reminded me of Ian.

"You don't happen to have seen my friend?" I said to Danuta. "We were supposed to meet back here at five, but she's not in her room."

"I'm sorry, no, I haven't." A frown briefly creased her forehead and then disappeared. "I wouldn't worry, though. I'm sure she's somewhere about. It's not easy to get yourself lost in a place this small. Have a drink while you wait for her, if you like? It's on the house."

"Thank you," I replied. "I think I'll just walk down to the harbour first, see if she's there."

"See you later, then." Danuta smiled, looking unconcerned. "We're doing a lovely chicken curry tonight."

I walked back down Wrack Lane towards the promenade. I was trying not to dwell on what might have happened—that Phrynne was still out on the headland, that she had fallen and injured herself, that she was alone in the gathering darkness and in need of help. I kept telling myself that such scenarios were far fetched, that Phrynne was most likely in the town somewhere, in another pub, probably. It even occurred to me that she might have returned to The Bell while I was asleep in my room, packed her bags and left—gone off, as Freddy would have said, in high dudgeon.

It would be just like Phrynne to punish me by embarrassing me in front of strangers. If there was one thing I knew about her it was that she could never bear not to have the last word. On anything.

The tide was going out again. A group of children—three boys and a girl—chased each other and threw seaweed along the widening strip of sand between the sea and the shore. The retreating ocean glittered dully. Now that the wind had dropped it lay completely calm. From the interior of the town I could hear church bells ringing. They're practising, I thought. I could not help thinking of Sudworth's murals, and remembering what Phrynne had said about the noise the bell towers made, remembering we had arrived in the town on the first night of their honeymoon. There was something eerie about it, I thought. So many bell towers in such a small place. It defied all logic.

"Hello."

The woman's voice, so close beside me, made me jump. I thought at first it was Phrynne who was speaking to me, because who else did I know in this town? But then I saw that the speaker was not Phrynne at all, but the thin woman from the cottages, the woman with the fair hair we'd seen hanging out washing in one of the long, windswept front gardens that bounded the path that led to St Barnabus's church.

"Hello," I replied. I realised she must have come into town via the cliff path. I wondered vaguely who was minding her child.

"The wind's dropped," she said. "Your friend not with you?"

"No," I said. "You don't happen to have seen her, do you? She said she wanted to explore the path a little further but she's still not back."

The woman shook her head. "Not seen her, but I wouldn't worry, she won't run off. She can't keep away from the place."

"I'm sorry?"

"I remember her from before. She's not someone you'd forget, is she, your friend? I was just a girl then. Worked for the Pascoes, waiting tables and so on. She was like a spotlight, your friend, like a movie star in one of those magazines my sister used to nick from out the doctor's. I could hardly believe she was here. I couldn't understand why anyone who looked like that would ever wind up coming to a place like this. It's dead, isn't it, this town? The whole place is dead. Especially in winter."

"I wouldn't say that. It feels friendly to me. Peaceful."

The woman laughed. "A body can get tired of peaceful, sometimes. Have you come far?"

"From London."

"Oh, London."

"Have you ever been there?"

Once again she shook her head. "Never will now, I reckon. Can't say I mind much."

We stood together in silence, looking out at the water. At one point she turned to me, and touched my sleeve, and I had the oddest feeling then, that there was something she wanted to tell me, something she but was holding back, whether for my sake or her own I could not tell.

Is it Phrynne? I wanted to ask. What do you know of her? *What happened?*

But I said nothing, and she said nothing, and the moment passed.

"Well, I won't keep you," she said in the end. She put two fingers in her mouth and whistled. The sound was keen and piercing and I was amazed at the strength of it. One of the boys playing down on the sand broke off from the game and came dashing towards us up the beach. He was neatly built and ruddy-cheeked, a normal-seeming, healthy child. His hair was as fair as his mother's.

"His dad's away at the moment, working on the oil rigs," the woman said. "The lad misses him, I reckon. Still, he does well at school."

She gathered the boy to her, and the two of them went off along the promenade. There seemed a closeness between them that made my heart ache, the more so because I knew it would not be so many years before the boy left, as Ian had left, as Gerald had, the way they all do.

———

I ran into Phrynne just outside The Bell. I was coming up the hill, she was coming down. Her expensive brogues were covered with mud, but otherwise she looked to be unharmed.

"Sorry to be so late back," she said. "Only I was visiting with the Colonel. We got talking and I lost track of the time."

"He's here in town, then?"

"Yes. Danuta had his address, after all. Didn't I tell you? He's quite close by, actually. When the Pascoes sold the pub he took one of the new bungalows close to the station. Would you believe he doesn't look a day older? Must be all that army discipline, or some-thing. He was sorry to hear about Gerald, G————————————————————starving."

It was fully dark by then, and in the dim glow of the streetlights it was difficult to read her expression. Was it possible that she was telling the truth?

I was so relieved to see her that I didn't give the matter too much thought.

Later, after Phrynne had changed her clothes and we had eaten supper, we went to sit in the saloon bar next to the fire. Phrynne had ordered brandies. She seemed less talkative than the evening before, but I could tell from the way she was behaving—the side-long glances and tight-lipped smiles, the too-eager laughter—that she was nerving herself up to making an apology.

After half an hour of superficial chatter, it finally came. "I'm sorry about earlier," she said. "I was awful to you." She swirled the remains of her brandy around her glass. I remained silent, mainly because I was unsure which part of 'earlier' she was referring to.

"I didn't mean what I said about Gerald," she continued. "I must have been out of my mind. I think it's only just starting to dawn on me that he's really gone."

That still doesn't mean you loved him, I thought. Get out of that.

As so often, it was as if she read my mind.

"I know I was terribly selfish," she said. "I could see from the start that you and Gerald were fond of one another. The two of you belonged together, really. But you were never going to do anything about it, that was obvious—not with Freddy being Gerald's best friend and everything—and so I just couldn't help myself. After Alec died I really wasn't myself for a while. And by the time I realised what I'd done it was too late, Gerald and I were already married. And Gerald was always good to me. You must know that better than anyone. Can you forgive me?"

I found I didn't know how to answer that. But if Phrynne imagined I was taking pleasure in her discomfort she was wrong.

"It must have been hard for you," I said finally. "Coming back to Holyhaven, I mean." Why the hell did you do it? I might have added. And why bring me? Was it weakness or compassion that made me hold my tongue? I didn't know then, and I still don't.

Freddy always said I was a pushover.

"I wanted to die, you know, that weekend," Phrynne said. "It wasn't until we got off the train that it hit me. What I'd done. Here we were, in this dreary cold place, and all I could think of was Alec, and the Italian sun. I don't know what would have happened with Alec in the long term—I've never exactly been a long-term kind of person, have I?—but at least it felt right at the time, it felt real. I lay up in that room the first night and thought about my life going on and on, always the same. I've never felt so terrible, before or since. I think that if it hadn't been for the Colonel I might really have jumped out the window."

"The Colonel?"

"Mike Shotcroft. He found me wandering around in the dark, out on the street. He said it was no good getting downhearted, that I had to soldier on. That was the phrase he used—soldier on. He sounded so serious, the way he said it, and that struck me as funny and kind all at the same time. I couldn't help but laugh, and you know what it's like once you start laughing, the fear goes out of you. He took me back inside and poured me a brandy and we sat in the bar. He told me about his time in India. Everything seemed more bearable after that."

"What were you doing outside?"

"That's the strangest thing—I can't remember. I can't even

remember how I got there. I was in a right state though, I can tell you that. One of my shoes was missing, apparently." She turned to face me than, and I realised it was the first time she had looked me in the eye since our reunion outside The Bell. "I've never stopped being terrified of this town, Iris. It's been like a shadow hanging over my life, all these years. I thought perhaps that if I came back here that feeling might disappear. Slay the dragon, isn't that what they say? But I couldn't have come alone. I needed you to be with me, I want you to know that. You're the only real friend I've ever had."

"And has it worked? Coming back here?"

She seemed to brighten. "I honestly think it has. I feel like a different person, and all thanks to you."

She reached out and took my hand, linking her fingers through mine as she sometimes used to do when we were schoolgirls. Maybe I should have felt relief, pride, that old glow of secret happiness I always experienced at her approval, at the thought of me and Phrynne, against the world.

I didn't, though. I didn't believe her story, and my mind kept returning to what Freddy used to say about Phrynne using me, about her need for a dull backcloth to shine against.

Something within me had changed, or died. I knew as certainly as I knew my own name that it would never grow back.

I slept badly again. Each time I drifted off I fell into the same dream, that there was someone outside my window, ringing a bell and yelling at me to come down, come down and pick up the milk bottles, but when I woke up the pub and the street outside were quiet as a churchyard. I went down to breakfast feeling headachy and out of sorts. When Phrynne did not immediately appear I felt a measure of relief, glad to sit by myself for a while, enjoying the strong coffee and reading a copy of *The Times* that either Robbie or Danuta had put out on the bar.

As more time passed and there was still no Phrynne I began to get worried. I finished my breakfast and hurried upstairs. Phrynne's door was closed, but when I tried the handle I found it was unlocked. I called her name and went inside.

The curtains were drawn neatly back and the bed was made. There was no sign of Phrynne though, and when I opened the wardrobe to look inside I saw it was empty.

I began to feel uncomfortable then, alone in her room, and as I turned to leave I almost tripped over something lying on the floor. When I bent to pick it up I found it was a shoe. Navy blue patent leather, with a tapering, medium-height heel and a neat silver buckle. I remembered that Phrynne had worn a pair just like it, as part of her going away outfit. I had thought the shoes most elegant, but then Phrynne always did know how to pick out clothes. It was one of her many talents.

I slept badly again. Each time I drifted off I fell into the same dream, that there was someone outside my window, ringing a bell and yelling at me to come down, come down and pick up the milk bottles, but when I woke up the pub and the street outside were quiet as a churchyard. I went down to breakfast feeling headachy and out of sorts. Phrynne must have slept badly, too—it was impossible not to notice the dark circles under her eyes. She poured herself a cup of coffee and leaned back in her chair.

"God," she said. "I've had it with this place. It's so *dull.*" She dumped a large spoonful of sugar into her coffee and stirred it around. "Let's fly to New York," she said. She took two sips of her coffee in quick succession, shooting me a mischievous grin over the rim of her cup. "You have to say yes, Iris. It'll be like old times."

"You're not serious?"

"I am completely serious. Name me one thing that's stopping us. After all," she said. "You're a long time dead."

THE
BOOK
THAT
FINDS
YOU

LISA
TUTTLE

Tʜᴇʀᴇ's sᴏᴍᴇᴛʜɪɴɢ ᴀʙᴏᴜᴛ ᴀ ʙᴏᴏᴋ ʏᴏᴜ ꜰɪɴᴅ ʙʏ ᴀᴄᴄɪᴅᴇɴᴛ, ᴀ book no one else seems to have heard of, a book that thrills and then becomes a part of you, when it's one you so easily might never have read at all—it almost seems like *it* found *you*.

For me, it was *Until the Stones Weep* by J.W. Archibald. The first time I saw that name and title was in cracked white lettering on the battered black spine of a used paperback, sandwiched between a novel by Eric Ambler and another by Evelyn Anthony in the Mysteries/Suspense section of the Southwest Book Exchange, a narrow box of a place with a concrete floor, fluorescent lighting, and the pervasive smell (to me, always sweet) of old paperback books.

I pulled it out. The cover was crassly at odds with the ambiguously eerie title, sporting a hyper-real picture of a leering, warty crone with bloodshot eyes, extending a yellow, claw-like hand in a beckoning gesture. It didn't look like a crime story, but like something much rarer in those days before Stephen King had sold his first novel. I turned it over and read:

Mystery . . . Desire . . . Madness . . . Death . . .

Six Strange Stories of the Supernatural by a Modern Master of the Macabre

"Mr Archibald can certainly make your skin crawl. His ghosts and half-seen monsters are as evocative as any by M.R. James."
—*Dublin Herald*

"A modern-day Poe, bringing fear and mystery into our modern world. No ghost-story aficionado should miss this treat."
—*Sheffield Telegraph*

"Better than H.P. Lovecraft."   —*Evening Standard*

since I'd discovered the works of Edgar Allan Poe at the age of seven. I'd read all of M.R. James, most of Lovecraft, and every genre anthology I could find, but I'd never heard of J.W. Archibald.

Of course I bought it, and read it from cover to cover that night, to be rewarded by an uneasy sleep punctuated by nightmares. Those six strange stories—which I only half-understood on first reading—made my skin crawl with a delicious, unreasoning terror.

I loved it.

The only problem was that there was no more, only those six stories by the writer who had shot to the top of my list of favourites. No one I knew had ever heard of him. As this was in the days before the internet, my means of searching were limited, but I tried my best, even putting through a request by the inter-library loan service, without success. I never stopped looking, but I never even came across another copy of the book I had found. It was as if I'd made it up . . . or it had been made up, created in an edition of one, especially for me. I knew that was silly. *Until the Stones Weep* was a British paperback, published by Fontana in London in 1966; it was by a great stroke of luck that I had come across one of the few copies that had found their way to America, but there must be others; somebody else must know about J.W. Archibald.

And of course there *was* somebody else, living about two hundred miles away, but it took me another seven years to find him.

Everybody called him Tommy, a boyish name that went with the twinkle in his eye, his unruly hair, his whole attitude that life was a game. He was a collector who made his living dealing in second-hand books. His store was on South Lamar, in Austin; it hasn't been there for a long time now, but old residents may recall it. I only discovered it in my last year at the University, when I finally moved off campus to share an apartment and a car with my best friend, Maudie. Even though I went in there nearly every week—browsing more than buying—I was too shy to strike up a conversation with the good-looking man behind the counter.

One day Maudie said, "We're going to Tommy's party tonight."

"Who?"

"Bookstore guy."

"What? Really? Wait, how do you know him?"

She rolled her eyes. "Same way you do. I scored a copy of *The Doors of Perception* from him yesterday, and he invited me. "

I felt a clench of jealousy. "Does he even know your name?"

She punched my arm. "He wasn't hitting on me! He said, Be sure to bring your little sister." She laughed. "I don't know if I should be offended that he thinks I look older than you!"

Tommy lived in a small wooden house on a big lot on Enfield Road. His front room contained free-standing bookcases and wall-mounted shelves; elegant glass-fronted bookshelves side by side with the casual brick-and-board arrangements Maudie and I used. As soon as I saw all those books, I relaxed, and forgot everything else in my eagerness to browse.

And there it was. The book I thought was my own private discovery, in a stranger's collection. I stopped breathing for a second, and put my finger on the familiar wrinkled black spine, to be sure I wasn't dreaming, then pulled it out and stared at the familiar, ridiculous, hideous old witch.

"Don't let the cover put you off; the stories are much better than—"

"They're *great*," I said fiercely, looking up with a frown into the face—smiling, interested, and very close—of the book's owner. I rearranged my own expression and said, "He's my favourite writer, Archibald, but I've never met anyone else who's even heard of him."

"Read anything else by him?"

When I only gaped, he led me into another room, where the walls were entirely covered in books. There was also a cluttered desk and a couple of chairs, one a leather recliner with a floor lamp beside it.

"It's a signed first," he said, holding up a small, hardcover book in a plain red and white dust-wrapper. "So I won't let you take it away—in case you're tempted not to return it. But you can read it here—any time you like," he added quickly as I sat down in his reading chair. "I didn't mean right this minute; you're more than welcome to come back."

"I'd like to look at it now—just to read a little bit," I said. "Please?"

His gaze softened; he gave me a sympathetic smile, and handed me the first copy I had ever seen of *The Secret Game* by J. W. Archibald and Sarah Anne Lyons.

"But it's—"

"A collaboration between two authors. Her second and his first published book, and the closest thing he's written to a novel. You know who she is?"

"*The Hound of God*, *The Servitors*, of course." Lyons was a respected English novelist, and wife of another, even better-known, novelist. I'd read one of her novels but had found it too dense with religious and literary allusions for my taste. "But she's—"

"Married to Albert Baker, yes, *now*, he's her *second* husband, but after the break-up of her first marriage, she was Archibald's, uh, girlfriend."

It was all too much. "No! But he must be so old—much older than her, and—well, I thought he was dead! The way he writes . . . " Archibald's stories, while avoiding contemporary references that would absolutely date them, had always struck me as belonging to the world of the 1920s, if not earlier.

"I can see why you'd think that. His style is very old-fashioned."

"But how old is he?"

"He's cagey about his age. He must be a good ten years older than Lyons—maybe twenty. She's, what, mid-forties now? So he could be in his sixties." He told me—enjoying my astonishment and awe—that he had briefly corresponded with Archibald. He was about to get out the letters when he finally realized that my interest, then, was all for the book in my hands, and left me to read it in peace.

I spent the next two or three hours in a kind of fevered dream, so rapt in story that it seemed to be happening to me. I could hardly have said what the book was "about"—I experienced it as a series of dreams and nightmares that flowed imperceptibly together. Incidents took place in London and Venice, in a Welsh village and on the Norfolk Broads, and, because I had never been out of Texas, as I read, the bleak stretches of Norfolk became the Texas coastal plains, the Welsh village was in the hill country, black cabs and red double-decker buses appeared on the streets of Austin, and the canals of Venice ran through Galveston.

The Secret Game was a novel in the manner of Arthur Machen's *The Three Imposters;* that is, a series of strange stories, loosely linked by several continuing characters. There were contemporary references that made it clearly a post-World War II production; mentions of bomb-damage and rationing and to movies and songs of the late '40s. It was copyright 1950. In both style and substance it was easy to recognize as the work of J. W. Archibald. I was not familiar enough with Lyons's writing to guess how much she had adapted her style to his, but I wondered how they had worked together. The tone and style was so thoroughly consistent, it seemed the work of one writer.

When I finished that enchanted first reading and stumbled back into the front room, I found a much diminished party, and no Maudie.

"Your friend wanted to leave. I promised her faithfully that I'd see you safely home—when you're ready. I thought you might want to talk some more about Archibald."

From the way he slightly slurred his words, I knew Tommy was in no condition to drive me across town, but I didn't care. I *did* want to talk about the book. We could talk all night, I decided, and drink coffee, and in the morning, he could take me home.

I was about half right. We *did* talk all night—not just about *The Secret Game* and *Until the Stones Weep,* but about all our favourite books, and our shared desire to write, and our oddly similar childhoods—and drank lots of coffee, which he liked just the way I did, with plenty of Half-and-Half and lots of sugar—until, by the time we were left alone in his house, we were both buzzing with caffeine and the thrill of finding a soul-mate. He was sober enough to drive me home by dawn, but instead we went to bed, to continue our conversation on another plane. And it turned out that our bodies connected as passionately as our minds. At one point while we were making love I fell into a sort of ~~dream~~~~ ~~

showing me one book after another, and they were all things I had been looking for, without knowing they existed, and he was giving them to me, to read and keep.

"Do you like this? How about this? No, wait, this is even better. This? Or this?"

I couldn't choose; I wanted them all, all at once. "Yes," I said, holding him tightly. "Yes, yes, yes."

After that, he never did drive me home—except to get my car and load it up with my things to take back to his house. *Our* house.

We had a blissful life together, for awhile. Neither of us was terribly ambitious—although we had our dreams, and wrote stories that we hoped to sell, really all we cared about, besides each other, was getting by, doing the things we enjoyed, reading and collecting and talking about the books we loved.

My sister thought it was the least romantic affair she'd ever heard of. She couldn't believe I'd rather be given an aged, yellowing paperback novel with a picture of a skeleton on the cover instead of a dozen red roses or a bottle of expensive perfume on Valentine's Day. But I've never liked cut flowers, and I'd rather choose my own fragrances. That wasn't just *any* crummy old paperback; it was an anthology that included a very rare, never-reprinted short story called "The Chill Touch of Your Hand" by J. W. Archibald. She thought I was crazy for thinking that driving to Oklahoma City to spend the weekend looking through the books in every Salvation Army and junk store was more fun than the "pampering spa weekend" she craved.

I'm not sure when or why it changed. I suppose it was a gradual thing, a distance that grew between us, a flame that burned out. At least on his side—I remember how shocked I was when, a month before what would have been our fourth anniversary of living together, he said, in that unmistakably heavy, resolute voice of doom those words all lovers dread: "We need to talk."

One week later, in a state of shock, I was living in my own one-bedroom apartment.

"Was there someone else?" Maudie and my sister both thought he must have been sneaking around with someone else behind my back. I did not think so. True, there was a new woman in his life before the month was out, but he'd always been fast like that.

Although of course I was miserable at first, the end of a relationship is not the end of everything. Other men found me attractive, and I had the freedom to pick and choose. And there were other things in my life. I had started selling my short stories—around the same time that I'd noticed Tommy's attitude towards me begin to change. Maybe the two things were not unconnected. My literary success did not amount to much—half a dozen short stories sold to magazines that paid less than five cents a word—but it was more than he had managed to do, and maybe he minded it more than he would say.

When I was twenty-eight, I came into an inheritance. I decided to use it to travel abroad. Friends of my family owned a flat in London I could use as a base for a month or two. London was at the top of my list—J.W. Archibald lived there. His reputation and career had received a boost with the coming of the horror boom, and he'd finally been published in America—thirteen of his old stories, and one completely new collection. An issue of *The Magazine of Fantasy and Science Fiction* with one of my stories also contained a brand new tale by Archibald, so I felt confident enough to call the magazine's editor to ask if he could give me Mr. Archibald's address.

His voice changed when he heard what I wanted, becoming lower and softer. "I'm sure he wouldn't mind, but . . . This isn't for public consumption but . . . he's not very well. In fact . . . I don't think he's long for this world. He's moved into a friend's flat—he couldn't really manage on his own any longer."

My heart sank lower and lower. "I see."

"But let me give you the address. You may as well write to him—I know he'd love to hear from you. I'm sure that if he's able, he'll write back."

J.W. Archibald was dead before my letter could reach him. Two weeks later, I received a note on black-edged paper, signed with a name I could not decipher.

I was sad, of course, but the idea that I might meet him had never been real. And what could one brief meeting have added to my understanding or my pleasure in his writing? It was his words that mattered, the magic he'd created on the page. The great sadness was that there would never be any more, that he'd never write another story, *not* that I'd never been able to shake his hand and tell him how much his stories had meant to me.

Before leaving on my travels, I reread *The Secret Game* and all of the short stories. They were just as good as I remembered, haunting, disturbing, and puzzling. Multiple readings did not dilute their strangeness; rather, it seemed the more closely you inspected them, the odder they became. Even now that I was older and more widely read, able to pick up on his references (he was big on opera, architecture, and obscure nineteenth-century artists), some things remained opaque.

I arrived in London at the beginning of November. It was cold and grey and looked exactly as I thought it should. This was before London became a multicultural, international city with futuristic, gleaming sky-scrapers, and enormous shopping malls, in constant flux. In those days, not so long ago, it seemed charmingly old-fashioned, a little grubby and run-down, but quaint; a city distinct from all others, like nothing I'd encountered except in fiction.

Although I was alone, I was too entranced by the novelty of it all to feel lonely. Living in a flat meant I could lead a normal life, shop and cook for myself and keep whatever schedule suited me. I walked all through the short daylight hours, sightseeing and storing up impressions, wrote in my journal and read in the evenings.

I'd brought only a couple of books with me, just enough to tide me over, for I anticipated the bookshops of London, where I was, as expected, overwhelmed by a variety of treasures.

On my first visit to Foyles, the new novel by Sarah Anne Lyons was prominently displayed, and that same day I read an interview with her in the *Evening Standard*, from which I learned that she was no longer married to Albert Baker. They had been separated for nearly two years, but the divorce was only now about to be finalized, having been waiting on the division of their property. Bert hated change, she said; he couldn't bear the disruption of moving, yet without selling their big house he'd been unable to give her half its value.

"It was much too big for him, of course, and he hasn't the least idea what has to be done to keep up a house, but he had become so stuck in his ways he was quite irrational . . . it was part of the reason I left him. I shan't be getting married again. When I was young, I seemed to feel I *needed* a man, to be complete, but now . . . now I find I enjoy living my own life. Rather like Lydie, in my new novel."

The interview was a two-page spread, including a large picture of a very beautiful mature woman. On an impulse, I wrote a letter, care of her publisher, asking to meet her. I said I was a writer myself, and mentioned my sadness at the recent death of J.W. Archibald. I gave her my address, told her I did not have a phone, but would be in London for at least a month and available whenever it was most convenient for her.

The very next day, in the bargain bin outside a bookshop in Cecil Court, I saw a familiar wrinkled black spine with white lettering. The cover (that leering witch) was even more battered than on my own copy, but the pages inside were clean, and I could not resist buying it.

Standing with it in my hand, I had a sudden idea. Why not use Archibald as my tour guide? The places where the stories were set could provide my itinerary. After seeking out the London streets and buildings he mentioned, I'd go to the Norfolk coast, the Yorkshire moors, Wales . . . .

I'd already purchased that indispensible guide, the *London A-Z*, and over lunch (in the Wendy's on Cambridge Circus—seeing it, I suddenly yearned for an American hamburger) I put the map-book and a pencil on one side and began to leaf through my new copy of *Until the Stones Weep* in search of place names. There were none in the first story, 'The Trembling Leaf' which . . . .

'The New Neighbours' likewise did not identify even the city in which its "mid-nineteenth century housing estate for merchants and professional men" was located.

In the third story, at last, I saw some familiar names—perhaps a bit *too* familiar. I'd already been along Oxford Street, and Bond Street, and was even now in Cambridge Circus, but the next reference perked me up a little: *Notting Hill*, where a strange event occurred inside a house on a nameless 'side street.'

There was a tube station called Notting Hill Gate; getting there would give me more practice navigating the underground, and when I got there, I did what I was already accustomed to doing in any new area: walked around and looked at things.

I found a second-hand bookshop within five or ten minutes of walking away from the tube station, down what surely was a side street—it didn't seem to have a name.

A bell over the door jangled as I entered; the man behind the counter looked up, but left me to browse while he continued talking to someone on the telephone.

"Oh, they'll sell, but it wasn't a great haul. He was only having a clear-out. Moaning about having to get rid of *everything* for lack of space, but I'm sure he's paid for storage. There wasn't anything special . . . No. Nor that.

"Oh, yes, *some* signed firsts, but nothing really . . . Baker's no fool; he's a collector himself. Let me have all his wife's books—those loving inscriptions! Obviously couldn't stand to look at them again.

You think? No, she's not collectible. Except that one with Archibald, and he didn't have that, of course. Uh-huh."

My skin prickled as I eavesdropped shamelessly.

"Seven boxes—no cherry-picking. Probably only a dozen I'd really—uh-huh. Uh-huh. Downstairs. I'll price them this weekend. If you want. Ok. Sure. Listen, you know that bloke in Camden Town . . . ."

I moved along the shelves, out of his sight, towards the back of the shop to the stairs leading down. Although there was no sign to invite customers to check out the stock on the lower floor, neither was there anything to say it was for staff only, so I descended, stepping lightly.

Downstairs it smelled of damp and dust and paper. The room had walls lined with metal shelving, double-stacked with books, and there were at least a dozen cardboard boxes on the brown and cream linoleum. The only lighting came from a single, low-wattage bulb dangling from a ceiling cord, and the corners were thickly shadowed. I took a step away from the stairs, then froze as one of the shadows moved. It looked like a man.

I opened my mouth to say something, anything to turn the sinister moment towards normality, but when the shadow reached the place where the light from the hanging bulb should have lit up his face and turned him into a person, there was no face. No longer a shadow, it seemed to be a life-sized figure of a man cut out of kraft paper, and it moved towards me too fast for me to scream—even if I had wanted to.

Then he was on me, arms wrapped about me, pressed hard against me; thin and light though he was, I could feel every naked, masculine inch of him. It was such an unexpectedly *welcome* pressure that I relaxed and melted into the embrace. I opened my mouth for his kiss, and arched my back and pressed myself against him, and as I did I remembered Tommy in our most intimate moments together, and the memory was so strong and physically irresistible that I groaned and lost myself in a convulsion of pleasure.

It was over in a second. Surely I had imagined it all, briefly overcome by the lingering effects of jet-lag in the poor light and bad air of the room. But there *was* a man—I couldn't see his face, for he was standing with his back to the light, but he was there, blocking my way to the boxes I was so curious about, holding a book. The book in his hands was a small hardcover, and he pressed it on me, pushing it against my breast.

I caught hold of it before he could go farther, and quickly darted up the stairs. Although I knew I'd felt hands on my naked breasts, I was fully dressed for the London winter, and my navy blue coat was buttoned up to my collar-bone.

The man behind the counter frowned when I thrust the book at him. "Where'd you get this? I haven't booked it in

yet. Oh, all right—"

Although I really meant to return it, it was easier to pay him the pound he asked and go. It was already dark outside. I rather wished I had let the man wrap my purchase, because the binding had an unpleasant, greasy feel in my ungloved hand, and for that reason I didn't like to put it in my purse.

The train was crowded. There was nowhere to sit, and I had no chance to examine the book I continued to clutch until I got home.

There was no lettering on the pale brown spine, no title or publisher's colophon. Inside, after two blank sheets, the title page:

The Rejected Swain's Revenge
"J.W.A."

Below those two lines, centred near the bottom of the page, was a sort of symbol or device that looked like two letters intertwined, but I wasn't quite sure what letters.

Turning another page I found another two blank sheets; between them, a folded square of blue notepaper. Unfolding it, I recognized the handwriting from the letters Tommy had shown me years before.

———

My sweet Lady Anne,

I've done what I can, but it was never enough to please you. You were a hard mistress. Will your new man find life with you any less difficult, I wonder?

Something in the pages of this book may move you as my own caresses never could. I wish you joy of it.

With all my heart, I remain

Forever yours

A.

I was both disturbed and excited by this unexpected discovery and I wished more than anything that I had Tommy to share it with. He'd produced a bibliography of Archibald's work, and I was absolutely certain it had not listed "The Rejected Swain's Revenge" even as a variant title. Could this have been produced by a private press? But then what had happened to the other copies? Why had no one heard of it? It seemed hardly possible that he had written, and caused to be printed, a book meant to be read by just one person, yet that is what I suspected.

Just thinking about reading it made me feel like a sneaking, spying, peeping tom—but how could I resist? I justified what I was about to do with the reflection that Archibald could not mind because he was dead, and Sarah Anne Lyons had not cared enough to take the book away with her when she left her husband—*anyone* might read it now.

Except, as I found as soon as I began to read the densely printed slabs of prose, it was hard to imagine anyone who would care enough. It was almost unreadable, an incomprehensible mess that reminded me of the automatic writing favoured by the Surrealists. There was no story and no argument. Whenever there was a sudden burst of clarity, it was to reveal a sexual scene, unusually graphic for the normally proper and tastefully suggestive author, and astonishingly unpleasant.

I flipped ahead, to see if things got any better, but it was all like that. I put the book aside, feeling soiled, and wished I'd never picked it up. (But had I been given a choice?) There were too many familiar turns of phrase for me to console myself with the thought that anyone other than Archibald had written it, but why? What had he thought he was doing? I wondered if he'd gone temporarily insane when his lover left him. He'd obviously regained his senses, because he'd been writing brilliant and mysterious short stories up until the final months of his life.

'Lady Anne' should have burnt it, I thought, with an irrational flare of resentment. She should have had more care for his reputation, even if she no longer wished to share her life with him. Yet I flinched at the idea of destroying it ~~if I~~ ~~it, it~~ and even if I neither liked nor understood it, it had been written by a very talented author.

Wrapping it in a shopping bag I stashed it out of sight in a drawer.

That night I slept badly. I woke frequently, heart pounding, convinced there was someone else in the flat; a man in my room, approaching my bed. The nightmares were connected to the book, but I could not think of how I could safely get rid of it.

In the morning, I packed my rucksack with clothes and books to last me a few days, took myself off to the nearest mainline station, and bought a ticket for the first destination that caught my fancy: Edinburgh. The Scottish city appealed to me for all sorts of reasons, not least among them that it had never, so far as I could recall, featured in anything Archibald had ever written.

The cold, wind, and icy rain did not bother me. I thoroughly enjoyed myself over the next four days, exploring the Old Town, seeing the sights and indulging in the bookshops—I even went on a ghost tour. I slept well at night and ate the hearty "full Scottish" breakfast provided by my motherly landlady every morning, and went back to London feeling much happier, with one bag full of my dirty clothes and another full of books I had not been able to resist.

There was a letter waiting for me at the flat; a handwritten note on headed notepaper from Sarah Anne Lyons inviting me to call on her, and suggesting a particular afternoon—now just two days away.

That night, I slept well, better than I had in Edinburgh. The simple trick of going away and coming back had given this borrowed flat the feeling of home. I did not open the book again, but told myself I'd been silly about it. All the same, I looked forward to returning it to its rightful owner.

Sarah Anne Lyons lived in a pretty, white-stucco-fronted house in a terrace near the river. She opened the door to me, gracious and smiling, and insisted I call her "Anne." Her beauty had not at all diminished with age, and she was even more beautiful in person than her photographs revealed. I felt quite overcome, almost in awe; she had that great charm and charisma that is the very definition of stardom.

Her sitting room might have been lifted from a copy of *The World of Interiors,* with its elegant, modernist furniture and white marble fireplace surround. Everything was black and white or shades of grey, including the framed prints on the walls, with a few perfectly judged touches of scarlet. There was no bric-a-brac and no clutter, nothing on the occasional tables but a white porcelain vase of red roses and an ebony bowl filled with apples.

The absence of books was especially striking, at least to me, but this was a room for entertaining visitors, not for curling up alone to read. Her office was probably lined with bookshelves.

While I was still gazing around the beautiful yet impersonal room, she brought in a tea-tray, and we sat down to cups of Earl Grey and crisp little chocolate cookies, and had our chat. I hardly knew how to begin to speak to her—I felt like an uncouth visitor from another world—but she was very skilled at drawing people out, and before I knew it I was telling her all about my original, fortuitous, discovery of *Until the Stones Weep,* the effect it had had upon my own writing, how it had led to the relationship that I'd thought would be the most important in my life—"but that's all over now."

She had listened to my outpouring dispassionately. Now she put her head on one side and gazed at me with her dark, inscrutable eyes. "Is it? Does anything—like that—ever *really* end?"

I stared back, unable to reply. I wanted to ask if she was speaking of herself and J.W. Archibald, but didn't dare.

She said, with a sigh, "I suppose you want to know about *The Secret Game.*"

Rather timidly I nodded. "If you don't mind."

"Oh, I don't mind. I don't mind talking about Archie—not anymore. There were years—far too many years—when I wouldn't, when I wanted to forget... You see, I hurt him very badly. Of course I was young, but that's . . . for . . . what I was doing, and there are always other ways of ending a relationship. I shouldn't be surprised—I wouldn't blame him—if for a time he didn't really come to hate me. Love can easily be turned to hate, you know; sometimes it's hard to tell the difference between the two passions. Whereas what I felt for him was indifference. That's a very hard thing for a lover to accept. But our relationship was never equal. He fell absolutely, passionately in love with me—really, with my looks. He wanted me, whereas I was never physically attracted to him. You never met him, did you? No, of course not. Even when he was younger, Archie was a very odd-looking man. Of course, what attracted me to him was not his body but his *mind*—he was just so clever! He knew absolutely everything about art, and music, and architecture, and so many other things. Knowing him was a great education—probably the best education I could have had; I was very badly brought up in that respect. So I was tremendously impressed by him, and eventually, although I was never in love with him *in that way,* he wore me down with the strength of his desire. We became lovers. He wanted to marry me—but that I would *not* do."

She set her cup down in its saucer, the little click providing punctuation.

"All that is past. I am very pleased to say that we finally made it up. He forgave me, and we became friends again—just friends, but *really* friends—in the last year of his life."

"This was after you'd left your husband."

She shot me a look that made me think I'd gone too far, but then gave a reluctant nod. "Yes . . . Bert, the fact that I'd married him, as well as who he was . . . that was salt in Archie's wounds, so . . . although I like to think we still might have reconciled, you're right: the fact that I'd left Bert undoubtedly eased the way. Made it easier for poor Archie to re-admit me to his inner circle."

"When did he send you the book?"

It was clear from her look that she did not remember, so I prompted: '*The Rejected Swain's Revenge.*'

She shook her head slowly. "I have no idea what you're talking about. The title means nothing to me."

So I told her about the bookshop in Notting Hill that had bought seven boxes of books from Albert Baker. "One was this very odd book. No publishing or copyright information. I think it must have been privately printed. I found a piece of notepaper tucked inside, addressed to 'My Sweet Lady Anne' and signed 'A.'

"No date?"

"No date. But because it was in with your ex-husband's books—"

She was frowning, the expression adding years to her face. "Oh, it was too bad of him!"

"Archibald?"

"Bert!" She shook her head sharply, lips tight with anger. "He must have intercepted it, seeing the return address. It was—unfortunately—just the sort of thing he would do. He was always jealous of my past, of any part of my life that did not include him. He was so ridiculously possessive. He didn't recognize the usual boundaries. He wouldn't stop at reading my diary or stealing my mail . . . and how dare I complain, unless I had something to hide." She stopped herself from saying more. After a few moments, the tension in her relaxed and she managed a wry smile. "One more crime to add to the ledger. Thank goodness, I don't have to put up with his spying and prying any longer."

"Would you like to see it now? I brought it with me."

"No!" Her eyes widened in alarm before she recovered her composure and said again but more gently, "No, thank you."

"But he meant it for you—"

"Whatever he meant by it, whenever it was sent, that time is past. It doesn't matter anymore. I'm glad that we were able to become friends before he died, and that's how I'd like to remember him—not as a rejected, vengeful lover, but as my friend."

So I kept the book, although I did not open it again. It had not been written for me to read, and, crazy or not, I had a notion that my bad dreams had been caused by my trespass into its pages. I spent some time travelling in England, France and Italy, but went back to Texas in time for Christmas, ready to settle down and write a novel. It was at a New Year's Eve party in Austin that I heard the news about Tommy.

The old cynic had finally been trapped into marriage by some young thing fresh out of college. They were having their honeymoon in Vera Cruz, but would be back home in another couple of weeks.

Why should I care if Tommy was married? I'd been leading my own life for years. I was over him. Why did it feel like a fresh betrayal, and the worst one; why did it feel like my heart was breaking? A line from one of Archibald's stories floated through my mind: the heart doesn't know what time it is.

I knew then that I could not live in Austin again, and made it my New Year's resolution to move. That very night I began asking about friends and acquaintances who had moved away to the west or the east coast, and when I had a handful of addresses, I wrote some letters. Within a week I'd learned that Maudie's best friend from high school, now living in Brooklyn, needed someone to help with the rent from March, because her present roommate was getting married. I applied for the position. The thought of living in New York was exciting; maybe I could get a job in publishing.

Before I left the city for good I mailed *The Rejected Swain's Revenge* to Tommy, with the original note from Archibald inside, and a Post-It note stuck to the cover saying:

Found in a London bookshop, from the collection of Albert Baker. Thought it would fit well in yours. Will repay close & careful reading.

I did not sign it (I expected he would recognize my handwriting) and I did not include an address, so it's not surprising that I never heard from him about it.

I scarcely gave him another thought as I was soon caught up in my new life in New York. But although I did not return to Texas for many years, Maudie kept me informed about what was going on. From her, I learned Tommy's marriage did not even last a year. It was not an amicable separation. Community property laws gave her a claim on everything he owned, and he wound up selling his business to pay her off.

Did I feel sorry for him? No. It was all his own fault. If he'd stuck to his position on marriage, as he had with me, none of it would have happened. Besides, I thought he'd bounce back as he had before. He probably already had a new girlfriend, and with his contacts in the book trade and his knowledge, everyone expected he'd soon open a new bookshop.

That did not happen. He went on selling books out of his house, even issued his twice-yearly catalogues, but people in town saw less and less of him—he seemed to have become something of a hermit.

It was only years later, when I was invited to a book festival in Austin, that I began to think of him again. The city was so changed, so much bigger and rebuilt I hardly recognized it as the sleepy, funky college town I'd known. The house where I'd once lived with Tommy had been knocked down, replaced by two tall, narrow townhouses.

I wondered what had happened to him, but my casual enquiries led to blank looks, and I did not pursue the matter. I might never have known of his fate were it not for a chance encounter on my last night in Austin.

I was in a group just leaving a restaurant on Sixth Street when I saw Tommy walking towards us. He was so terribly changed by age, I think I recognized him more by his stance and loose way of walking than anything else. He didn't notice me; his eyes were cast down, and I did nothing to attract his attention.

It was what I saw when he went past that haunts me. There was someone walking behind him, so close it was unnatural, and a collision seemed imminent, yet because they continued in this manner for as long as I could follow their progress with my eyes, I knew it was deliberate, and Tommy well aware of, even allowing, this pursuit.

The person behind wore a long black overcoat—a completely unnecessary garment in the stifling warmth of the Texan night—and a slouch hat, which should have made him nearly impossible to identify. But what I *could* see—the parchment-coloured cheeks and chin, the long, incredibly thin, flat hands—and perhaps above all the odour, faint but unmistakable, carried to me on the faint breeze of his passage, of cheap pulp paper—convinced me that I had encountered him before, in the basement of a second-hand bookshop in Notting Hill.

The feeling of guilt for what I've done, what I've inflicted on poor Tommy—

Is it guilt that I feel? Or jealousy?

CONTRIBUTORS

Editor Simon Strantzas is the author of *Burnt Black Suns* (Hippocampus Press, 2014), *Nightingale Songs* (Dark Regions Press, 2011), *Cold to the Touch* (Tartarus Press, 2009), and *Beneath the Surface* (Humdrumming, 2008), as well as the editor of *Shadows Edge* (Gray Friar Press, 2013). His writing has been reprinted in *The Mammoth Book of Best New Horror*, *The Best Horror of the Year*, *The Year's Best Weird Fiction* and *The Year's Best Dark Fantasy & Horror;* has been translated into other languages; and has been nominated for the British Fantasy Award. He lives in Toronto, Canada.

Nina Allan's stories have appeared in many anthologies, including *Best Horror of the Year 6, Strange Tales* (Tartarus), and *The Mammoth Book of Ghost Stories by Women*. Her novella *Spin*, a reimagining of the Arachne myth, won the British Science Fiction Award in 2014, and her collection *The Silver Wind*, a story-cycle on themes of time and memory, won the Grand Prix de L'Imaginaire in the same year. Her debut novel *The Race*, set in an alternate future England and featuring bio-engineered greyhounds and island-sized whales, is out now from NewCon Press.

Nadia Bulkin writes scary stories about the scary world we live in. She moved from a Muslim society to a Christian one when she was eleven, although she remains unaffiliated and unabsolved. She now lives in Washington, D.C. and tends her garden of student debt sowed by two political science degrees. Her fiction has recently appeared in the anthologies *Letters to Lovecraft*, *Phantasm Japan*, and *Sword & Mythos*. For more, see nadiabulkin.wordpress.com.

Michael Cisco is the author of novels *The Divinity Student* (Buzzcity Press, 1999, winner of the International Horror Writers Guild award for best first novel of 1999), *The Tyrant* (Prime, 2004), *The San Veneficio Canon* (Prime, 2005), *The Traitor* (Prime, 2007), *The Narrator* (Civil Coping Mechanisms, 2010), *The Great Lover* (Chômu Press, 2011), *Celebrant* (Chômu Press, 2012), and *Member* (Chômu Press 2013). His short story collection, *Secret Hours*, was published by Mythos Press in ~~appeared in *Lovecraft Studies, The Weird Fiction Review, Iranian Studies*, and *Lovecraft and Influence*. Michael Cisco lives and teaches in New York City.

Malcolm Devlin's stories have appeared in Black Static and Interzone. He currently lives near the canal in Oxford, England.

Brian Evenson is the author of a dozen books of fiction, most recently the story collection *Windeye* (Coffee House Press 2012) and the novel *Immobility* (Tor 2012), both of which were finalists for a Shirley Jackson Award. His novel *Last Days* won the American Library Association's award for Best Horror Novel of 2009. His novel *The Open Curtain* (Coffee House Press) was a finalist for an Edgar Award and an International Horror Guild Award. He lives and works in Providence, Rhode Island, where he is a Professor in Brown University's Literary Arts Department.

Richard Gavin is a Canadian author in the realms of horror and the esoteric, oftentimes cultivating the borderland where these worlds meet. To date he has released four short-story collections, including *At Fear's Altar* (Hippocampus Press, 2012). His tales have also appeared in *The Best Horror of the Year, Year's Best Weird Fiction*, and the *Black Wings* anthologies. His occult writings have been featured in *Starfire* and *Clavis: Journal of Occult Arts, Letters and Experience*. He welcomes readers at www.richardgavin.net

Yaroslav Gerzhedovich was born in 1970 in Leningrad (St. Petersburg), and studied at the Serov Art College. During his 20-year career his style has undergone some changes, but the foundation remains the same—small size works, many small parts, muted colors, meticulous manner of execution, which has developed under the influence of Gothic and Renaissance art.

John Howard was born in London. He is the author of *The Defeat of Grief,* and *Numbered as Sand or the Stars*, and the short story collections *The Silver Voices, Written by Daylight,* and *Cities and Thrones and Powers.* His collaborations with Mark Valentine have appeared in the collections *The Rite of Trebizond and Other Tales,* and *The Collected Connoisseur.* He has published essays on various aspects of the science fiction and horror fields, and especially on the work of classic authors such as Fritz Leiber, Arthur Machen, August Derleth, M.R. James, and writers of the pulp era. Many of these have been collected in *Touchstones: Essays on the Fantastic.*

John Langan is the author of two collections, *The Wide, Carnivorous Sky and Other Monstrous Geographies* (Hippocampus 2103) and *Mr. Gaunt and Other Uneasy Encounters* (Prime 2008), and a novel, *House of Windows* (Night Shade 2009). With Paul Tremblay, he has co-edited *Creatures: Thirty Years of Monsters* (Prime 2011). One of the founders of the Shirley Jackson Award, he lives in upstate New York with his wife, younger son, and a houseful of animals.

Helen Marshall is an award-winning Canadian author, editor, and doctor of medieval studies. Her debut collection of short stories, *Hair Side, Flesh Side* (ChiZine Publications, 2012), was named one of the top ten books of 2012 by January Magazine. It won the 2013 British Fantasy Award for Best Newcomer and was shortlisted for a 2013 Aurora Award by the Canadian Society of Science Fiction and Fantasy. Her second collection, *Gifts for the One Who Comes After,* was released in September, 2014. She lives in Oxford, England where she spends her time staring at old books.

Daniel Mills is the author of *Revenants: A Dream of New England* (Chômu Press, 2011) and *The Lord Came at Twilight* (Dark Renaissance Books, 2014). His short fiction has appeared in various magazines and anthologies including *Black Static*, *Shadows & Tall Trees*, and *The Mammoth Book of Best New Horror 23 & 25*. He lives in Vermont.

David Nickle is the author of the novels *The 'Geisters*, *Rasputin's Bastards*, and *Eutopia: A Novel of Terrible Optimism*, and co-author of *The Claus Effect*, with Karl Schroeder. His stories are collected in ~~Knife Fight and Other Struggles and Monstrous Affections~~ in Toronto, Canada, where he works as a journalist covering municipal politics.

Lynda E. Rucker is an American writer born and raised in the American South and currently living in Dublin, Ireland. She has sold more than two dozen short stories to such places as *The Mammoth Book of Best New Horror*, *The Year's Best Dark Fantasy and Horror*, *The Best Horror of the Year*, *Black Static*, *F&SF*, *Shadows & Tall Trees*, and *Nightmare Magazine*. She is a regular columnist for *Black Static*, and her first collection, *The Moon Will Look Strange*, was released in 2013 from Karōshi Books.

Lisa Tuttle has been writing strange, weird stories nearly all her life, making her first professional sale in 1971. She is a past winner of the John W. Campbell Award, the British Science Fiction Award, and the International Horror Guild Award. Her short stories have been widely published and reprinted, and gathered into five published collections to date. Her first novel, written in collaboration with George R.R. Martin, *Windhaven*, originally published in 1981, is still in print, and has been translated into many other languages. Her other novels include *Lost Futures*, *The Mysteries*, *The Silver Bough*, and, forthcoming in 2016, *The Curious Affair of the Somnambulist and the Psychic Thief*. Born and raised in Texas, she now lives with her family in the highlands of Scotland.

D.P. Watt is a writer living in the bowels of England. He has two collections of short stories, *An Emporium of Automata*, (Eibonvale Press, 2013) and *The Phantasmagorical Imperative*, (Egaeus Press, 2014). Recent and forthcoming works include, *The Usher*, (Dunham's Manor Press), 'Honey Moon' in *A Soliloquy for Pan*, ed. Mark Beech, (Egaeus Press), and 'Myself/Thyself' in *Terror Tales of the Highlands*, ed. Paul Finch, (Gray Friar Press). Why not visit him at theinterludehouse.co.uk

Michael Wehunt spends his time in the lost city of Atlanta. His fiction has appeared or is forthcoming in such publications as *Cemetery Dance*, *Shadows & Tall Trees*, and the Paula Guran-edited *Mammoth Book of Cthulhu*, among others. You can visit him at www.michaelwehunt.com.

YEAR'S BEST
WEIRD FICTION
VOLUME ONE

EDITED BY

LAIRD BARRON
AND MICHAEL KELLY

Year's Best Weird Fiction, Volume One

"Well, it's a triumph. A really well-assembled collection,
which succeeds in distinguishing itself from the best horror and
best fantasy anthologies with an eclectic table of contents."
—Nathan Ballingrud, author of *North American Lake Monsters*

Oct. 2014   www.undertowbooks.com

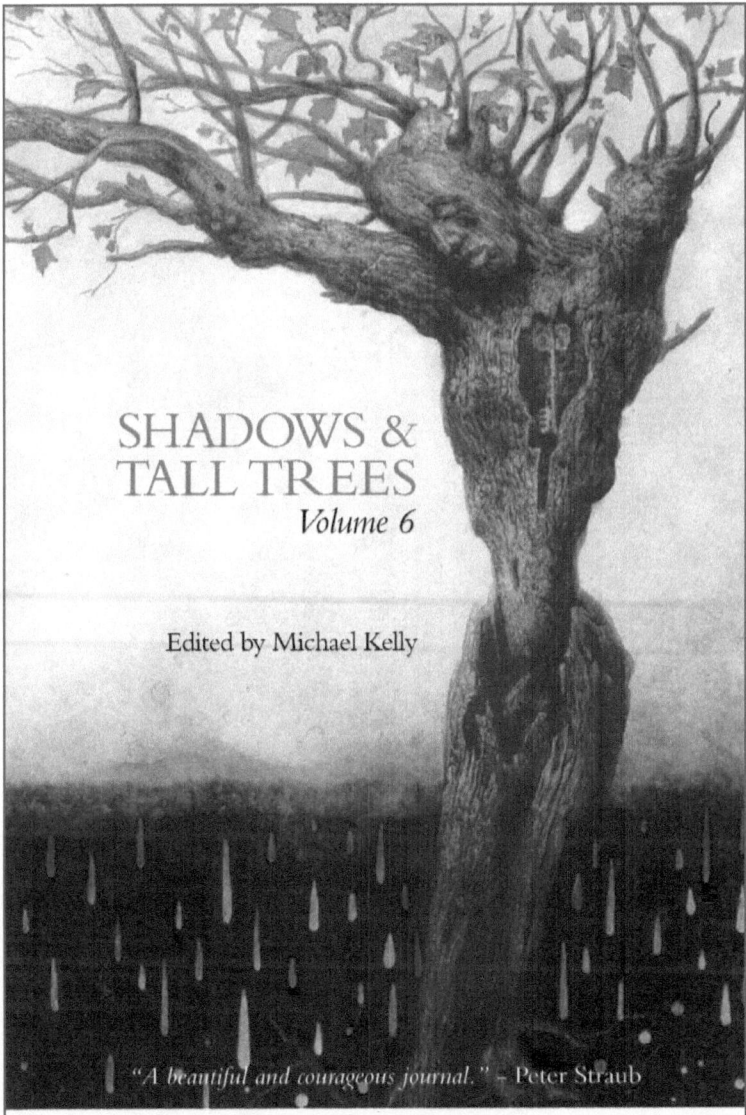

SHADOWS &
TALL TREES
Volume 6

Edited by Michael Kelly

"A beautiful and courageous journal." – Peter Straub

Shadows & Tall Trees, Volume 6
(Shirley Jackson Award Nominee, Edited Anthology)

"A beautiful and courageous volume."
—Peter Straub, author of *Ghost Story*

March 2014   www.undertowbooks.com

V . H . L E S L I E

SKEIN

AND

BONE

Skein and Bone

"An absorbing and gorgeously unsettling collection."
—Alison Moore, *The Lighthouse*, (Short-Listed for the Man-Booker)

August 2015   www.undertowbooks.com

YEAR'S BEST
WEIRD FICTION
VOLUME TWO

EDITED BY
KATHE KOJA
AND MICHAEL KELLY

Year's Best Weird Fiction, Volume Two

Forthcoming Oct. 2015   www.undertowbooks.com